Against The Stars

Serpentine

Book 1

Angela Castillo

To Marina Sirtis
And Gates McFadden.
Thank you for your inspiration.

1
Forcebot

Captain Periwinth Zephyr sucked in a breath and leaned against the corridor wall. "Another worthless meeting of the Kindreds."

"Don't say that." Commander Bradstorm Helms folded burly arms over his navy dress uniform. "At least almost everyone attended this time."

"Only to issue complaints." Periwinth moved away from the wall and strode down the corridor, realized she was stomping, and decided she didn't care.

"Captain!" A thin, high voice floated down the hall. "I will speak with you."

Periwinth ran a hand over her eyes and swiveled to face her vocal assailant.

The leader of the Grimshim Kindred, a willowy woman with cobalt braids, swept towards them, golden bracelets jingling from both arms.

Periwinth suppressed a sigh. "Yes, Magistrate Eunice, what can I do for you?" The woman had already monopolized far too much valuable time during the afternoon meeting with her endless quibbles.

"I've told you; I prefer Empress." The woman fanned out her long fingers across her neck, showing off an impressive array of rings. "I waited for you to address the Bloomwraith leader, but you didn't, despite my numerous correspondences. Their proselytizing missionaries come every day to warn us of our evil wasteful machines. It's the most ridiculous thing I've ever heard. Where would they be without our tech? Burnt to cinders by the sun, that's where!"

Periwinth suppressed an eye roll. "As you'll remember, more pressing matters filled our time today. I'll bring it to Magistrate Colin's attention the next time I speak to him."

"Bring it to his attention? He's the one sending the missionaries!" Tiny wires sprouting from the woman's elaborate headdress shook with each word. "We must shut down the tethers, or at least limit access to authorized travelers only. I've been saying this for months."

Periwinth rubbed the bridge of her nose and silently counted to five before answering. "Empress Eunice, I see your frustration, and I can understand how these 'missionaries,' as you call them, could be a distraction. But if they aren't physically harming your crew or impeding your work, there's not much we can do. The people of all ships are free to speak and act within the scope of their beliefs for the length of this journey. We will not restrict movement through the tethers. Not now, and not for the remaining ten months we must travel together. As we've reminded everyone on numerous occasions, cooperation is required for the health and safety of all Kindred groups. However, I will address the matter with Magistrate Colin."

The woman opened her mouth but before she could say another word, Bradstorm held up his hand. "The captain must go now," he said. "She is weary from the long meeting." He rested a hand on Periwinth's elbow and gently steered her towards the command chambers.

The empress snorted but thankfully did not follow.

"Thank you," Periwinth said when they were safely out of earshot. "I wanted to toss that headdress on the ground and stomp it to smithereens."

Bradstorm's lips twitched under his silvering mustache. "Probably not the most dignified action for the captain of seven starships."

"Perhaps not." Perewinth gave a short laugh. "But I do wish we'd thrown the Ortemp magistrate into the brig. If nothing else, for extreme lack of table manners."

Bradstorm chuckled. "Poor Solstice Marrow! She kept getting sprayed by juices when he bit into fruits."

"I'm certain I'll hear of it later," Periwinth said. "And you're right. Five out of six ship leaders attended. That's the best we've done so far." She smoothed down the front of her blue and silver dress uniform, adorned with a ridiculous amount of fringe. It itched around the collar and sleeves, and she longed to change into more practical attire. "I wish the Cholter leader had come."

"You know how I feel about that," said Bradstorm. "Their treatment has been abysmal for a very long time."

Periwinth dipped her head. "I hope we can soon repair our relationship with them. We will need their unique skill set more than ever in the coming months and years, especially when we reach Fortress." She sighed. "I'm not sure I can do this, Bradstorm."

Bradstorm reached to touch her shoulder like he might have when they were in grade school together but frowned and pulled his hand back. "We all have faith in you. The only way you can fail us is by losing faith in yourself."

"I know," said Periwinth. "But …" she lowered her voice. "This wasn't my choice. I would never have taken this position if I hadn't felt pressed to do so."

Bradstorm glanced behind them, then up at the forcebot camera that stared down at them from the corridor's ceiling. "Yes, but we must keep that between us. Promise me you won't breathe another word about it."

"I won't." She bowed her head. "At least you understand. If it wasn't for you, I'd be completely alone."

Bradstorm's jaw relaxed, but he said nothing.

Swift footsteps approached, and Periwinth sighed. "What now? If it's the Empress again–"

Bradstorm straightened his shoulders. "I'll think of a distraction

Captain."

"How could you possibly distract her? Blast a hole in her hat?"

"Maybe I'll pull out a card deck and perform a magic trick."

"Sure, that would be–interesting." Despite the tedious nature of Periwinth's job, Bradstorm always managed to bring an element of amusement to her day. *He probably knows it's the only thing that keeps me sane.*

A soldier dressed in the black and silver headship uniform sped around the corner, almost running into Bradstorm's folded arms.

"Sorry, Sir. I thought you'd be in your quarters." His eyes met Periwinth's and he saluted. "Captain!"

Periwinth blinked and smiled. "At ease. Trayford, is it?"

"Yes. Yes." The soldier pressed his hands against his chest and inhaled. "We tried to reach you through the comm–"

"Turned off for the meeting." Bradstorm frowned. "You were to contact Ulder if the need arose."

"Yes. He's the one who sent me." The soldier took another gasping breath. "A forcebot is out of control on Level Ten. Ulder's wounded. The station's a mess."

"Not again." Periwinth sprinted to a nearby panel and shoved the flat of her hand against the surface. A wall slid open to reveal a row of blast rifles in various sizes. She threw one to Bradstorm, then grabbed one for herself. "Keep up!" she yelled over her shoulder to Trayford. Bradstorm would need no further instruction.

She ran down the corridors to the lift. The two men smashed in behind her, and Bradstorm's fingers flew over the command panel.

The doors slammed shut, and the lift hummed.

"Is the breech terrible?" Periwinth asked between gasps. "How much damage has been done?" Blood pulsed in her temples, and the blaster jiggled in her hands.

Trayford wiped a stream of sweat from his face. "I don't know, Ma'am, but I fear it's much worse than before. The bot locked itself in. Pretty close to the primary power–"

The lift came to a shuddering halt. The doors slid halfway open, then stuck.

"Grid," Trayford finished.

"Didn't take long." Bradstorm pushed past the opening, his shoulders barely squeezing through. "At least we aren't trapped between levels," he hollered through the crack. "Let's go. Be prepared for anything."

Trayford followed, then reached back to help Periwinth.

She stepped into the corridor, nerves tingling through her skin like writhing snakes.

"Tell me there's a Grinshim team down there," Periwinth said to Trayford.

"I don't know, Ma'am. The main team's been in section four repairing the breach from last week."

"One year." Periwinth groaned. "We must survive for one year. These bots are supposed to be infallible, and they are glitching everywhere. What is going on?"

The hall lights flickered like a final gasp for air, then powered down.

Bradstorm switched on his comwatch light. "Come on," he called, light bobbing through the corridor.

Terrible whines and snapping sounds, like a giant eating a grisly meal, came from behind the closed doors of power room ten.

"Hurry, get the doors open!" shouted Periwinth.

Trayford punched buttons on the control panel. He shook his head. "Nothing's working."

Muffled shouts and screams rose over crashes from the next room.

"That doesn't sound good." Periwinth leaned forward and tapped in her command code. "Manual override, Zephyr 77508."

The doors slid open. An acrid, electrical smell burned through Periwinth's senses, and she yanked the itchy uniform over her nose.

The grid rose before them, a three-story, u-shaped wall of screens. The surface consisted of lights and wires that should pulse and hum but now sulked like a dormant, prehistoric beast.

Lights flashed from walkways and command stations where people darted through machine-lined corridors. Officers barked frenzied orders that no one followed.

Power room ten was the smallest grid and only affected the bottom level of the headship. *Fortunate. If this had happened in level one and somehow shut down the life support–* Periwinth shuddered.

She sprinted to the railing and stared into the chaos that filled the lower level.

There it is. Twenty feet tall, giant steel arms churning like windmills. The forcebot's eyes glowed from a bulbous head, shedding a greenish hue on everything around it. The machine seemed to have a personal vendetta against the power grid, pulling out tubes and wires by the massive steel claw full.

"Captain!" Ulder limped to her side, clutching a blooming red stain on his shoulder. "We've tried everything to stop it. Somehow the bot shorted out its own command response."

"These things were supposed to be perfectly safe!" Trayford cried. "The Grindshim team assured us–"

"We don't have time to speculate about the cause right now," Periwinth's blood pounded in her ears. "We must keep that thing from reaching the main power grid."

"Flannagan's in trouble." Bradstorm gestured to a white-faced soldier far below them, cowering dangerously close to the forcebot's car-sized feet.

"Creator help us," Periwinth muttered. "All right. Ulder, can we access the lift on the lower level?"

Ulder shook his head. "Not enough power to open it. But even if we get in there–"

"The bot's command response is shorted out." Periwinth scanned the perimeter wall. "We must find a way to disable it."

"We would have shot the thing with a blaster, but the stream could ricochet of the bot's shields."

"That's always been the concern with the bigger forcebots and why I didn't want the machines working in the same space with people in the first place." Periwinth sighed. "All right, we'll have to take the risk."

"Captain?" Bradstorm's eyebrow shot up.

"Bradstorm, I need you and Trayford to go to the other railing." Periwinth gestured to the side. "Try to get that thing's attention. Just make a ruckus. Ulder, can you help the soldier escape?"

Ulder nodded. "If the bot's distracted, I could sneak down to the outer shell and pry a side panel open. If the soldier's injuries aren't too severe, he might be able to run out."

"All right." Periwinth studied her surroundings. A metal cabinet faced her. One door the size of a serving tray dangled by a hinge and she wrenched it free. "Gentlemen, let's go."

Bradstorm and Trayford rushed to the other side of the balcony and pounded on the plexiglass panel. The forcebot's massive head rotated, one luminous green eye fixed on the men. It ambled forward.

Periwinth leveled the blast rifle at the metal railing and used the continuous laser stream to cut one side of the plexiglass, then the other. She steadied herself, tossed the metal door over the side, slung her blaster over her shoulder, and dropped eight feet to the floor below.

The robot's attention was still on the two men. It slammed a steel fist, still clutching a handful of wires, against the plexiglass.

Flannigan gazed at her with glassy eyes, oblivious to the now-open panel behind him and Ulder's frantic waving. A giant wire snaked past him, emitting sparks and missing him by inches.

Periwinth gritted her teeth. *Too late to catch his attention.* She hefted up her make-shift shield, readied her blaster, and pulled the trigger.

A blue stream of light radiated from the gun, catching the forcebot square in the chest. It turned and stared at her.

She held steady, the weapon warming in her hands. A small alarm by the hilt buzzed a warning. She shoved the gun out as far from her body as possible, still squeezing the trigger, and pulled her shield close.

The forcebot's chest exploded, and metal and sparks rained through the air. Pressure slammed against her body, and she flew back and hit the wall.

Darkness enveloped her in a peaceful shroud, and she settled into nothingness.

Periwinth's skin itched. Her eyelids fluttered open, and she stared down at a thin white gown instead of her dress uniform.

Monitors beeped around her, and she willed herself to sit up on the narrow cot. Pain stabbed into her left temple.

"You should rest a while longer."

Marrow sat beside the bed, a leather-bound book in her gnarled hands. Her shimmering blue hood was pushed back, fastened at her throat by a gleaming silver broach. Smooth, white braids circled the prominent forehead in perfect order, as always.

Periwinth's arm throbbed under a thick flesh-colored bandage and her ankles ached where they'd taken the brunt of her leap. A burning sensation streaked up her left leg. *I don't even want to see what happened there.*

"Healing will take until lightfall," said Marrow. "Not too bad, considering they brought you from the brink of death. The light surge backfired at full strength."

"Ulder and Flannerly?" Periwinth croaked through parched lips. "Bradstorm?"

"All fine, thanks to you." Marrow's lips pressed together in a manner Periwinth knew all too well from when Marrow had taken her under her wing as a young pilot.

"You shouldn't have taken that risk." Marrow touched the surface of a drinking glass, where water had perspired to the ridge. "Everyone is counting on you. Humankind depends on you for their very existence."

Periwinth sank into the cot's flattened pillows with a gusty sigh. "Sure they do. But what if that forcebot had taken out the main grid? Or killed someone? Trust is already so thin."

"Grindshim techs were dispatched to the three ships that utilize level four forcebots. All will be dismantled and checked thoroughly for glitches."

"That makes sense," said Periwinth. "But you waited to tell the magistrates, right?"

The corners of Marrow's lips stretched down. "Of course we alerted the magistrates."

"No, no, no!" Periwinth pressed her hand against her forehead.

"Under whose authorization?"

Marrow folded her arms and straightened her shoulders. "Why, the Solstice, of course. The doctor wasn't sure when you'd awaken. We couldn't wait in this dire situation. Be at peace. We only told the magistrates about a vague system repair. Just the techs know about the forcebots specifically."

A tired excuse buzzed through Periwinth's mind. Every muscle in her body ached, and she fought the rushing in her ears that tried to convince her to sleep. She pounded her fist into the thin bed covering.

"You should have waited for me, Marrow. The Solstice chose me to be captain and the leadership needs to hear from me when there are problems. I can't show a hint of weakness, or the seven ships will lose faith in our leadership. And you must have decided without consulting Bradstorm. He never would have agreed to it without me. He's my second, Marrow. The Solstice is third."

"Commander Helms suffered injury as well, though he fared better than you. He was in no condition to make such a decision." Marrow's chin quivered. "For once in your life, could you consider what I have been through myself? You are as dear to me as a daughter, and you almost died. Again. We did what we thought was best. For the safety of all. We chose," she laid her hand on Periwinth's shoulder. "the option we believed you would have chosen."

"What's done is done." Perewinth ran a hand over her eyes. "So many small fires. One of them is fated to destroy these fragile threads that hold us all together."

Marrow rose, making tiny adjustments to her many draperies. "Almost dying has caused you to become out of sorts." She gestured to the bedside table. "I've made you fablegrass tea, your favorite. Get some rest."

She left the room.

Periwinth sighed but obediently sipped the tea. It was a comfort, served in one of Marrow's personal clay mugs. How many cups of tea had the older woman served her when she'd come to her home for encouragement and advice?

If I can't trust her, who can I trust?

The room's hanging divider parted, and Bradstorm came to her bedside.

Periwinth scanned his face and arms, her gaze landing on a small bandage that covered his bare shoulder. "Marrow said you were badly injured. I was worried."

"Only a scratch." He arched an eyebrow and brushed her arm with his fingertips. "Are you going to live?"

"I suppose." A tingle ran through her skin. Human touch was rare, everyone treated her like a fragile doll. Or maybe a thorn-covered citadel, she wasn't sure which.

He drew his hand back and cleared his throat. "Captain, I'm glad you're safe. We have scanned the seven ships for problems. Every level four forcebot has been powered down for repairs."

"So I've been told," Periwinth said. "But Marrow said you weren't consulted in the matter."

Bradstorm's shoulders slumped. "And neither were you. I never lost consciousness."

"Unacceptable," said Periwinth. "But we'll have to deal with that later." Even as she spoke, the words seemed weak and futile. "Please continue with your report."

"Very well," said Bradstorm. "A team is deciding what manpower can be redirected to replace the bots until the machines have been returned to working order."

"Aren't the machines irreplaceable?" asked Periwinth.

Bradstorm rubbed the back of his neck. "Almost. But the damage caused by the one today is much greater than the inconvenience. I agreed with the Solstice's decision, though I should have been consulted before they chose to inform the magistrates."

He sat beside her, running a hand through his hair that had become more silver since the beginning of the voyage.

Lowering his voice, he leaned closer. "I'm worried, Captain. I examined that bot myself."

He tucked a piece of paper in her hand, then slid out of the chair. "I'll be nearby if you need me. And Captain." A muscle twitched under the three-day beard. "I'm thankful you're awake."

"Thank you, Bradstorm."

Periwinth waited until he'd left, then moved to her side, away from the curtain's view. She opened her hand just enough to read the one word on the paper. *Sabotage.*

Oh Creator, anything but that. Bad enough the glitch had occurred, but what if someone on the ship intentionally caused it?

Ten thousand, five hundred and sixty-two souls.

Periwinth closed her eyes. Six faces flashed before her, photographs from the files of people she'd researched so thoroughly but never met. *Creator, please lead them here. I can't lose another life. Please keep these ships together, for the sake of all.*

2
Hummingbird

Main lights dimmed to announce the approach of evening. Machinery vibrated, a constant hum pulsing through the metal-formed world, causing a womb-like hypnosis.

Tansy watered the last plant in a line of herbs, measuring the liquid to the last precious drop. The greenhouse, one of four on the Embroid ship, had become her responsibility as Mother's illness worsened. An ache hit the back of her neck, and she rubbed it away. *Need some of that arnica balm when I finish here.*

A flash of green caught her eye from the floral section. She placed her watering can on a ledge and stared.

An impossible winged thing flitted from blossom to fragile blossom. The bird's straw-like tongue, barely visible, darted from its beak, reaching for precious nectar.

A hummer. How can it be a hummer? The simple beauty of the creature brought tears to her eyes. Most of the birds brought to

Gyron generations before with the original Earth colony had never been released into the wild for fear of their utter extinction. The Embroid people rarely made the journey to visit the cities boasting of these sanctuaries.

"How did you get here?" Tansy whispered. Perhaps these birds were allowed to fly free in the headship, who knew of the wonders those people enjoyed. But that wouldn't explain how this creature managed to navigate five ships and the tethers to sip nectar before her at this moment.

She reached out a tentative finger with a child's inclination to stroke the silken wing.

MORM MORM MOOORRMM.

The unfamiliar animal noise jolted her from the reverie. The hummer fluttered to a further flower.

"Stupid Mootrat! Can't you be quiet?" a man's voice hissed.

"Is someone there?" Tansy went to the door of the greenhouse and peered out. Her neighbor's barrier was only a few feet away. Above her was darkened nothingness, as the evening lights weren't bright enough to see the inevitable ceiling of the impossibly large ship.

She moved to the edge of the thick plastic green divider and stood on tiptoe, straining to see over the ledge. "Hello?" she whispered.

A furry creature popped over the wall and slid down the smooth surface, landing at Tansy's feet. The animal's body was about the size of the squirrels on Gyron, but with floppy, rabbit-like ears sprouting from its head. It stared at her with luminous eyes while scrabbling at her toes with tiny hands.

Tansy gasped. "A mootrat! Two animals in a row I've never seen on this ship." She leaned over. "Where did you come from?"

"Hey, would you please let me in?" the man whispered through the panel. "This wall's crazy slick, and Smirk is a better climber than me."

Tansy hesitated, fingers hovering over the button. "Who are you?"

"Look, I'm not going to hurt you. I'm after my pet, that's all."

Never open a door to a stranger. How many times had the rule been repeated to her as a child?

I'm a grown woman. Almost twenty-one. I can make my own choices. What danger could someone possibly pose to me here? I scream and dozens will hear me. It's not like he'd have anywhere to run.

Heart pounding, she pressed the button. The panel slid open.

A man slipped in, so tall that his thick dreadlocks brushed the arched top of the entryway. A scruff of beard flecked his chin and silver hoop earrings glinted in each ear. Eyes of the lightest crystal blue she'd ever seen gazed into hers.

"Hey." He gave her a lazy smile. "I'm Camp."

"Tansy." She backed away, fresh panic clutching at her gut. "Where are you from? I've never seen you before."

"Not from this ship, obviously." He clicked his tongue at the mootrat, who scampered up the sleeve of his duster jacket, settled on his shoulder, and chattered at Tansy.

"Then where…" her voice trailed off as she realized. *He must be a Cholter.*

"Yeah, yeah. I'm from the tail." He shrugged. "Brought a delivery a few doors down and Smirk here got away from me."

"Isn't it illegal to have a pet mootrat?" Tansy asked.

Camp pulled out a fistful of bright orange papers from his pocket.

Infraction slips. Tansy had never received one, but every person on the seven ships had been grilled about them.

Camp stuffed the slips back into his pocket. "Yeah, the headship knows all, don't they? Stupid forcebots don't hold secrets." His voice dropped to a whisper. "But the powers have enough on their hands, keeping everyone alive and tethered. They don't enforce infractions. Mostly."

"I wouldn't know," said Tansy. *Now I sound like a snob.* She held out her hand to the mootrat. The creature grabbed her arm and examined it, as though it suspected hidden treats.

"Oh, he is cute. I'm a little envious. I always wanted a pet. My mother tried to save up to buy me a brighten-bird." She pointed to the hummingbird, which had darted from the greenhouse opening and now hovered over a potted plant by Tansy's dwelling. "But I decided I couldn't bear to keep a winged thing cooped up."

"Lor–would you look at that?" Camp whistled. "I haven't glimpsed a wild creature since launch. And I've never seen one of those, not even on the surface. Have you?"

"Never. I'm trying to decide if I should report it."

Camp gave her a sideways glance. "Ah. You must be one of those law-followers."

Tansy shrugged. "The little thing could get caught in an exhaust fan. Besides, I can't think of any reason to hide it."

"Except that they'll bring out a net, catch it, and put it in a cage again," said Camp.

Tansy's lashes fluttered. "But maybe it would be safer."

"Safer isn't always better." Camp rubbed his hands on his knees. "It's okay. I can see how you might find comfort in obedience. The law hasn't harmed you or anyone in your family."

I wouldn't say that. But out loud Tansy said, "I think I'll keep it a secret, this one time." She hoped Camp didn't catch the slight tremor in her voice. It wasn't from fear, she decided, but excitement. "Maybe it will come back to visit again."

"I bet it's too smart to get caught in a fan," said Camp. He patted the mootrat's head. "I know Smirk is."

They watched as the bird flew over the barrier and out of sight.

"Tansy." Her mother's soft voice floated from their dwelling.

"Almost last meal." Tansy twisted her hands. Her Embroid upbringing to never refuse the needy pushed through her quiet doubts. "Would you care to join us? Mother won't mind."

"If you invite a Cholter to dinner?" Camp tightened his jacket. "I wouldn't be too sure."

At once Tansy realized how shabby his clothes were, the gauntness of his cheeks. *Cholters don't take handouts.* They barely accepted food rations.

"Of course not." Dryness hit Tansy's throat, and she swallowed, heat creeping up her neck. "We're not racist like that. Mother's not well, but she's having a good day."

"Oh, sorry to hear that." Camp bounced on his toes, as though preparing for a school footrace. "Look here, I'd better not come inside. Don't want Smirk kicking up a fuss. Thanks, though." He gave her another quick smile. "Who knows? Maybe you'll need something delivered from the Cholter ship someday."

"Maybe." Tansy barely squeaked out the word before he disappeared.

She pressed her fingers against her heart, the frantic beating almost matching the rhythm of the hummingbird's wings. Back on Gyron, men from other cities and cultures visited her remote village at times. Mostly in the markets when they came to barter for herbs and vegetables. But for the last two months on the ship, she'd only seen Embroids, and her own Kindred were far from exciting. Priority rested on staying calm, living as a vessel where peace was welcome to dwell. Seldom was a voice raised, or a child seen running in the ship's grid paths.

Camp is simply the most interesting person I've ever met.

With reluctance, she put away her watering device and went to the front door of her home.

A spicy fragrance rose to meet her senses. Her mother, Lanis, reclined in a corner on a pile of pallets and cushions.

Shelves lining the rounded walls held books and trinkets,

mostly figurines her father had carved. Dishes, bunches of herbs, and cleaning brushes hung from hooks. Tansy had painted the few chairs and tables in bright blues and purples with flowered designs running rampant on legs and surfaces. The place was stuffy and small, and Tansy much preferred the greenhouse.

"Tansy, last meal is on the table," said her mother.

"Thank you, Mother." Tansy tried to keep the surprise from her voice. Mother rarely made dinner these days, the effort of standing beside the cooking receptacle was mostly too much. Tansy had fully expected to reheat a vegetable medley she'd made yesterday. But Lanis had prepared freshly baked rolls and a seared fish with broccoli.

Lanis leaned over the diffuser on the stool nearby and inhaled the steam, closing her eyes.

Tansy glanced at the device. "Thieves oil again?"

"Inhalation purifies the lungs," said her mother. "That's what the elder told me."

A trickle of irritation mixed with drops of sorrow burned in Tansy's mind. *Yes, Thieves oil helps with germs and infection. But nothing can be done about the cancer. The medical clerics tried every cure they knew.*

Lanis unfolded herself from the cushion and pushed herself up with shrunken, stick-like arms. Her once shiny, bouncing curls hung in strings over her thin, white face. The only hints of her original beauty were coppery eyes, glowing from sunken depths.

Tansy shook away the sorrow invading her mind.

"Picked a handful of plumquats," she said brightly. "I'll wash them up to go with our soup."

"How nice, darling." Lanis staggered to the small table. "I didn't think they'd ripen until Wednesday."

Tansy frowned. "Mother, it is Wednesday."

Her mother waved a claw-like hand. "Yes, yes. I'm glad it is too, or we wouldn't have the plumquats." The too-bright smile Tansy had grown to hate stretched over her lips. She'd begun smiling that way years ago when rumors of the supernova had reached their village. Tansy had been ten. Father was still alive, and every night she'd heard whispered conversations through the thin walls of their house. She'd huddled in bed, wondering if they'd ever know how much more the whispers scared her than if they'd actually told her the truth.

After the quick meal, Tansy scanned the dishes with a sanitizer and wiped down the table.

She thought of the trembling whiskers of the mootrat and the buzzing wings of the hummingbird.

"Mother, have you ever seen a hummingbird?" she asked. Not long ago, she would have helped her mother outside to share such a sight. But now the slightest exertion would affect Lanis for several days.

Lanis tipped her head to the side, squinting. "Only once. My school took a field trip to Skawling City to tour the zoo there. I always wanted to take you." She sank back on her cushion with a deep sigh. "My great-grandmother lived with us for some time growing up. She would tell us of our ancestors who lived on Earth in a place called Colorado. They'd keep feeders for the birds, and the hummers came in swarms. What made you think of them?"

"No reason." The lie burned Tansy's tongue. She didn't want to sadden her mother about missing the rare beauty. Plus, Lanis might insist she report the bird to the headship.

In the two centuries since colonization, all Kindreds had tended the creatures brought from Earth. They'd studied the planet's environments for the best natural habitats and released various species at careful intervals. But the work of decades was undone when plans had to be made for yet another planet evacuation.

Teams of people had been given the task of preserving as many Earth and Gyron-native animals as they could, providing comparable environments and diets to keep them alive for the year's journey to Fortress.

Many people kept dogs and cats in their dwellings, of course, and some owned smaller creatures like snakes and lizards. But these were mostly descendants of pets the first Earth colony had brought. They possessed a sameness, similar shapes and colors, with few variations.

Maybe I should notify the aviary keeper in the headship. But how would I get permission to go? Does one simply ask? Perhaps Father Sharood could tell me what to do.

Tansy rose and went to her own small room. She sank into her bunk and flipped open the cover of her favorite book, staring at the pages but not reading. She longed to see more creatures, faces, things she'd never experienced.

Shapes and shadows flitted into her head, and she closed the book to concentrate. These visions were a continued part of her life, and to fight them was useless.

Weightless, she hovered in the air like the hummingbird, looking down at a group of people in her mind. *Is that me down there? Yes. But who is that beside me?* Camp, the young man she'd met today. Without the mootrat, she noted. A group of people she didn't recognize stood nearby. They were gathered beside a tether station. She frowned. *Perhaps I'll get a pass to the headship after all.* Her head pounded and she opened her eyes. Since launch, the days of travel had been so monotonous. *Could I even dare to dream of such a wondrous opportunity?* But the vision wouldn't come to her if it wasn't going to happen.

Gifts like these visions had been bestowed upon many of her people. But her abilities were special.

Tansy went back to the room where Mother lay, head tipped back on a cushion, small snores coming from the withered lips. She hated to wake her, but her headache intensified. Mother was the only person who understood, the only one who could help ease the ache. She patted the withered hand.

"Huh, what's the matter?" Lanis's eyes fluttered open.

"I had a vision." Tansy's head spun faster, as it often did when a sight-dream landed with sudden force. She longed for her mother to be strong again, to stroke her hair and bring comfort through the pain like she used to.

"Was it a bad happening?" her mother murmured.

"I don't think so. My head aches, though."

"I'm sorry, dear. But it is the way," said Lanis. She threw an arm over her eyes. "I will pray for Spirit to cover you in peace."

Tansy sank into the cushions next to her mother. *What could the vision mean?* Some Embroids saw shadows of the future, some heard snatches of words or shadows of character discernment. But Tansy's visions were vivid and detailed. Unless something was done to prevent it, the happening would certainly come to pass.

If anyone discovered the true strength of her gifting ... She pushed the horrible thought down into the depths of her mind, where it usually stayed.

"I'm going to bed, Mother," she said, patting the thin shoulder, already rising and falling in slumber.

3
Stowaway

Camp pressed the button and the tether-tube door slid closed with a satisfying 'snick.'

Though hard for his prideful heart to admit, the Embroid's ship contained a beauty and wholesomeness a part of him longed for. The words of his father, who'd passed away a year before, came to his mind. *"Son, you're a Cholter. Other Kindreds want what we can do for them, but they don't want us. Don't long for stars you can't touch."*

Boursin, the guard in charge of checking in tether travelers, gave Camp a bored stare from his console. "Did you bring any illegal contraband with you?" he said in a monotone voice.

Camp patted his pouch where Smirk was sleeping. "Nothing today," he said, though Boursin knew about his pet. Boursin was a born and bred Cholter, and they stuck together like Garble wrappers in the sunshine.

Persneep, the Cholter's leader, strode through the door. "Oh, you're back," he said to Camp. He licked his lips with a bright red tongue. "Get anything good? The Embroid greenhouses are bursting with fruits ready for the harvest, or so I've been told."

"My orders were to deliver only, Sir. If you'd like me to arrange a trade next time, you'll have to provide the papers." Camp didn't feel the need to share about the hummingbird. He doubted Persneep would know what he was talking about anyway. Persneep was a small, shifty man who'd been born into his leadership position. Though his morals might be questionable, no one could touch him in his glory days. He could still shinny in and out of a refuse tube in ten seconds flat and had invented many scavenging tools the entire community used.

"Eh, more's the pity." Persneep shrugged and turned to Bourson. "Came to ask about that intake chip you promised me."

"Oh yes, right here." Bourson ducked down behind the console and came back up with a paper-wrapped parcel.

"Have a good day," Camp said over his shoulder as he went on through the next panel to a room with a row of four check-in comscreens. He waved his comwatch in front of the first one. Blue light bloomed across the screen. "State your mission," came the synthesized voice.

"Returning from delivery of empty containers to Embroid ship," said Camp. "Scavenger, Class Two."

The computer screen blinked permission to move forward.

"Why, thank you," said Camp as the next panel slid open.

Voices rose from behind the door he had just come through. He paused. *Yancy must be trying to bring in spittleweed again.* The medicinal herb, also used in a habit-forming tea, was legal for Embroid use but not on the Cholter ship, like many resources. The law stated that since Cholters were more 'prone to addiction,' they must observe heavier regulations than anyone else.

Though plenty of the Kindreds drink it in privacy. The hypocrisy would have been unbelievable if Camp hadn't lived with it his entire life. Cholters suffered stronger fines for infractions than other groups. His people had been outcasts for a hundred years on the planet. But at least on Gyron they'd lived in a town far from others, preferring to travel further distances for trades, so their village could remain a place of refuge. Now the little band was forced to journey with everyone else in the world, in a place of forcebot scrutiny. The stress was evident when he spent time with neighbors and friends. Lines of worry replaced those created by laughter, and deep sighs took the place of snatches of song and wild tales.

Bourson's voice rose again, a smidge louder this time. "I don't have the authority!"

Camp shook his head. *Why won't Yancy let it go? Even if Bourson let him through, the forcebots will report him and he'll have to turn it in. Spittleweed possession is a far more serious infraction than a mootrat pet.*

An unfamiliar voice replied in a clipped accent. "Sir, we are begging of you . . ."

I haven't heard talk like that since we left Gyron. Camp froze. *Must be one of the smaller Kindreds from the headship. But what would they be doing here?* He squared his shoulders. *I hope it's not someone from the top coming to make trouble.* Doubtful, since the other Kindreds avoided the Cholter ship at all costs.

Still, better make sure Bourson doesn't pop an artery. He slid his pack off his shoulder and ducked back into the tether station.

Despite his intent to remain nonchalant, his step faltered when he saw the small group standing at the desk. A tall man with piercing gray eyes and dusky brown skin waited at the counter. Beside him stood a woman with bright blond hair tucked up in a cap. He almost missed the girl, perhaps four, staring at him from the folds of the woman's skirt. *From their clothes, they look like Quient Kindred. Why aren't they on the headship?* Camp threw Bourson a look.

Bourson shrugged.

Persneep drummed pudgy fingers against his frown-creased cheeks.

"As I was saying," the man continued, slapping the flat of his hand against a stack of papers on the counter. "We would have boarded the ship with everyone else."

"My father wouldn't come," the woman murmured. "He wasn't right in his mind. We couldn't leave him, you see."

They'd risk their child? Camp slid a step closer to Bourson.

"Why are you here now?" Persneep rolled his eyes, his scowl intensifying. "How did you get a zoomer? Steal it?"

"No, nothing like that," the man said in a firm, authoritative tone. "The zoomer belonged to our neighbor. An old craft he'd used to give space tours before the discovery. He went with the Serpentine. Left the zoomer for us in case we changed our minds since we had a child and all." The man patted the little girl's shoulder, and she stared up at him, thumb ensconced firmly in her mouth.

"My father passed away three days after the Serpentine left," said the woman, brushing her eyes. "We decided to try for the journey, though our chances were bleak. The sky had already brightened."

Camp nodded. The last days on Gyron had been dreadful. The Cholters were the last group to board, and had been rushed by the burning sky, the forwarning that all would soon be lost. Even then, when he'd stared out at the lush mountains, the forests stretching past the barren fields where the seven ships were constructed and tethered, it had been hard to believe.

Worst had been the time when the green and blue planet they'd always called home finally disappeared from sight. And then weeks later, when probes had reported the supernova's completion. The cruel finality. The world, along with the thousands of souls who'd opted to stay, had been blown into utter nothingness.

Bourson's sleepy lids flipped open. "So you're telling me

you've been chasing us for the last two months? In a daytrip space zoomer?"

The woman nodded. "We followed the Serpentine's trail of cosmic dust. Good thing we caught up because we ran out of food two days ago, and our water system was near to failing."

"The biggest challenge was keeping that junk pile going," said the man. "There were times …" He paused and swallowed. "There were times I didn't think we'd make it."

"The docking process was terrifying," the woman put in. "We weren't sure our zoomer was equipped for such a task. Fortunately, the beacon found the ring dock by the front of your tether. The automatic system worked like a dream, but the process was rough." She held up her arm, covered from wrist to elbow in the sickly yellow beginnings of a bruise. "Look, I know you need to get information from us, but could we please have water? At least for my daughter? It has been so hard."

The child's stomach rumbled, quite loudly for such a little thing.

Pity stirred Camp's soul. Thanks to his parents working their guts out, he'd never known hunger, but it had always been his greatest fear. *Poor little mite.* "There's a water dispenser." He waved to a panel in the wall. "You can have as much as you want."

The woman rushed to the panel and poured cups for her daughter, her husband, and herself. "Small sips," she said to the little girl, who replaced her thumb with the cup.

Bourson's shoulders heaved almost imperceptibly. "What do

you think, Persneep?"

"As leader of this ship," said Persneep, "I grant you with the decision."

Bourson held up his hands. "Look, I can send a request to the headship, they've probably already spotted your zoomer. Shouldn't take long to hear back."

The man darted Camp a glance, then looked at his wife. "Ah, can we hold off reporting in, maybe for a day or two?"

Bourson rubbed his chin. "I'm not sure why you'd make such a request. The forcebots will report you. We'll have to acquire family rations, and those must be assigned–"

"I have extra," Camp cut in. "Been gone for the whole day, and the Embroids were generous with their vegetables." He turned to the man. "My name is Camp, and your family are welcome to stay in my quarters for a day or two. It'll be a tight squeeze–"

The man turned, his eyes widening as though he'd noticed Camp for the first time. He beamed and held out his hand. "Dashner Rind. This is my wife, Jayne, and our daughter, Raven."

Camp took the man's hand, and instantly confirmed his suspicions. *These people are hiding something.* Just as he'd figured. He'd inherited the truth touch from his father, and it had saved his life more than once. *Everyone has secrets. Can't hold that against them.*

The woman's eyes pleaded with him.

"Let's go, folks," said Camp. "Bourson, can you take care of the computer?”

Bouson raised an eyebrow. “You take full responsibility?”

“For what? A refugee family? Haven’t you heard, Bourson? Our captain Zephyr is merciful and just. Besides,” he turned to Dashner. “It’ll be at least a day or two before the Headship bothers to make their tedious way down here. Word is they don’t like us Cholters too much.” He gave what he hoped was a reassuring smile. “Folks, if you’ll follow me, your luxury accommodations are right this way.”

Dashner appraised the entryway as the double doors slid open. “Interesting technology. I’m still wondering why they couldn’t build one ship big enough for everyone.”

Camp shrugged. “Maybe they could, but I figure they just wanted to keep us apart to avoid wars. Don’t know how the headship gets along with all the smaller-party Kindreds stuffed in one place.”

“We’re hoping some of our family is up there,” said Jayne. “Do you know of them? They’d have blond hair like me.”

“Lady, I’ve only been through the Embroid and Tark ships,” said Camp. “The headship has five thousand people alone. So no, I’m sorry.”

“We’ve never met a Cholter, either” said Dashner. “But we are very thankful for your generosity.”

“Wait ‘till you see my pod before you go thanking me,” said Camp. “I’m not being modest. It’s tiny.”

The larger doors that led from the tether tubes gaped open, and

Camp beckoned the family through. Raven hung back, her face pale under the freckles she'd inherited from her mother.

"I understand, little one," said Camp. "It's not the happiest place. Or the cleanest."

Corridors created maze-like paths around the home pods. Like the other Kindreds, the Cholters had been responsible for setting up their living arrangements, besides the basic layout and husks of the dwellings. The grid of corridors was the same as the other ships, but there the similarities ended. Bright paint, mosaics of broken glass, and scraps of cloth and metal decorated the pods' exteriors. Surrounding most homes were stacks of remats, broken sundries workers scavenged from the refuse tethers to fix.

In the center of the hundreds of home pods, the inner hub squatted like a purple toadstool. This is where the Cholters gathered to trade, swap stories, and work on projects that called for more help than their home units could manage.

In addition to being the last in the string of seven, the Cholter ship was also the smallest by a third. Talk had circulated at first. Why drag the seventh ship along at all? The Cholters could easily be absorbed by the main ship, along with all the smaller people groups. In the end, it was decided they needed the space for their ever-important repurposing projects. But Camp knew the truth. No one in the headship wanted them there.

The ship's ceiling rose a hundred yards above them, dotted with pan lights and clusters of tubes, each large enough for a man to crawl through.

Dashner tilted his head back. "So each ship has the same oxygen system as the zoomers, I'm guessing."

Camp nodded. "While oxygen and water circulate through the tethers, each ship also contains the individual ability to sustain life, in case something separates them." *Or someone.*

Janey trudged through the corridors, tugging at Raven's hand when the child ventured too close to a pile of remats. Camp could tell Jayne was trying to hide a look of disgust, though everything in the piles had been cleaned with detergent and treated with special rust removers.

I wonder if Tansy would act the same way if she came here? He shook the thought from his mind like dust. The last distraction he needed right now was any thought of the Embroid girl. Something gnawed at him. Something that he'd normally have thought all the way through by now.

He turned right, then left. His tiny home pod was back in the corner, just the way he liked it. They didn't have the fancy barrier walls like the Embroids, so he'd constructed a fence from scraps of metal and wood. He went to the gate and pulled out his pulse-key.

Dashner looked over his shoulder. "Is that Grindshim made?" he asked, a tinge of wonder in his voice.

"Sure," said Camp. "Found it in the trash tether. Just needed a new chip. People who have everything throw away anything."

"Can't argue with that," Dashner grinned. "I mean, we got a

free spaceship."

Chase opened the gate and led them through the yard. Piles of remats, some as high as his head, were stacked throughout the yard. Mostly machinery and metal, since that's what he focused on.

A small garden had been plotted in the corner, the leafy vegetables sagging in the artificial lights. *Oops. Forgot to ask the neighbors to water.*

"You have a garden?" asked Janey.

"Required for every citizen, even though we receive food rations from the Bloomwarths, Tarks, and sometimes Embroids. I had turkeys over there," he nodded to a small building on the other corner. "But they escaped, and I haven't had a spare second to round them up again. Neighbors have a fish tank."

He went to the bright blue front door of his home pod and swung it open. "Come on in. Hope we all fit."

They squeezed into the tiny house, Camp's head inches from the hard plastic ceiling. The home pod consisted of three rooms, relatively clean compared to his yard. Bathroom to the right. Table and chairs in the main room, with a couch and a small viewscreen where he watched centuries-old Earth movies and received daily notices from the headship which he mostly ignored.

He pulled Smirk out of his pocket and set him on the table.

Smirk blinked and wiggled his ears. He proceeded to address the group in high-pitched chatter, gesturing with his tiny paws. He ran up Camp's shoulder and buried his face in his dreads.

Janey gasped and stole a glance at Dashner.

Ravan took her thumb from her mouth, clapped her hands and laughed. "Silly monkey."

"That's not a monkey," said Dashner.

"Smirk, mind your manners," said Camp, pulling him off his shoulder and placing him back on the table. "Here, you can feed him a treat." Camp handed Raven a withered carrot.

He smiled at Dashner. "Don't worry, he wouldn't hurt a fly. But I would keep your bags closed tight unless you want the contents scattered about."

"Good to know," Dashner said, his eyes never leaving the mootrat.

Camp nodded to the inner door. "Speaking of which, you can put your things in my room. You and your wife can have my bed. Little one can fit on the sofa, and I'll sleep in my hammock out in the yard."

"We can't ask you to sleep outside." Jayne held out her hands.

"If I truly slept outside, I'd be floating in space, so yes, that would be a lot to ask of someone," said Camp. "But here in Serpentine, the temperature is regulated throughout the ships. We have no seasons. Lights are controlled to simulate night and day. The worst thing I could experience is an errant turkey coming back and roosting on my face."

Dashner rubbed his beard. "Well. If you're sure."

"S'fine." Camp went over to his pantry. "Let's see. I have bread and peanut butter. There's leftover stew in the cold cupboard, but I'm not sure if there's enough to go around. How about I put everything out and you eat what looks best?"

He set the food on the table with plates and silverware, lugged out his water pitcher and the three cups in his possession, and stepped back. "Huh. Now that I think of it, that couch looks a tad uncomfortable, even for such a little mite. Think I'll run to my neighbors and see if they have an extra blanket or two."

"Please–" Jayne began, but she was interrupted by Dashner, who reached out a hand and grabbed Camp's arm in a surprisingly strong grip.

"Sir, we'd appreciate it if you kept our presence here quiet." The man spoke through gritted teeth, the grin gone as fast as it had come.

"Not a nice way to treat your host." Camp firmly removed the man's hand from his arm. "I can assure you this entire ship is aware of your presence. Even if Persneep hadn't been in the tether station, I'd estimate no fewer than ten pairs of eyes watched us come in, probably many more. Everyone knows each other here. Anyone who wants information will run to the tether station and inquire. Cholters don't keep secrets. We couldn't if we tried."

Dashner exhaled gustily. "Right. I'm sorry. We can't risk being sent–back out there."

"That would be crazy," said Camp. "No one would ever suggest such a horrible thing."

Jayne closed her eyes and leaned against her husband's shoulder. "You have no idea how terrifying it was–with a child. We didn't know if we'd make it in time."

Camp's shoulders slumped. "I can only imagine, ma'am. But I think when you are found–and you will be–you might be surprised by the way things are done around here. Captain Zephyr is doing her best to keep everyone tethered together, and that's no exaggeration."

Dashner rubbed the nape of his neck. "Got it. But we'd still like to lay low for a few days. To catch our breath."

Camp nodded. "Let me see about those blankets."

He slipped out the door. *I'm sure everything will be alright. What could they possibly steal? I have nothing of value. The forcebots can sniff out theft from ships away.*

Candy answered the door the moment he knocked. "Good day, Camp. What brings you over? Frank isn't here right now."

Camp gave a tiny bow. "Good day, Candy. I came to beg you for a few extra blankets if you have them."

"Blankets? Well, yes, I might have some extra ones. I collect textiles to weave and knit into new things. I've saved back a few that were in better shape for market day. You may certainly borrow them if they aren't used too roughly." She narrowed her eyes. "And keep them away from that mootrat of yours."

"Actually." Camp lowered his voice. "I have unexpected guests."

Candy raised an eyebrow. "Oh?" She gave him a sly smile.

"New girlfriend?"

A harsh blush hit Camp's cheeks. "Oh goodness, no. Look, you'll probably find out anyway. A family is staying with me. Three refugees docked on the Cholter ship in a zoomer. Man, wife, and their little daughter."

"Oh my." Fingers crept to her mouth, drumming her lips. "Frank thought this might happen, but maybe before now. We didn't think a zoomer could last this long."

"Almost didn't. They're starving."

"Do you have enough food? I can spare some."

He shrugged. "I had leftovers, and my garden is producing well enough."

"You're always so generous, Camp. Been that way since you were a child. Hang on a minute."

She went inside. In a beat she returned, her arms full. "Here are the blankets. And some cookies I made this morning. And I found this." She gave him a rag doll, limp, with one arm dangling by a thread. "A bit worn, but still has lots of play in her. Belonged to Jenny, but she didn't want her when she got married. She'll be glad dolly is getting a good home."

"Thank you," said Camp. "And please, let's keep this quiet for today."

Candy's eyes narrowed. "The headship doesn't know?"

"Not yet, but of course they will," said Camp. "Give these folks a bit to catch their breath. They've been through a scary time."

"I understand." Candy patted his arm. "Be well, Camp. Let me know if we can help with anything else."

4
Silver Seal

A pounding at the dwelling's main door jolted Tansy from slumber. She sat up and glanced at her mother.

Lanis slept with an arm flung over her face, her chest rising and falling in a peaceful rhythm.

Tansy pushed a cushion to the side. *Guess I fell asleep here after that vision.* She stretched and stood, avoiding her reflection in the mirror by the door. *Whoever it is will have to take me as I am. Their own fault for coming by without notice.*

She pawed at the security panel, her eyes blurry. *Is food disbursement early this week?*

An Embroid man she didn't recognize waited outside. His silvering beard curled over his chest, and a thick leather pouch hung across his body.

Tansy's mind fumbled through half-awake fog to reach for his name. It floated, feather-ish, from his psyche to hers. *Griffin. One of the lesser elders. What is he doing here?* The old familiar fear of discovery, of her world shattering to pieces, clawed at her stomach and she tamped it down, hushing it like an ornery child.

He blinked at her, probably from the shock of her disheveled-beyond-belief self. "Tansy Pellum?"

"Uh-huh."

Griffin held out a thin, silver envelope. "I'm here by instruction from the Headship to deliver this." He leaned closer, his goldenrod hood almost brushing Tansy's forehead. "Captain Zephyr sent it herself. At least, that's what it says on the envelope. Hard to believe, but there it sits." He squinted at her. "Noticed you're an herb-keeper. Do you think it's a special request? Medicinal? Wasn't aware the captain is ill."

Tansy released the breath she'd been holding in a gusty sigh. "First I've heard from her, so I have no idea." She took the parchment envelope with trembling fingers and stepped back into the doorway to escape the man's beady gaze.

Her name was embossed in silver across the crisp white envelope, the flap sealed with a thick crust of wax in a way she'd never seen, only read about. A thin scent of ancient ink and mysteries wafted from the envelope. She'd never seen a piece of paper so lovely, not even the books holding the Embroid's sacred texts.

She gave Griffin a slanted glance. He cleared his throat and looked from the envelope to her, raising his eyebrows.

"Thank you for bringing this. Give me a moment." She ducked

into the house, placed the envelope on the table, and grabbed two plumquats. "Fresh from the greenhouse. Good day to you."

Griffin plucked the fruits from her open palm, stared at them, and stuffed them in his pocket. "Thanks," he mumbled. He shuffled away in his old sheepskin shoes. He looked back once, shrugged, and went on.

Probably hungrier for gossip to spread than fruit. Tansy stifled a laugh. She'd rather die than share the contents of the letter with the nosey old man.

She went inside, slamming the door and locking it. Now that the snoop was gone, her own curiosity burned within her. She picked up the envelope and held it to the light. *Almost a shame to destroy the beautiful shape of the seal in the wax.* Two swooping lines wound into a resting dove.

"Good morning, honey." Her mother staggered to the table and sat down heavily. The morning hours usually consisted of what she called her 'energy times' where she showered, ate, and on very good days, went out to the greenhouse for short spurts.

"What's that?" Lanis touched the corner of the envelope.

"I don't know," said Tansy. "I received it from the headship. From Captain Zephyr herself."

Lanis laughed, a raspy, tired sound. "She couldn't send you a message on the comscreen? What is it, a silly reassurance she's copied out for everyone on the seven ships? Last week they sent that announcement about the Bloomwraith pipe concert we all had to endure. Remember that?"

"Ohhh, I can still hear that tinny, off-key whistle at the end." Tansy pressed her fingers against her temples. She laid the envelope on the table. "I'll read it after I mix the cereal. You must be hungry."

Her mother's mouth quirked up at the corners. "Not very, dear, I can wait. I want to know what the letter says, too."

"Okay, I'll open it." As Tansy ran her finger under the flap, gently loosening the wax to cause the least amount of damage to the seal, a slight thrill ran through her arm, almost like an electric shock. *This letter is important. It will change my life forever.*

Her mother's eyes were wide, expectant. For the first time in months Tansy saw a glimmer of excitement on the tired face.

She pulled out the letter and unfolded it. Lovely handwritten words traveled across the page in perfect script, a feast for her eyes as she read.

"My Dear Miss Pellum,

You are invited to join me, along with six others, for a special dinner in my private conference room on the headship. Clearance has been arranged for you to journey through the ships to the Grimshim tether station, where you will convene with your guide at 1100. No penalty will be given if you choose not to come, but please note, it is vital for the good of the ship that you come to this meeting. Do not speak of this letter to anyone. Bring the paper with you, but keep it hidden. I will see you in the morrow.

Cordially,

Captain Periwinth Zephyr

"Huh." Tansy sat back in her chair, her braid mashing into her spine.

She glanced over at her mother, whose face was even more ashen than usual. "What's the matter?"

"You don't think they're–that she's discovered your gift, do you?" Lanis said.

"Oh, Mother, no. Not possible." Tansy said, though her own heart had crawled up into her throat. She reached for her mother's thin fingers and squeezed them, hoping her tone was reassuring. "No one could know. We've kept it a secret for so long."

"But the legends–" Lanis murmured. "Many of our kindred suspect. I've noticed them staring. During waits."

I know all too well. Tansy had found it difficult to evade prying eyes and questions since they'd begun the journey. But Lanis didn't need to know that. "Don't worry, Mother. Members of other Kindreds barely recognize our giftings anymore. Remember what Grandma used to say."

"Truth is in the beholder's eye, and faith in a skeptic's heart melts into ruin," said Lanis. "This has strengthened us, for we hold these secrets dear, and they have preserved our people for decades. But Tansy–" her fingers tightened around her hand, so the knuckles turned bluish-white. "Our own people would seek your death."

Tansy gave a shaky laugh. "Mother, you shouldn't worry about ancient superstitions. Besides, no female child waits to inherit my powers if I'm lost." Tansy patted her mother's hand as she gently pulled away. "I've decided to make you honey cakes instead of dry old cereal. You need something to tempt your appetite."

"You'd better hurry, or you'll miss morning Wait," said Lanis.

"Wouldn't want that," said Tansy. But as she went to the shelves to grab the ingredients she needed; her head swam.

Lately, the community gatherings at the Clarity building had been overwhelming, the cacophony of thoughts thundering around her like Kremwalth Falls back home. Like the foaming purple water, the ideas, hopes, and dreams pummeled her mind relentlessly. The closer she came to her twenty-first birthday, the stronger they were.

Lanis had assured her that she could control them in time, but Tansy found this tough to believe. This fear reminded her of when she'd lost her first tooth at five. Her father had promised her over and over that a new tooth would grow in the bloodied space, but she'd cried for days anyway. If she'd still been in the small Embroid village, she'd have retreated to the sacred caves of solitude until she learned to block and control the constant wave, but where could she hide on a spaceship? At least in her quarters, she had some relief, but if she remained at home during the time of Waiting everyone would grow suspicious.

The honey cakes went into the heater and out again, baked in seconds. She placed them on the table. "These will be cooled in a few moments," she told her mother, who'd returned to her corner cushions. "I'm going to prepare for the Wait."

She went into the tiny bathroom and ran a quick shower. After dressing in her Waiting robe and taming her tangled, curly hair into a braided bun at the nape of her neck, she slipped into a pair of thin sandals. Her Embroidian Life Beads hung from a special peg. As was the custom before a Wait, she touched each engraved bead. One for her first Wait. One for her first uttering of the Embroid Creed. Her necklace held over twenty hand-carved, unique beads, but elders owned more elaborate strings, some boasting more than one hundred. She fastened the beads around her throat and went into the common area.

"These cakes should be cooled now." Tansy placed one on a plate. "Here you are, Mother."

Lanis took an offered cake and inhaled. "The aroma alone strengthens me. Thank you for going to the trouble."

"Of course." Tansy kissed the top of her mother's head and went out the door.

Most Waiters had already gone inside when Tansy reached the large double doors of the central building, taken from the Clarity Hall in the Embroid city of Falton. Furniture, tapestries, and sacred texts had been brought and set in place during the last months of preparation. Right before launch, families had simply journeyed to the ship every three days to attend the Waits.

Father Sharood dipped his head, his vermillion hood slipping over his eyes, as she walked by. "Good Waiting to you, Daughter Tansy."

"And good Waiting to you, Father Sharood. Gratitude and reverence."

She found it remarkable that the Opulence, the men and women responsible for the upkeep of the Clarity Hall, were unable to sense the power she possessed. Mother had explained it was always so with an Emergent in past generations. Somehow, they could shield their powers, but even so, Emergents lived dangerous lives. While some, like her great-grandmother, had gone on to serve kings and leaders, many others had been assassinated by jealous family members or other Kindred who hoped the inheritance of power would be passed to another, more deserving soul.

Straggling Waiters moved around her, unhurried strides belied by the frenzied thoughts filling their minds, like schools of fishes rushing downstream. No one wanted to arrive last in the Clarity, to become a disturbance to the precious peace, held above everything else in their lives.

A familiar thought pattern caught her attention, and she brushed her hood aside.

Aunt Cora and Uncle Tam shuffled past, their two young sons trailing behind them.

"Good waiting, Aunt Cora," Tansy murmured.

Aunt Cora paused and turned, giving her a quick smile. She smoothed her robe over a belly swollen with child. Her lovely face was a painful reminder of Tansy's mother's past beauty, as they were twins. "Good waiting, Tansy. How is my sister?"

"The same," said Tansy. A sudden thought came to her. "Would you be able to check in on her tomorrow? I must go on a journey."

Aunt Cora's eyes snapped. "A journey? Wherever to, my dear? Has a Tark requested a healing potion?" An eager light, similar to Griffin's, brightened her eyes.

Tansy remembered the letter's caution not to share the contents. "Something like that."

Her aunt opened her mouth, closed it again, and shrugged. "Of course. I'll check on my sister. I've been meaning to stop by for a visit."

A clash of cymbals sounded inside the building, and the outside stragglers moved through the door, their robes brushing the floor like so many brooms.

Tansy allowed herself to be swept in by the human wave. She found her way to the cushion with her name embroidered on the top and sat, cross-legged, her robe tucked beneath her knees.

Five musicians played at the front of the building. Harp, drums, cymbals, flute, and lyre. Five women dressed in white tunics swayed to the rhythm in a hypnotic dance, hands outstretched.

Golden walls shone over the congregation. To Tansy's left was a stained-glass window depicting the yellows, blues, and whites of the rounded sun, while to the right, purple, pink, and white pieces of glass formed a crescent moon.

In the center of the room rose a marble carving. A pair of white hands, five times larger than life, held a bright blue globe. A reminder that Spirit would never allow the human race to die out.

Chalk scrawlings covered the entire west wall. Embroids wrote of their needs, illnesses of family members, and general hopes and dreams. "My health" stood out in pink letters, written by Lanis's careful hand.

Tansy closed her eyes and prayed. She prayed for the needs written on the wall and her mother. Lastly, she concentrated on the morrow's journey. As she did, the thoughts of others invaded her mind. Mostly prayers like the ones she'd composed. But swirling throughout, like ink in milk, were darker thoughts of lust, mayhem, even murder. She'd learned long ago that everyone possessed evil thoughts, even moon-faced Father Sharood. They couldn't be held against anyone. Out of respect, she struggled to push them away and focus on her own wonderings.

What would happen in the headship? Could Zephyr know that I am the Emergent?

"You will tell him." The Voice she knew so well sounded in her spirit.

Tansy knew better than to ask questions. She waited.

"He will help you. The walls will crumble, and you must twist away."

Tansy snorted in frustration, so loudly that the people sitting closest to her gave her curious looks.

She smiled an apology and closed her eyes again. *Tell him? Tell who?* She couldn't imagine telling anyone of her gift.

When she shifted her foot it prickled, and she wiggled her toes, trying to bring the feeling back without making too much of a stir.

For the final thirty minutes of the Wait, she kept still, straining to hear, praying for a vision, for more. But after the first speaking, she heard nothing. It was the quietest Waiting she could ever remember.

The gong finally sounded, rung by a girl so tiny she could barely swing the hammer. The people rose as if one, quietly moving out, in case one more word was spoken into their minds. No one wanted to miss anything.

If a person heard an important word, they were encouraged to meditate at home for a time, speak to Father Sharood, and bring it before the congregation at the next Waiting. This rarely occurred, but when it did, the words mostly consisted of love and affirmation for the Embroid Kindred as a whole. Tansy could still remember the day four congregation members had cried out at once, one of them being her mother, when they'd received visions of the supernova. They'd informed the Prime Minister of the Capital city of Predica, who'd ignored them until, months later, his astronomers had confirmed their fears.

That was before she'd known of her giftings, for those had not manifested so powerfully until she'd reached her teens.

Tansy staggered home. Most Embroids reported feeling refreshed and renewed by their time of Waiting, but Tansy always felt like a deflated balloon.

No time to rest. I must prepare for tomorrow.

5
Mushrooms

Camp awoke to a furry paw patting his cheek.

"MORM MORM MORM."

He stared into Smirk's bright eyes.

The small creature chirruped and tugged at his hair.

Camp yawned. "Why do you always insist on waking me twenty minutes before I'm actually supposed to be awake?"

Smirk chattered louder and gave a meaningful glance at the dwelling.

"I know, I know. You're hungry. But you're always hungry."

Camp stuck a leg out of his hammock, struggling for coherent thought. *Why am I outside? Did we fumigate for lamp roaches again?* A light snapped on inside his dwelling and everything flooded back to him. *Dashner and family. Right.*

Sitting up, he smoothed back his hair. He hoped there'd be enough water left from his allotment for a rinse-off shower.

Probably. If anything, these people didn't seem selfish.

Wonder what Tansy's doing? The thought rose unbidden, and he allowed his thoughts to drift to her. The warmth of her smile. The brightness of her hair.

"Good morning."

He raised his head to see Persneep's wizened face peeping over the fence.

"Why are you sleeping out here?" Persneep asked, pulling his beard from the top of the fence where it had become snagged in a rusted forcebot claw.

The best way to avoid answering a question? Ask one. "Are you standing on something?" Camp asked, walking to the fence line and peering over it.

Persneep's head bobbed up and down. "Let me in. I have a delivery for you."

Instead of following the little man's demands, Camp opened the gate and went outside. *No need for Persneep to barge in here and grill the family first thing in the morning. I'm sure they don't need the added stress. Plus he might see that Darse Engine I scavenged last week and demand it for the common Cholter good.*

Camp closed the gate with a satisfying clang before the little man could glimpse the contents of his yard. "So, what do you have for me?"

Persneep licked his lips and pulled an envelope from the recesses of his bright purple robe. "A summons from the headship."

He handed it to Camp.

"Wow, my name's written on the front." Camp flipped the envelope over and frowned. The seal had been broken, the flap loose. He glared at Persneep.

"Eh, it was open when it arrived. I thought it was for me," Persneep stammered.

"Sure, because the names Persneep and Camp look so much alike, right?" asked Camp. "Pretty lousy of you, but what should I expect?"

"As ship's magistrate, I have a right to know–"

"When a letter is marked private? Sure you do. Thanks for bringing it by." Camp went through the gate and slammed it in Persneep's face.

He scanned the contents of the letter, a shroud of gloom thickening over him with every word. He sat down heavily on his hammock. *Why in the world would Captain Zephyr invite me to a meeting? Could news of the refugees have reached the headship so quickly? Could this be about Smirk? She chose me from thousands of people. Something else is going on here.* His entire life had been about living under the radar. Doing enough to get by, but never creating a noticeable fuss. Maybe if he'd been born into another kindred he would have become an officer. Or even a teacher. But he'd accepted his place and tried to make the best of it. Suddenly the world was tipping, the weight slipping to one side. *What if everything falls apart?*

He stuffed the envelope in his pocket and picked his way through the stacks of machinery, piled plastic bits, and empty containers.

The sizzle of frying food met his ears as he walked through his front door, and a delicious aroma filled his home.

Dashner was at the cooking unit, stirring a pot of oatmeal, while Jayne fried something in a pan.

"Are those ... mushrooms?" asked Camp. "Didn't think we could grow them here. Maybe on the Bloomwarth's ship, but they'd never make it through the other ships without being pounced on by someone else."

"We brought them," said Dashner. "One of the few things we had left, but they were dehydrated. Wouldn't taste that great without water to fluff them up."

"How long did you go without water again?" Camp asked.

Jayne turned, eyes wide. "In the last days, we managed to gather a few drops of condensation from the storage tanks. We were trying to figure out ways to produce more, but the system had failed. Without knowing if we'd have the power to dock with the ship–" she pressed her fingers against her cheeks. "I don't want to think about it. We're here now, and that's what counts."

Raven scooted over to Camp, holding the doll that Candy had given her. "Thank you for the dolly," she said, her words coming out with a slight lisp due to a missing front tooth.

"You can thank my neighbor for that," said Camp, tampering

down the anxiety clawing at his soul. "And here's a sewing kit." He plucked a packet off a shelf and handed it to Dashner. "I'm not super handy with a needle and thread, but if you'd like to repair the doll's arm you can give it a try."

"On it," said Dashner. "Raven, let's fix your toy."

Camp remembered his summons and pulled the envelope from his pocket. He tapped it against his hand. "Listen, folks, I don't want to cause any alarm, but I've just received a summons from the headship. I'll have to journey through the ships all the way to the headship early tomorrow morning."

Dashner's mouth fell open. "A summons? No offense, but for a Cholter? Does that happen often?"

"Only for our magistrate, as far as I know," said Camp. "And he never goes. I am curious to see what they want." *And why they chose me.*

Dashner frowned. "Do you think it's about us?"

Camp shrugged. "I doubt the captain would have time to prepare correspondence in this ancient form and send it through six ships since you docked on the Serpentine yesterday. I'm flummoxed. Why did she choose me? Will there be other Cholters there? I don't know. I'm not supposed to discuss it with anyone else." He put his hand over his mouth in mock concern. "Oops. Well, everyone on this ship will know about it anyway, since Persneep read the letter. He possesses the loosest lips of anyone I know."

Jayne reached out and touched Camp's hand. "Please don't

mention us. I know you can't do anything if they already know."

Camps shoulders sagged. "Look, I am happy to assist you folks. People helped me when my father died and I was left on my own at twelve years old. But there are trackbots and small screens and other means of watching us that we don't even know about. Hundreds of ways the headship keeps tabs on us. We've been assured that every tracking tool has been revealed to all Kindreds, but no one here believes that. And we don't really care. We just want to get to Fortress and carve out a new village for ourselves."

He took a bite of mushrooms, savoring the new flavor. "Pretty good for dried rations."

Jayne nodded. "The mushrooms are my favorite. I hope I can find someone who grows them."

"Like I said, you can check the Bloomwraiths, or maybe the Embroids." Camp's thoughts went to Tansy and her greenhouse. "I know someone to ask."

Jayne's face brightened. "That would be nice. I might try to cultivate them when we get settled."

Dasher looked up from his work, needle in hand. "Don't count on them giving us our own place, Jayne. They might throw us in the brig."

Why would he jump to that conclusion? Camp pressed his lips together. "I really don't see that happening. The headship has left most rules and laws up to each Kindred, and you've met our leader. As long as nothing threatens the survival of all, and as long as each ship continues to contribute their part, the headship doesn't interfere. Which is why I still have Smirk."

At the sound of his name, the Mootrat climbed up his arm and settled on his shoulder, chattering as though he was contributing to the conversation.

Camp gave him a bite of oatmeal.

Smirk smashed it between his paws, then threw it into Dashner's hair.

"Smirk! Behave yourself!" said Camp.

Dashner sighed and pulled the brown goo from his hair. "I suppose there's nothing to do but lay low here and wait things out. Jayne and I have much to talk about."

"Yes, we never planned out what we'd do when we arrived," said Jayne. "Truth is, we didn't think we'd get here."

"Perhaps if you'd tell me why you're nervous about discovery," said Camp. "I could try talking to the captain, or at least approach her team."

"Sorry, I'm not ready to do that," said Dashner.

Camp held up his hands. "Fine. Well, you all take care. Help yourself to whatever scraps you can find. I have work to do today. Tomorrow, I leave at first lights."

"So early?" said Dashner.

"I have no idea how long it will take me to get through the six ships. Each one has its own set of regulations. I've only been as far as the Tarks."

Dashner squinted one eye. "That's what, third from here?"

Camp held up a hand. "The order is as follows: Cholters, Embroids, Tarks, Ortemps, Bloomwarths, Grindshims, and of course, the headship."

"I still can't believe they talked the Tarks into coming." Jayne shook her head.

"The mystery is really why they didn't put their ship on the end," said Camp. "If they decide to part off, three ships will drift away into space, and there's nothing we can do about it."

Jayne wrinkled her nose. "I thought each ship possessed its own navigation system."

"Maybe," said Camp. "But what good would that be if we have no idea where we're going? Most of us don't even have our own team of pilots or techs. Most of our food is provided by other ships, and the Grimshims control the forcebots and air circulation systems for everyone."

Dashner pursed his lips. "They made sure everyone would have to rely on each other. But high emotions can be deadly to rational thought."

Jayne patted her husband on the shoulder. "Perhaps we should go on to the headship with Camp. Might be safer."

"Not yet," said Dashner.

"Well, you folks can stay put for now," said Camp. "As for me, I suppose I'll find the reason for all of this by tomorrow."

6

Tether Trip

Tansy's feet ached, and her pack, too stuffed to fit in the tiniest extra pea, hung heavy on her shoulder.

Takes at least three hours to get there and back. I'd better gather my gumption, as Mother says.

The Embroid woman standing at the tether controls smiled as she walked into the tether station. "Tansy Pellum? I've been expecting you. I'm Nimcy." She gave the customary greeting, two curled hands beneath her chin. "I hear you're going all the way to the headship."

Tansy returned the greeting. "Yes. Have you been there?"

Nimcy shook her head. "Not yet, but I'd like to go someday. My duties give me little time for site-seeing." Her smile brightened a watt. "I hear you're in charge of a greenhouse."

"Yes, the smallest one," Tansy replied, trying to decide if Nimcy was making kind idle chatter or if she was being judgmental of Tansy's decision to neglect her duties. "I'll only be gone for the day. Should return before light fade." *Hopefully.* Now that Tansy thought about it, the captain's letter hadn't mentioned the time of her return. She shrugged. Aunt Cora knew to check in on her mother, while a neighbor had been asked to water the plants. She could always contact them through the comwatch if she needed help for a longer time.

The tether doors slid open. "Should be a smooth ride," said Nimcy. "Have fun."

Her words and tone remained warm, but Tansy still felt a slight sting of guilt. *The captain requested me. Me, of all people. What could she possibly want?* Fear welled up once more, and she pushed it back. *I'm not allowing my adventure to be spoiled by something that might not even be true.*

Two rows of cushioned seats met her eyes in the tether car. She counted ten sets, all empty. She sank into the first one and waited, wondering how long the ride would take. The last several years of school had been filled with details about the ships and what the Kindreds could expect, as they'd waited for the completed construction and prepared for the long journey. But she'd never been interested in the mechanics of such things and her mind had wandered during topics like tether-tube length.

The car moved forward with a gentle tug. A quiet hum surrounded her. No windows lined the sides of the vehicle; she was completely enclosed, like the lifts in tall buildings back home. The whole journey reminded her of a lift, except longer, and sideways instead of up and down.

She closed her eyes and pushed her extra senses, straining for a glimpse at what was to come. But today the future was a dark and formless void.

Tansy forgot to check her comwatch at the start of the journey, but the trip didn't last long. The car halted and she rose. *Next time I need to pay better attention so I'll know how long it will take to get back home.*

She'd been told the length of the journey would depend on what she'd find with the different Kindreds. What moods they were in, which officials were running the tether tubes, and their general attitudes of the day.

The Tark who waited in the next tether station was wholly different from anyone she'd ever met, on the ship or back home, but she wasn't completely shocked; she'd seen pictures of Tarks in her schoolbooks.

The man was about her height, with wide muscular shoulders, his chest completely bare except for a fur slung over his shoulder. His hair, bright white like most of the Tarks, gleaned in the station lights, and several thick-lined tattoos made from green ink ran over his arms and bare shoulders, each design comprised of sharp angles and grimacing creatures she'd never heard of.

"Hello," she said. "I'm Tansy Pellum. I'm passing through to the headship."

The man said nothing, only glared and smashed a button at his console with a meaty fist. He nodded to a cushioned bench by the ship's entrance.

Oh dear. She sat where indicated. *I hope this doesn't take long.*

The ship's double doors opened, and a woman stalked into the tether station. She also wore the usual Tark raiment, except her dress was much more elaborate, with patterns of emerald and purple beads on the light tan material. The dress fell to her knees, ending in a thick ruff of white fur. Perhaps ermine, one of the many species of animals the Tarks raised.

The woman raised a severely painted eyebrow at Tansy. "You seek passage through our ship?" she said in a low but commanding voice.

"Yes, if you please," said Tansy. "The headship has requested me."

The woman shrugged, her long silver braids, which had been fashioned in a sort of crown around her head, shaking. "We do not concern ourselves with things of the headship here. However, there is no other way but through." She peered at Tansy, looking her over. "You may go," she said. "My guards will escort you to the next tether station."

"Oh, I'm sure that's not necessary," Tansy said. "It's pretty much the same layout as the Embroid ship. I shouldn't have trouble finding my way."

The woman folded her arms. "I am Chieftess Lahara. If I say there will be guards, there will be guards. Besides, you may face dangers. Some of our animals roam freely, and the guards can handle them if you happen to meet up with say, a gork, one of the giant pigs." She tilted her head. "Do you know how to deal with a gork encounter?"

Heat rose to Tansy's cheeks. "I beg your pardon, ma'am. I'm sure I would have no idea what to do."

"My daughter is already on her way to the tether station, or I would send you with her," said the chieftess. She waved at the door. "Now you will go."

Tansy scurried through the door, feeling like a scolded schoolgirl. *Her daughter? Does she mean her daughter is going to the same requested meeting?* But she didn't dare press the matter.

As she walked into the main ship's gridwork, a rush of new thoughts and emotions overwhelmed her mind, coming from the swarming crowds that moved along the paths. This always happened when she'd gone to other villages or towns. She took deep breaths. Her fingers crept to her life beads, and she focused on each event, attempting to picture each day as they'd happened, until the crashing waves died down to the usual dull ache that always settled there.

The two guards waiting for her near the doors were dressed much like the tether operator, though the choices of fur and necklaces were different, and one wore a tall hat embellished with a pair of antlers from an unknown beast. The first man gave her a nod, his face void of expression, then turned and began to move through the ship. As she followed, the second soldier matched their stride a few steps behind.

Animal odors filled the ship, though not to an unbearable point. Children who looked to be in their teens and younger scurried through the paths with brooms, shovels and buckets. *Must be the reason the place looks so clean.* Even still, she watched the ground, and had to detour around a few foul-smelling piles of manure.

A great beast bellowed from several dwellings over, and this was answered by a cacophony of bleats, roars, and clucks.

How can they stand the noise and odors? They must be used to it.

The first soldier turned to face her. "We will walk through our market now. You are permitted to buy things, but do not take long in your selection."

"Oh, I don't have any mon–" she began, but the guard had already swiveled on his heel and was moving forward once more.

The construction of the market booths would have made Camp, that Cholter man, proud. They were haphazard, some leaning to the side, all made of various ship materials like thick cables and sheeted plastic. A line of crafted pouches swayed above a young man's head, while a stout woman held out a bowl of meat, the heavy spices singeing Tansy's nose.

"You." A raspy voice came from a small umber tent. "Girl, come to me."

Tansy looked around but saw no one else.

"Yes, you with the sunshine hair. Come here."

She glanced at the first guard, who gave a swift nod.

Crouching down, she lifted the tent flap and scooted inside. Her eyes adjusted to the thick darkness.

A tiny light appeared, then brightened as a lamp was lit with natural fire. The gnarled face of a very old woman peered at her.

"There you are, dear. I have been waiting a very long time." The woman cackled. "You're special, aren't you?"

Tansy swallowed. "I'm Tansy Pellum, ma'am. And I'm just an Embroid. Maybe you thought I was someone else?"

"No, no, I know who you are. I could feel it the moment you stepped on this ship. I've always had the gift of feelings, you see. Passed down from my father's side."

Is this true? Do other Kindreds have special gifts? Tansy had never even considered the possibility. Yes, Embroids were aware that other Kindreds worshiped Spirit, but their rituals were all wrong. Especially the wild Tarks, who were considered pagan at best. *But if Spirit made every Kindred, why wouldn't he give them all gifts? If this woman can discern who I am . . .* sweat beaded on her forehead.

As if reading her thoughts, the woman gave a dry chuckle. "Do not worry, Tansy of the Pellums. Your secret won't leave the walls of this tiny tent. But I have something for you."

She pulled out a round object and placed it in Tansy's hand.

Tansy squinted at it in the dim light. A scarlet flower with thin, tendril-like petals had been embedded in a clear material, maybe glass. The whole object was perfectly round and maybe two inches long.

"A poppinwinkle," said the woman. "The last of them withered away decades ago. But my grandmother had this one preserved somehow."

Tansy turned the smooth stone over in her hands. Such trinkets were rare; most had disappeared or been repurposed long ago. Something like this would be worth a fortune back on Gyron, maybe the cost of a family transport vehicle.

"Why would you give me something so precious?" she said.

The old woman shrugged. "My family chose to stay behind. I have no one of my blood remaining. So I decided to give it to someone with an understanding of our Creator. Of our gifts. We must unify, Tansy Pellum. The journey ahead is far more dangerous than anyone could know. Surely you have felt this."

Tansy gave a sharp nod, then remembered the guards outside, "Thank you. I will treasure it always. I must go for now, but maybe I'll come through again and visit with you, if that's all right."

The woman gave a hoarse laugh. "I would like that."

Fresh air wafted over Tansy's skin as she exited the stuffy little tent. She tucked the stone in her pocket and nodded to the guards. "I'm ready to go."

###

The Ortemp's ship was much plainer and drabber than the colorful home of the Tarks. The gray, cookie-cutter dwellings had been left pretty much as they'd been created. The mechs the Ortemp people were known for squatted in enormous mechanical heaps on the far side of the ship, towering above all else.

Tansy walked through the grid paths undisturbed, though a few children stopped to stare at her before being admonished by adult guardians. Tansy found it difficult not to gawk in return, for some of the children had mechanical limbs, and one little girl's stare was partially made up of a mechanical eye, glowing from a face of flesh.

The Ortemp people had dealt with a genetic disorder running through the Kindred that caused people to be born with missing limbs and other disfigurements. Over time, they had developed cybernetics to 'fix' these maladies. The mechs had been created as part of a long-ago feud with the Tarks, but both sides had declared peace long ago. These mechs had been repurposed for use once they reached Fortress.

Tansy shuddered as a man clanked past on two mechanical legs. *I'd rather be blind or limbless. Not being faced with the situation, I can think that way. But what if something happened to me?*

As she moved to the Bloomwraith's tether station, she checked her watch. *Still making good time.* She was glad she'd left an hour earlier than the prescribed schedule.

The Bloomwraith's ship was best of all.

She stepped out of the tether station, into an earthy, humid space. Inhaling deeply, she smiled. The greenhouses on her ship were nice, but nothing compared to the tree-lined path before her. *I wish Mother could have come.* She would have loved to see the growing things, the full-height willows and oaks and elms, and the vines flowing over the pathways and dwellings in such a tangle she could barely see the ceiling in places. She'd heard that the first thing the Bloomwraiths had done when given their ship five years ago was to begin the growing process, for they refused to fly through space without their beloved forest surrounding them. Bees buzzed past her, and a bright yellow butterfly fluttered by.

The Bloomwraiths were a solemn people, dressed in plain, earth-colored robes. Men and women alike let their long hair flow over their shoulders or fastened it at their necks in tight rolls. None of them wore hats.

Most of them nodded and smiled as she passed. The Embroids and Bloomwraiths were mostly friendly with each other, as both Kindreds celebrated a simple life and the love of growing things.

Finally, the Grimshim ship. *Hard to believe I'm going to have to do this all over again tonight.* Tansy's feet already ached, and it was with a grateful heart she slid into the cushioned tether car seat.

The Grimshim's ship was much like the Ortemps. Not a leaf or twig was to be seen. No rocks, wood, or plants decorated the outsides of the people's home pods. Children walked by, their eyes fixed on screens grasped in their hands. The sounds of chatter and laughter, which had filled the other four ships, had been replaced by hums and beeps of various machines.

Tansy crept through the crowd, attempting to escape notice, but it was hard to do in her very obvious Embroid robe and hood. Despite her worry, her presence didn't seem to create much of a stir. Perhaps because this ship was closest to the Headship, and they were more accustomed to seeing people from a variety of Kindreds. Her feet carried her through the ship quickly.

A woman beckoned to her from the tether door. Her long, white robe was gathered at one shoulder by a purple jeweled clasp.

"Tansy Pellum? Good to see you. I have been instructed to direct you to the tether room on the other side. I am from a small Kindred called the Mornsgrobes. Once you reach the tether station, your guide will be waiting for you."

The woman gestured to the large, transparent door, orange lights pulsing around the edges. "This tether craft is larger and faster than the ones in the other tubes, so please do not be alarmed. Once you've arrived, a guide will be provided to lead you to the meeting area."

"Thank you."

This tether craft was much larger than the ones she'd used earlier that day. The windows revealed three decks, filled with seats, instead of the usual one. Tansy's stomach jumped with excitement and curiosity. *I'm going to the headship.* She closed her eyes and allowed herself a teensy moment to revel in the new experiences she'd had throughout the day.

The tether craft jolted to a halt, and the doors slid open.

7
Moody Meeting

A towering man, even taller than Camp, stood inside this check-in room. He wore the smart blue and silver uniform of a headship soldier, but his muscular arms were bare and the ornate silver insignia on his shoulder told of a high rank.

Tansy was accustomed to seeing soldiers dressed in this fashion. At the beginning of the voyage, many were stationed on the Embroid ship to guide people through the grids and help them learn how to use the ship controls and check the life-support systems. But after the Kindred had been sufficiently tutored, they'd returned to the headship and left the Embroids alone. Which, she suspected, suited Father Sharood and the other elders just fine.

"Welcome, Tansy Pellum." The man held out a hand, smiling beneath his thick black and silver beard. "I am Commander Bradstorm Helms."

I've seen this man before. In pictures. He was Captain Zephyr's second in command. *This meeting must be even more important than I thought. But what on earth would they want with me? Unless they've discovered my powers. What else could it be? I was foolish to come.* She gripped the strap of her pack and glanced back at the tether doors.

Commander Helms cleared his throat. "I can assure you, there is nothing to fear. We are glad you have come and will try not to keep you too long today. Everyone on the Embroid ship has important duties, and greenhouse tending is among the most vital."

Am I the only one on the seven ships that doesn't know everyone's job?

As the man led her to a control panel and entered a code, she strained to read his thoughts, to discover why she'd been summoned to this meeting. But, as generally happened when anxious, all thoughts were murky, running into those from her own mind. She huffed in frustration.

Commander Helms turned, raising an eyebrow. "The wait won't be long. Three others have already arrived. They are anxious to meet you."

Tansy exhaled. *That woman on the Tark ship. She said she had special giftings as well. Were the people here also chosen for their giftings? Why would the Embroid elders say that no other Kindred possessed them?*

The door slid open to reveal a pleasant moss-green hallway, lit by pale yellow lights along the ceiling. Somewhere, water trickled, and Tansy craned her neck, searching for the origin. There, along the wall. A copper water fountain with an abstract sculpture, a glowing, fluid shape.

She wondered idly if it held some religious symbolism. In the Embroid culture, every design had purpose, from the patterning of their clothes to the carved trim on chairs and tables.

Perhaps they keep it because it's pretty, and no other reason. In school she'd learned that many of the kindreds created art for aesthetic purposes alone.

Suddenly she felt naive and ignorant and twelve years old. She shook her head and continued to follow the man through a smaller door, this one not locked by a panel.

The spacious room stretched larger than any tether station. Three people sat among overstuffed sofas and chairs. A center table, ornately carved, held an assortment of beverages and snacks, some Tansy recognized, but many she did not.

"Please, make yourself comfortable." Commander Helms gestured to a chair. "Help yourself to any refreshments. The last two members of this group should be here momentarily, and then we will all go to the captain's meeting room. Captain Zephyr wanted you to have a chance to encounter each other before you met with her. Please let me know if I can do anything else for you. I'll return in a moment." He bowed and went out the door.

In the Embroid kinship, one only dipped a head to those in higher stations. Tansy shook away the strangeness of having such an important man bow to her, gave his retreating figure a quick two-handed Embroid salute, and went to the refreshment trays. She selected a round, pink cake from the table and a cup of clear, purple liquid. *Might be grape juice.* She'd tried it once, at a family holiday. She chose a chair to perch in and surveyed the other people in the room.

A petite girl with short dark hair and a tattooed snake running up her slender wrist caught her eye and waved. "Glindel. From the Grimshims."

Tansy smiled. "Tansy. Embroid."

Glindel nodded. "I thought so."

The hulking young man across from them shuffled his feet. "Tracer. Ortemps."

A second girl shifted on the edge of her seat, her eyes darting from side to side, as though looking for a means of escape. Her head jerked slightly as she surveyed the room, long white braids jumping with the movements. She didn't seem like the sort of person who'd offer any information about herself. She wore a Tark-style dress. *Must be the daughter of the chieftess. Makes sense that she'd be among the chosen; at least she has ties to important people.*

The door slid open, and Commander Helms entered. "Our final two have arrived. Camp, Falstaff, please choose something to eat and sit wherever you'd like."

A short young man with bright green hair shuffled to the refreshments tray, grabbed a plate of cakes, and slid into a corner chair.

Camp entered the room, bright eyes taking in his surroundings. His dreads were slicked back into a ponytail, and his arms dangled easily by his sides. He did not go for the snack tray.

Tansy sat straight in her chair, her hands tingling around her glass. *The Cholter with the mootrat.* She'd guessed, of course, that a Cholter would be among the group since there seemed to be a representative from each ship. *But what are the odds?*

Camp sat across from her. Their eyes met, and he gave her a wink.

Behind his nonchalant air, she sensed it. *Why, he's afraid. Even more than me.* She crossed her arms. *Probably worried they'll take away his pet. Hope he didn't have the nerve to bring it with him.*

Commander Helms opened his hands. "We will be leaving for the captain's meeting room momentarily. Please know you are most welcome, and no one here has been called in for admonishment."

There was a whooshing sound as several people let out sighs of relief.

Tansy was one of them.

"I'll be right back." Once more, Commander Helms left the room.

Tansy took another sip of her drink. "Does anyone know what kind of juice this is?" she said in a desperate attempt to break the silence. Feelings had begun to sort themselves out of the massive tangle, and her mind needed a distraction from the scramble of thoughts that would undoubtedly invade.

"You've never tried it?" Glindel's eyes widened. "It's ton-fizz. I thought everyone had access to drinks like this."

"Embroids are careful about what they put in their bodies, much like Bloomwraiths," the young man with green hair said. He nodded at Tansy. "You are an Embroid, right?"

"Yes," said Tansy. "You're a Bloomwraith? You don't dress like one."

"Name's Falstaff." The guy shrugged. "And yeah, I'm different."

"Why are any of you surprised about the drink?" Camp spoke up. "Everyone knows some ships have better access to certain types of food than others. It's not like life here is much different than back home." Though his words were bitter, his tone was level and matter of fact.

"Why are we here?" The tall girl leaned forward, her eyes glowing a jaded green. "My beasts require care. It's birthing season, and Father needs my help."

Everyone glanced at each other.

"No one knows, right?" asked Falstaff.

The tall girl rolled her eyes. "Specifically, why is HE here?" She pointed to Tracer.

Tracer straightened his shoulders and lifted his chin. "Look, if I knew, I'd tell you. Besides, I have the same right to be here as you do."

The tall girl sniffed. "Everyone knows Ortemps can't be trusted. I'm surprised you were able to get away. I thought you'd be too busy oiling your children."

Tracer squinted at her, the muscles in his cheek tightening. "Our mechs and cybernetics will be vital for everyone when we reach

Fortress." He wrinkled his nose. "I'm also wondering how you came to be here. I thought you'd be shoveling dung. Maybe even rolling in it."

The tall girl leaped to her feet, knocking over the refreshment table. Food scattered and drinks splashed over the beautiful furniture.

"I am Kafla, daughter of the Tark leaders," she said, fists trembling at her sides. "You will not speak to me in such a manner."

Tracer rose as well, revealing that he was almost as tall as Kafla. "You spoke the insults first." He folded his arms against his chest.

Kafla screamed out a slur and grabbed his arm. She let go just as quickly. "A cyborg abomination! How could they allow you here with all of us?" Her hand went to an empty sheath at her side, which Tansy assumed usually held a weapon.

Tansy shot Camp a look. *What should we do? Isn't someone watching us?*

Camp stretched and rose slowly. "Take a look around, Kafla. Quite a collection of souls have been assembled here, and we are all uncertain why, unless someone is lying. There's no need to call names."

"Filthy Cholter." Kafla spat on the floor. "How dare you speak directly to me."

"Fine." Camp turned to Tansy. "Miss Tansy, can you please tell Miss Kafla here that there's no need to call names?"

Something warmed Tansy all the way from her head to her toes, despite the situation. *He remembered my name.* She opened her mouth to say something, she had no idea what, (though she knew it would not be a reminder to Kafla to mind her manners), but–thank Spirit–the door slid open once more and Commander Helms came back into the room.

His eyes flicked over the mess, then from Kafla to Tracer to Camp.

They all stared back, and Tansy had to suppress a giggle at the barrage of thoughts that entered her mind. Miraculously, she kept her composure.

"I trust no one needs to see a medic?" Commander Helms said.

Everyone remained quiet.

"Then please, follow me. The captain is ready for you."

He strode out the door without glancing behind him.

Falstaff followed, then Camp, Tracer and Glindel.

Tansy waited for Kafla, who nodded to her.

"I will go last," the tall girl said, adjusting her cloak. "Only a fool turns their back to an enemy."

"As long as I know where we stand," Tansy muttered.

8
The Headship

Camp pulled his jacket tighter. He wasn't expecting the tether corridor to be this cold, but the water lines whooshing above him might have something to do with it. Despite the Headship's size, this tether tunnel seemed smaller than the others. *Might be a private tube used by dignitaries and leadership only. You'd think they would find a way to heat it more effectively.*

He glanced back at Tansy, who seemed snug in her Embroid robe. For the first time he considered the practicality of such a garment. *I wonder why she's here? Coincidence? Could there be such a thing? No. But who am I to question the Creator's will to put us together again?* Something in him had brightened when he saw her in the waiting room, and he wondered if she felt the same way. *Or they brought her in as a witness against you.*

Should have gone around the room and shaken everyone's hand. Then maybe you'd know if someone was lying. He grimaced.

That Tark princess would've gladly removed his arm if he'd attempted such a thing, weapon or no weapon.

The Tether doors opened, thankfully to a burst of warm air. The group of six followed Commander Helms through several corridors that all looked the same, with no windows or decoration.

"We're going to the main lift." the Commander said over his shoulder. "For those who haven't visited the headship, this takes us up through the core. The captain's meeting room is located on the top level. Right eye, in fact."

A vision popped into Camp's head, the diagram he'd seen of the headship. The outside looked much like its namesake, the head of a serpent, with two massive observation panels on the front and a mouth-like mooring deck for the exploratory ships they planned to send out once they reached Fortress. *The Headship mooring deck is huge and would have posed no problem for a zoomer. Why did Dashner choose to take such a risk and dock on the Cholter ship?* He'd said he wanted to lay low as long as possible. The man had been hiding something. He hated to jump to the most negative conclusion, but now he regretted his blind trust. Cholter law could be quibbly in places but held no mercy for those who harbored serious criminals. *Of course, you'd have to add Persneep and Bouson to the list.*

But I took full responsibility.

The next door opened to a larger room filled with stations and screens. Soldiers in blue and silver uniforms scurried around with comscreens, adjusting knobs and levels.

"What are they doing?" asked Falstaff.

"They're in charge of making sure the tethers move smoothly, so all seven ships receive water, power, and oxygen," Glindel said. She folded her arms as everyone stared at her. "What? I'm a tech. I've been here before."

Tracer's cheek muscles tightened, but he said nothing.

Camp figured he must be upset by Glindel's advantage. But she still seemed clueless as to their reason for being there.

Why were we chosen? They were all so different. Glindel with her petite figure and crop of dark, curly hair. Tansy with her shyness and sweet spirit. The massive Tracer and his cybernetic arm. *Why could the captain have called us? Have we all amassed the same number of infractions? Will she lead us to a giant room of judgment and punish us as a group example for all the ships?*

Most of these people seemed incapable of committing a crime of any sort, except for Tracer and the Tark Princess. *I bet Kafla could run a sword through a man's gut without a second thought.*

They marched past the soldiers, who appeared far too busy to notice the rag-tag procession. *Either they were advised of our coming, or they're accustomed to the various cultures who lived on the headship, and they'd learned not to gawk.* It was a nice change after being stared at, questioned, or even roughed up by people who didn't trust Cholters, which had happened to him a few times back on the planet during his delivery days.

Wouldn't it be nice to stay here, on the headship, with people who didn't mind where I came from? He shook his head. He already lived with people like that. His people. And even if some people on the headship were accepting, it wouldn't be true across the board. That would be impossible.

The group followed Commander Helms through a door at the end of the long control room, stepping out into an open area. This, at last, seemed to be the central hub of the headship.

The group of seven milled out onto a long walkway. As one, the six newcomers moved to the polished, silver, chest-high railing, and gazed through the thick glass at the new mini-world.

Instead of being spaced out on one-level grids like the other ships, these dwellings were stacked on each other, much like the high-rise apartments found in the bigger cities of Predica and Falton. When Camp strained to see over the railing, he counted five levels below, and perhaps three on top. These modules reached up like thickened soda straws to the ceiling above.

Snaking around all these buildings were walkways and narrow tracks, where small vehicles puttered about. On the ground, barely visible, were more vehicles, and tiny little people who looked like the antique toy soldiers he'd played with as a boy.

Commander Helms came to stand beside him. "It's something, isn't it?" he said quietly. "Above the transparent levels are five more decks where more people work to keep everything running. I can't comprehend it myself."

Camp exhaled. "I knew the headship was big. They talked about it at school and showed us diagrams. But it's hard to picture until you see it."

Commander Helms clapped a hand on his shoulder. "My mother was a Cholter," he said. "Her name was Balta. Cholters don't hold well with people separating and marrying outside the group. That's why she never returned home."

Camp shrugged. "I believe the old ways hurt us more than help. I'm pleased to meet a relative, no matter how distant." He shook the commander's hand.

The corners of Commander Helm's lips turned upwards. "Mr. Camp, I think you are just the sort of person we are looking for."

Tansy, too far away to have heard their conversation, turned towards him, her forehead creased.

Camp moved to where she stood. "Hey. Good to see you. What do you think about all of this?"

Tansy bit her lip. "I don't know. I'm still wondering what we're doing here."

"I don't think we should be too worried," said Camp. "I believe it's a good thing."

"Hope so," Tansy gave a half-smile.

Stars aligned, she's beautiful.

Tansy blinked, and her cheeks reddened, just a tinge.

Wait, can she read my thoughts? Camp turned and stared out the window. She *was* an Embroid. But as far as he knew, most Embroid's could only read strong feelings. A few could possibly receive faint impressions of futuristic events, though many scoffed at such a notion. *Must have read it all over my face. Get yourself together, Camp.*

He couldn't help but send one more glance in her direction, but she had turned away to stare down the chasm.

"Time to go," Commander Helm's voice thundered across the walkway. He led them up the winding terrace to a lift, where they all squeezed inside.

Camp closed his eyes, attempting to regulate his breathing. He'd only been in a lift a few times, back on Gyron when he'd made deliveries to some of his father's richer clients in the big cities. He didn't care for enclosed spaces, and it had taken everything in his power to agree to come on board in the first place. Spaceship, or instant death? The choice had been more difficult for him than most. Thank the Creator, he'd worked through it, but being in this tiny box with six other living, breathing beings brought it all back in a rush. He felt as though a fist were squeezing his heart tight in his chest.

He took deep breaths and opened his eyes.

Tansy was closest to him. Her lips trembled, and she glanced his way, deep green eyes filling with concern.

"Are you alright?" she whispered.

"Yeah, yeah. Just don't like lifts," he answered.

"Here." She pushed up his sleeve above his leather glove, grasped his bare arm, and closed her eyes.

His fingers tingled at her touch, and he fought the impulse to pull her closer. A peace flooded through him. Along with this peace came the knowledge that he could trust this girl completely. But he'd already felt that from the moment he'd seen her in the greenhouse last week.

Her eyes opened and she smiled. "Feel better?"

He nodded. "What did you do?"

"Prayed for Spirit to fill you with peace. Do you wait for Spirit? Embroids do."

He tilted his head. "If you mean Creator's Spirit, some Cholters still believe. Many turned away at the great separation. Still more left the faith when the sunblast was discovered. As for me ..."

He was interrupted by the great sliding doors.

Tansy pulled her hand away. "We can talk later. I want to hear more."

"Me too," said Camp, as they swept out of the confining box. "I mean, I want to know more about you as well."

This last sentence was caught by Falstaff, who nudged him with a pointy elbow. "That Embroid's a pretty girl, even swathed in those thick robes, isn't she?"

Camp pressed his lips into a thin line. *Pretty isn't even close.*

Commander Helms stopped outside of a shimmering silver door, bordered by flashing lights that glowed on the hall walls. A tank filled with a variety of fish, stingrays, and sharks filled one wall from floor to ceiling. The hum of the pump vibrated through the air, and the aquarium lights sent rippled patterns across the walls and floor.

Camp set his jaw to keep it from dropping. Most of the swimming creatures were descendants from Earth. He only recognized three that were native to Gyron, as most species from the two planets were incompatible and would war to the death, no matter what size or type they were. From what he'd read, the headship had brought along hundreds of aquatic species, so this must be only one tank of many.

These fish swam in peace, with no thought of the chaos surrounding them. The swirls of colors and patterns mesmerized him, and he wished he could watch them all day. Aside from a goldfish a childhood friend had owned and the fish they caught in the feeding tanks; he'd never seen anything like them. *Will they survive once we reach Fortress?*

"We have arrived." Captain Helms announced. "I'll make sure the captain is ready to see you now."

He disappeared through the door.

Camp watched the colorful forms as they swished by. Blues, reds, yellows. Fish of all colors and sizes. *If they can live together in that small tank, then why can't we make it through one year? Once we get to Fortress, we can spread out again. At least that's what they say.* A cold doubt filtered into his mind, but he couldn't put his finger on the reason. When Commander Helms had touched his shoulder, he'd sensed an unease. *These people are hiding something. Something big.* The same feeling had entered his mind every time the leadership appeared on a view screen, especially the three members of the Solstice.

The doors slid open at last, and they entered the room.

9
Captain's Table

Camp blinked in the cool light, made up of blues and purples instead of the stark white of the hallways. A large silver desk sat to the right, along with shelves of books, vases, and smaller fish tanks. The left section of the room was taken up by a glass table, edged in silver and in the shape of a half-moon. On the outside of the crescent, in the center, stood a woman Camp recognized from the screens on every ship and in every home. The face who'd addressed everyone on first launch and briefed them for every important milestone and event.

Captain Zephyr was shorter than he'd thought she'd be, even tinier than Tansy or Glindel. Shoulder-length hair as black as space matched the color of her large eyes, rimmed with dark lashes. A firm smile was accented by high cheekbones. From what Camp understood of Earth, her ancestors were from a country called India. Of course, such things were long gone from daily consideration. Her

Gyron Kindred were called Kimsta, and only a small number remained.

As the group filed in, Captain Zephyr indicated the blue, cushioned chairs on the inner rim of the crescent. "Welcome. Find a seat and get comfortable. We may be here a while."

Camp stole a look at Tansy, but her eyes were fixed on the captain.

Everyone chose a seat. Kafla folded her long legs beneath her, perching on the edge in a crow-like fashion, like in the previous room.

The captain gave her a slanted glance but said nothing.

After everyone had seated themselves, Captain Zephyr glanced around.

"Everyone settled? Good. Bradstorm, are we ready?"

Commander Helms bowed. "Marrow and Crenth are inspecting the aviary today."

The captain lifted her chin. "And Platmoth?"

"Finalizing his report on the L-4."

"Good. And we have fully checked this room for listening devices and disabled every feed? I don't care for the Solstice to know what we're discussing today."

Commander Helms scratched his jaw. "I don't think they'd ever guess."

"That's true." Captain Zephyr exhaled sharply and smiled, wincing. "Oh, that rib needs another go-over from the bone-mend scanner. Remind me to talk to the doctor."

What happened to the captain? Surely if she'd been seriously injured the ships should have been informed. Camp shifted in his seat.

Commander Helms lifted his comwatch and pulled up a holo screen. He typed a message and reduced the screen. "Reminder set."

Kafla cleared her throat. "Some people have beasts to care for."

Captain Zephyr gave the princess a wide smile. "Of course you do. Every member of the seven ships has an important job, and I do not take any of yours lightly. I promise not to keep you here longer than necessary. I asked you all to keep the contents of your letter a secret, but I know there are always trip ups in the delivery process. Who here received their letters with the seals intact?"

Everyone but Camp raised their hands. Heat rose to his cheeks, to his deep chagrin.

Captain Zephyr patted the screen in front of her. "No matter. The most important thing is that no one knows why you came, and if anyone asks, you've been brought here as part of an educational program designed to teach young members of each kindred about the wonders of the headship." This last part was said in a sarcastic tone.

Falstaff cleared his throat. "If I may be so bold to ask, Captain. Why are we really here?"

Captain Zephyr stared at him. "Oh, it's so very important. At least, it's my prayer that it will become important. I believe in the validity. So does Bradstorm."

Commander Helms grunted an assent.

"Anyway." She glanced around the room. "Did you all have a chance to become acquainted in the refreshment room?"

Kafla grunted. Everyone else stared down at the table.

"First of all, I beg you, implore you, not to allow what we discuss today to leave this room," said Captain Zephyr. "I realize I'm asking a lot of you. I promise I will never command you to betray your people or do anything to harm them. And I will not ask for an oath or pledge. You either choose to keep this, or you don't." She met each person's eyes. "We are in a dangerous way. The leadership on each ship has, I'm afraid, behaved as expected. They stubbornly refuse to see the importance of unity." She dipped her head. "Since the chosen leaders of the Kindreds will not listen, I have selected a new team."

Falstaff lifted a hand. "Forgive me, Captain. Wouldn't this be a betrayal of the Solstice? Since you and the commander are here, and obviously, they are not."

"It would be fair to think so," said Captain Zephyr. "I have put much thought into this meeting. Much thought and prayer. Again, I do not believe any harm will come from this assembly." Her mouth twitched up at the corner. "Have you ever heard the saying 'it's better to ask for forgiveness than permission?'"

"Sure." Falstaff shrugged. "I guess I never thought I'd hear it from the captain of seven starships."

Captain Zephyr strode along the curved side of the table, running a finger along the smooth, silver edge. "As many of you may know, I was the captain of the original zoomer sent on the slipstream to explore Fortress. Though we'd sent out exploratory probes and gathered what information we could, we ran into difficulties beyond measure. Eleven members of the team of twelve were lost. I was the only one who returned."

She paused, and silence filled the room, only broken by the never-ending hum of the ship, and the restless movements of the people waiting for her to continue.

As she glanced back up, her eyes widened, as though she'd been transported to some other faraway place, and she only now remembered her true surroundings. She blinked. "Despite this great loss, our mission was accomplished. We did find a livable planet, and in many ways, it will offer more than Gyron ever could. For instance, we discovered alien beasts on the surface, and new types of flora and fauna. These findings exceeded our wildest dreams, since we thought we would have to enrich and seed a new planet, and that would take many years, if it was even possible. On the other hand, we'll have poisons to identify, dangerous animals to fight and avoid, and the possibility of unknown sicknesses to combat. To face these challenges, we must have unity. And that, my dear friends, is something we cannot fabricate.

"Throughout history, all cultures have striven for unity. For some, the cost of unification meant allowing a dictatorship to arise and leading a culture as one, unified in fear of disobedience. As happened to the original Gyron colony two hundred years ago, some groups have attempted to branch off into smaller groups, only trusting those who believe exactly the same way." She locked eyes with Camp. "As we've found, this only leads to fractures, dividing groups into tinier pieces.

"Seven ships. Seven ships tethered. Seven ships in complete reliance on each other." She tapped her chin. "The trust must be infallible."

Glindel raised her hand. "Captain, doesn't each ship have the power to break away on its own? I mean, if the ship's elders so choose. Each ship has the schematics and the power source. It might get tight with our gardens, but we could survive. We could ride the slipstreams on our own and even arrive there faster."

Captain Zephyr gave a dry, mirthless chuckle. "Oh, I pity the elder who'd try to lead his people to Fortress by themselves. You couldn't imagine the horrors that await. None of the smaller ships are equipped to handle them. And they all know it."

"What you speak is not the truth," Kafla said in a contemptuous tone. "My parents are the leaders of the Tarks. The Tarks possess the power of the gods. They can do anything."

"With all due respect," said Captain Zephyr, folding her arms, "They cannot."

Kafla leapt from her seat, diving across the table towards the captain.

Commander Helms flew between Kafla and Captain Zephyr with remarkable speed for a man of his size, and Kafla was deposited back in her seat so fast Camp barely registered the movement.

Commander Helms stared at Kafla, his chest heaving. "I trust you will remain in your seat for the duration of this meeting."

"You are fortunate I do not have my sword," said Kafla darkly.

The commander folded his arms and leaned against the wall. "You can spend the night in the brig, if you like."

"No one is spending the night in the brig." Captain Zephyr smoothed back her hair. "I wouldn't have spoken the words if they weren't true, and I did not mean them as an insult. I respect the Tarks as I respect all the Kindreds. But take it from someone who has been there. The strongest, most capable man on our team was torn to pieces before my eyes." She brushed a slim hand over her face. "The techs wouldn't have spent an extra year perfecting the tether system if we didn't need to stay connected."

Glindel stared down at her hands. "I've always believed that separation would be suicide, especially for the lower ships." She glanced at Camp. "No offense."

"Few share your belief," muttered Tracer. "Minister Flyton gives us a lecture on how we should prepare for sudden tether-break every day."

"I didn't call you here to discuss the feasibility of such a happening, but I truly hope I've impressed upon you the importance of preventing it," said Captain Zephyr. "I'm afraid we don't have more time for me to share my war-stories, and they would bring a disheartenment to the day, so let's move on." She glanced at the door. "We must speak of other matters, and I was hoping the last member of our party would arrive before I went into it. Bradstorm, any word?"

Captain Helms glanced at his comwatch. "A lost child stopped her on the lift. It took time to locate the parents. Should be here any moment."

Camp shared confused looks with Tansy. *Who else could be coming?*

Captain Zephyr pressed her chin against steepled fingertips. "The person will have to be informed when she arrives. The main purpose of this meeting is hard to share." She gave a deep sigh. "We have reason to believe there is a saboteur among the seven ships. Several strange incidents have occurred since launch day. Most can be explained by human error or typical machine malfunction. But exactly four could only have been caused on purpose. By human interference."

"Do our leaders know of this?" asked Kalfa. "My parents ..."

"Have been informed. All of the magistrates have, though the information has not been put out for public knowledge," said Captain Zephyr. "But the leaders are glutted with the problems of their Kindreds. So far, the glitches have only affected small areas, and no human life has been lost. But things could escalate. I'm positive they will if we can't find the culprit."

"Wouldn't the forcebots catch them?" asked Glindel.

"This is someone who must know the forcebot network and every covered area," said Commander Helms. "Somehow, they've found chinks in our armor."

Camp's tongue stuck to the roof of his mouth, and his neck burned. Judging from his companions' expressions, they were just as shocked. Tansy's eyes pleaded with him to say something. *But what do I say?*

He finally rubbed his hands together, and hoped his words sounded nonchalant, "This is quite a revelation, and of course we hope you find the instigator. But it doesn't answer the most important question. Why have you called us here?"

"In hope," said Captain Zephyr. She pursed her lips and glanced at the screen in her hand. "You all have two things in common. You are between the ages of twenty and twenty-five. I need fresh new minds, unsullied by the bitterness of age."

"Okayyyy," said Tracer. His joints clinked as he flexed the fingers of his metal hand.

"And I've discovered that each of you possess a special skill, unique to the Kindreds."

Camp rubbed his sweaty palms on his knees. "So, are you going to have everyone share their supposed special gifts? Should I have had a song or an interpretive dance prepared?"

Tansy and Glindel giggled, and Tracer smirked.

Captain Zephyr glanced at her touch screen. "Let's see. Campion . . . oh, that's right, Cholters don't possess last names. You work in delivery, grew up in the Cholter city of Coomp. Before me are essays from school, health patterns, a list of infractions from the forcebots, your complete family line, their accomplishments and professions. Basically, your life's history." She glanced down. "It does say you're outspoken and have received numerous warnings for mouthing off to force-bot handlers, which your Kindred have refused to address."

Camp opened his mouth, but she smiled. "Don't worry. I think we can all handle a few smart-alec remarks here."

"I'm not going to spill any of your secrets," she continued. "And no, I don't have some special power to read minds." She gave Tansy a pointed look. "I do, however, have acute skills of research and observation. Secrets belong to the individuals unless they choose to share them with the group. Just remember. This venture could be the key to the survival of the human race."

"I'd like to know what makes me special," Falstaff muttered.

Tansy turned to smile at Falstaff, though she was too far away to possibly hear what he said.

An instant dart of jealousy pierced Camp's heart, and a realization. He didn't like seeing Tansy give that smile to anyone else.

She has a right to smile at anyone she wants. She's not going to fall for you, filthy Cholter.

"As I was saying." Zephyr raised her dark, thin eyebrows. "My mission for you is simple. I wish for you to observe . . ."

"You mean spy." muttered Tracer.

"I mean observe," said Zephyr. "I am begging you to watch, think, and learn. Try to find ways and ideas to unify these ships. Anything could be helpful. Perhaps an event could be planned between yours and a neighboring ship . . ."

Kafla muttered a string of words Camp didn't understand. That didn't sound like a Tarkan blessing.

"Maybe a gathering, or a contest," Zephyr finished. "But the most important thing. If you see any signs, any at all, that your people wish to untether, I must know. Keep watch for sabotage. I suppose I am asking you to spy . . . but only in this way. I'm not interested in defying any integral laws. The leaders of the Headship have no say over day-to-day life, what constitutes a crime amongst kindreds . . . we can't even stay an execution. I will be respectful in every way except for this. These ships must stay together for the entirety of this journey." She pursed her lips. "Spy is the wrong word. No, you are guardians. We cannot afford to lose a soul on this journey. No one is replaceable."

Putting her touch screen down, she glanced around the room. "I thought I was the one who selected you all for this group. But after meeting you, I believe the Creator chose for me."

She nodded to Commander Helms, who handed each person at the table a small object.

Camp turned the comwatch over in his hands. Smaller and lighter than the one he already wore, the device was blue, with a silver bird on the band.

"I'm aware you already own comwatches, like every adult on the seven ships. But these are special. They will open almost any door on the headship, except for main vaults and the highest security units. Most importantly, they will connect you directly to me, Commander Helms, and any other team member here. No one else has access."

She rose. "Please feel free to stay awhile. A meal has been prepared for you. This is a time of sharing and getting to know each other. If you choose to leave the team, please do so now. I'll request that you leave your comwatch on the table as a sign that you don't wish to be a part of this vital team that could save so many lives."

The sound of plastic crinkling and leather straps being fastened filled the room. No one placed their comwatch down, not even Kafla, to Camp's surprise.

He studied his comwatch before tucking it into his bag. The one he possessed only allowed him to speak to the other members of his own ship. *A way to contact Tansy whenever I want? Not a bad deal.*

Zephyr rose. "I must leave to meet with the Solstice, or they may suspect the reason for my absence. Thank you all for agreeing to join this great experiment."

Commander Helms cleared his throat. "The other one has arrived. Are you ready for her?"

Zephyr's face lit up. "Oh yes. Please tell her to come."

Commander Helms opened the side door.

A girl entered. Her slight figure, the size of a young child, glided into the room. Her pale skin was nearly translucent, and her hair was whiter than the moon. She gazed at each person with violet eyes fringed with thick white lashes.

Zephyr put an arm around the thin shoulders. "Everyone, this is Halsey."

Halsey smiled at each of them, revealing a small gap in her two front teeth. "Forgive my lateness, Captain. I'm pleased to be here."

The captain handed her the remaining comwatch, and Halsey fastened it to her wrist. Her fingernails glowed with a purple polish, a color Camp had never seen before.

After her comwatch was in place, Halsey said, "I am from the Duluth people. I am the only one remaining of my Kindred. Therefore, I live on the headship."

Tracer hissed, and Kafla bristled in her seat. "You would bring this child to join us? From the headship?"

Halsey dipped her head. "I might be older than you."

Zephyr clasped her hands together. "Halsey is twenty-three. Looks can be deceiving. We believed it would be good for you to have someone nearer your age from the headship to work with and perhaps help make plans."

Commander Helms brought in a cart with steaming dishes.

Tantalizing aromas of spiced meat and fresh bread hit Camp's senses. He had planned to refuse the food, as was Cholter custom, but he was starving. *And you're sharing rations with an entire family. Better fill up.*

None of the rest of the group hesitated to eat, except for Tansy, who closed her eyes for a quick prayer. Clinking sounds of silverware against the real porcelain plates filled the room.

Captain Zephyr stood. "If you all would be so kind as to excuse me, I will leave you to get further acquainted. You may take your leave after lunch at any time."

She rose and walked to the door.

Turning back, she gave everyone a smile. "And thank you so much for coming."

10
Shaky Spirits

Periwinth stomped down the center deck, bruised ribs grating with pain.

Bradstorm followed, his long legs catching up with her in a few strides.

"Captain, forgive me, but you need to take a breather. You've had a long day. May I remind you that the doctors recommended complete bed rest for the next seven days."

She exhaled, tilting her head back. "I appreciate your concern, but this is so important to me. It's a long shot, Storm, really, it is, but what else do I have left?"

He huffed loudly, his warm breath hitting the skin of her neck. "You haven't called me that in a long time."

"Sorry, Commander. This formality has been an adjustment. Remember, the last time I hurled through space I commanded a tiny ship. We were all like siblings. No room for privacy or ceremony."

"Siblings except for one."

"Yes, except for Jordan." She couldn't keep her voice from trembling. Eight years hadn't been enough. She could still see his face through the escape pod, the fear in his eyes.

"I'm sorry," said Bradstorm. "I've been distracted by all these tech malfunctions, but that's no excuse for my insensitivity. Please accept my apology, Captain."

"It's fine," said Periwinth. "We have more pressing things to discuss right now."

She hit the panel to an empty control room and gestured him in. "Here, these screens shouldn't be hot."

He entered, and the door closed behind him.

"The Solstice is expecting us," he said.

"I know, I know. But I need a moment to gather my thoughts. So many things to remember. And after the stunt they pulled, choosing to address the bot issues without my consent. I wonder if they truly want peace among the ships." She closed her eyes and pressed her forehead against a cool metal panel.

When she opened them again, Bradstorm's eyes were fixed on her face, his forehead an ocean of creases. "I'm taking you back to the clinic."

"No, please. I'm fine. As you said, the Solstice awaits. The only reason they didn't suspect anything when I begged off inspection this morning was because they assumed I'd be in bed. But now that I'm meeting them, I'll have to show a tough face. Crenth and Platmoth will look for the tiniest hint of weakness."

"Only because they want your position," Bradstorm muttered.

Weariness enveloped Periwinth, and she put her face in her hands. "Do you really believe that? Why would they have nominated me for captain if they thought one of them would do a better job? Marrow I understand, she thinks of me as her prodigy, and an extension of herself. But Crenth and Platmoth? They wouldn't have a chance."

Bradstorm pursed his lips. "A snake does not collect chicken eggs to hatch a brood," he said. "Any fool could see you were the right one for the job. The assembly had no other option but to vote for you. But those three . . . Crenth is greedy for power, it's written all over his face. And Platmoth . . . wants to possess . . ."

"You can say it, Bradstorm. You're the only person in this world I trust. He wants me."

Bradstorm bowed his head and slammed a clenched fist against his palm.

Periwinth smoothed down a wrinkled shirt sleeve. "If only I knew this plan would work. Gathering this 'unity' group might seem ridiculous. But Bradstorm," she clasped her hands. "If we can't unify seven, we will never unify ten thousand."

"I hope you're right." Bradstorm strode across the room, his hands clasped behind his back. "The seven could be useful to us in more ways than we've discussed, especially if we can keep them a secret."

Periwinth's heart thudded against her ribcage. "I don't like what you're suggesting. Surely, we will never come to need a Conveyance."

"Don't speak it out loud. Even when you think we can't be heard." Bradstorm swung back around, his honest eyes filled with worry. "This group. You've already told them about the sabotage. Secrets can work to bind or sever. This information will show us which of them can be trusted. But seven pairs of loyal eyes, or three, or even one could be an asset to help us find the people responsible for what's happening before someone gets killed."

He pressed his fingertips against the bridge of his nose. "My men reported finding devices planted in two more forcebot's frontal lobes, just waiting to go off. If the saboteur is someone from another ship, they might be making a power play. If it's one of us …"

Periwinth's chin quivered, and she hated it. "We ARE us, Storm. We are all us. There is no 'them.' We need every single person here. How can I get you to understand?"

"No one comprehends this more than I do," said Bradstorm. He moved closer, holding her in his steady gaze. "You experienced terrible things on that first journey. Things most people wouldn't recover from. Your heart is brave and unbelievably fierce. That's what I believe in. Your heart will guide us home."

"Your faith in me is touching, but perhaps too strong," she muttered, looking away.

"Hey, we're going to make it," Bradstorm said, reaching out, but stopping right before his hand brushed her cheek. "We must trust ourselves, and Creator. It's all we have. This group looks promising. Yes, they're hardly more than kids, but that's why we chose them. You've been working on this idea for weeks and I never would have agreed to help if I didn't think it was a good one."

She laughed. "It's a stab in the dark, and we both know it. But thank you. I don't know what I'd do without you. Now let's go meet with our honorable Solstice"

Periwinth stepped through the panel door, almost running into Halsey. "Goodness, excuse me! I didn't realize you were out here!"

The tiny young woman dipped her head. "Good day, Captain Zephyr, I'm sorry if I startled you. I came to let you know the Solstice have changed their meeting place from transfer room five to conference room seven. Marrow was concerned when you didn't answer her call.

"Thank you, Halsey. I appreciate you telling me." Periwinth sighed. "Please keep in mind, we're not mentioning the unity group to the Solstice for now. It's not worth talking about until something comes of it."

Halsey's long, pale eyelashes fluttered against her cheeks. "Of course, Captain. And thank you for your trust in choosing me out of everyone on the headship to be a member of your special team."

Periwinth smiled. "In the two months since we've left Gyron, I've felt connected to you. Like me, you flew through your classes and gave the graduating speech in your school. Those of us who have few Kindred remaining must stay together. You have proven to be extremely intelligent and trustworthy. I am honored you've chosen to join us and I know you will be a valuable asset to our group."

"May it be so," Halsey replied. She waved her arm. "And these comwatches. What a thing to entrust the group with. Do they truly unlock any door or device? On all the ships?"

"No," said Bradstorm. "We would be utterly foolish to equip strangers with such power. But they will work on anything with level three clearance or lower."

"Level three," Halsey murmured. "All right, good to know." With that, she skipped away down the corridor, like the child she resembled.

"Amazing how someone who has lost so much can stay in such good spirits," said Periwinth. "We should all learn from her."

"Indeed," said Bradstorm, but he did not smile.

11
Torn Tether

Tansy followed Camp through the sliding doors of the tether ship, Kafla's eyes burning into their backs as usual. The trip had been a quiet one. Camp had asked a conversational question here and there, but Tansy had been too occupied by her thoughts to give more than short answers and the Tark princess, unsurprisingly, remained in stony silence in the furthest back seat of the vehicle.

As they entered the main part of the ship, Kafla moved away with swift steps.

"Nice to meet you," Camp yelled as she disappeared into the crowd.

"Lovely person," Camp said to Tansy. "Guess she couldn't be bothered to escort us through the ship." He nodded. The two guards who'd originally brought Tansy to the tether tube waited for them with grim stares.

"Isn't she though?" said Tansy. "I think we might be the bestest of friends."

Camp grinned.

Tansy and Camp stayed together through the Tark's village, their required guide stomping ahead, the second guard behind them.

Tansy wished so deeply to discuss the meeting with Camp, but not here, with guards hanging on to their every word and action. *What could it all mean? What are we expected to do?*

"Look at that tapestry." Camp pointed to a brightly colored design depicting a woman warrior wielding a shield and perched high on the back of a giant creature. "Is that a raffi?"

"What's a raffi again?"

"One of those horse-giraffe animals. I think they were originally from Earth. They're the biggest living land mammals. The Tark's had to jump through some serious hoops to get them on the ship."

"Pretty neat," Tansy murmured.

"I'd love to see a real one, wouldn't you?" said Camp.

"What, a raffi or a woman with a spear?"

Camp chuckled. "Well, I think we've spent the last few hours with a woman like that. She wasn't carrying a spear today, but I'm sure she's perfectly capable of using one. I meant the raffi. I remember reading about elephants and buffalo and rhinos in school, but those animals died out way before we were born. I've seen horses and cows. But a raffi . . . those things are fifteen feet tall, easy. I'm not sure how many they have left." He pivoted on one heel, scanning the buildings. "I suppose they're kept in those tall sheds in the far corner. They must have special stables for them or something. Maybe next time I come through they'll let me check them out."

"That would be something," said Tansy, still in a distant tone.

Camp shrugged and looked away.

I'm being rude and hurting his feelings. The thought filled Tansy with chagrin, but she didn't know how to pull herself out of this fearful place. *The captain might know of my powers after all. That look she gave me—surely it's not coincidental?* But the captain had alluded to everyone present having secret gifts. They passed the market tents, now silent for the end of the day. *That old woman acted like she had a similar gifting to mine. Could it be true?* She longed to ask Camp, but again, the risk was too great. *I'll have to speak to Mother.*

The rest of the walk remained silent. They continued through the Tark's second tether station without incident.

Tansy settled into the tether-craft seat and fastened the precautionary seatbelt, which she didn't understand because the craft went at a smooth crawl. he ride, which she'd finally bothered to calculate, lasted less than fifteen minutes on each tether.

Camp sat beside her.

As the gentle hum buzzed around them, Camp spoke up. "Is everything all right?"

Tansy nodded. "I'm sorry if I've been quiet. I'm not upset with you or anything." She lowered her voice. "After everything that happened today, I'm worried about saying the wrong thing out loud.

I don't know what security devices they've installed in these tether cars."

Camp groaned. "I know what you mean. The next ten months promise to be long ones. And this request from the captain . . . well, I've never seen myself as the special ops type."

"Really?" Tansy squinted at him. "I don't know, you could always hide behind your dreads, use them as some kind of covert camouflage."

"So, you're making fun of my hair now." Camp settled back into his seat.

"No, no, I was only joking." She ducked, so he couldn't see her warmed face, which was probably as red as her best tea chrysanthemums. "I like your hair."

"Good." He twirled a dread around his finger. "Because I'm not changing it."

A flood of feelings came from his mind, washing through her like a mild-season rain. She put up her mental shield, cutting them off as they swept in. *It's not fair to read his feelings like this. Especially since he has no way of knowing mine.*

How do I feel about him? She'd never thought about how she'd manage romance, since she'd never been faced with such a situation. She'd caught the fancy of a few boys in her class, yes, and inappropriate thoughts of older men from time to time. But she'd never faced the management of feelings from anyone she also cared about.

She pressed her fingers against her temples. An influx of

thoughts like these, especially such strong emotions, made it difficult to figure out how *she* felt. Camp definitely intrigued her, but she'd need time away from him to sort through her own feelings. *Would he really want to be with me if he knew about my abilities? Could he keep them a secret? Can I trust him?*

"It's been quite a day," she said at last.

"You're right about that." Camp leaned back in the seat. "I thought the headship summoned me because I was in trouble or something."

"Because of Smirk?" asked Tansy.

"Aw, you remembered his name. No." He pursed his lips. "I'm going to tell you, but I need you to keep it in confidence. Though it's not going to do any good."

"Sure," said Tansy. "As long no one could get hurt."

"No, no, nothing like that." He shook his head, so the beads in his hair clinked together. "At least, I don't believe there's any danger. Not sure what to think, to tell you the truth. A family is staying with me."

"A Cholter family?"

"Nope. Let's just say they aren't on the roster. Though I'm positive the forcebots know they're here. Might've even sent soldiers down to our ship to check them out by now." His fingers tightened on his armrests.

"Not on the roster? You mean, they're stowaways?"

"Kind of. They docked on the Cholter ship, day before yesterday. Stragglers from Gyron in a private zoomer. A couple and their little girl."

"I didn't think a zoomer could make it that far," Tansy said. "Do you think there might be others?" So many people from her village had decided not to come. *Could some of them have also survived?* A pinprick of hope quivered in her mind. Faces she'd thought to be lost forever, captives of their stubborn fears. One old man had refused to leave his greenhouse, another woman was deathly afraid of flying through space and would rather be 'burnt up in a supernova,' as she'd said to Father Sharood. Then there were the naysayers that thought the report was a government lie meant to herd them all aboard at the mercy of the main city's control.

"This family barely made it," said Camp, dashing her seed of joy that had sprouted so suddenly. He must have noticed her expression, because he softened his tone. "Who knows, though? We left hundreds of smaller ships on Gyron, and some folks said they'd try to come on their own. More might have attempted the trip."

Tansy closed her eyes and pushed her thoughts past the tether ship, past the tube, out, out into the vast expanse. But she could only see the blinking lights of the Serpentine, and then the inky blackness that was space.

The tether car shuddered to a stop, and she opened her eyes.

Camp's crystal gaze settled on her face. "Are you sure you're okay?"

"Yes. Sorry. Why did we stop? Didn't this trip seem shorter than the others?"

Camp scratched his chin and stood, stretching. "Now that you mention it ... "

As Tansy stood beside him, a terrible screeching filled her senses, and she clapped her hands over her ears. The tether car jerked and jolted, as though it were being dragged ... *backwards*. She staggered and clutched at Camp's arm to keep from falling.

"Hey, why don't you sit down and let me go see what happened?" said Camp. Another jerk threw him to the floor. He was back up in an instant, anger blazing in his eyes. A trickle of blood dripped from his head above his right eyebrow. He touched the blood. "Great."

Another jolt threw her back into her seat. "Camp, what's happening? What can we . . ." A picture flashed through Tansy's mind, unbidden as always. "An electric line. Someone must have cut the power propulsion system. We're being pulled back by suction." She wrenched herself back to a standing position. "Here, I think I know where it is." She moved to the front of the car, holding onto the seats as the craft continued to jump backwards.

"Tansy, wait, how could you possibly . . ." Camp followed her, slipping and sliding along the floor.

She made it to the front where a glowing panel was situated. Lights on the top pulsed and she placed her hand over the green one.

"Embroid civilian detected," came a computer's voice. *"Civilians do not have access to control panels. Wait for assistance."*

The car jerked back again, and the color drained from Camp's face. "What if that chiefess lost her ever-loving mind, pulled the lever, and untethered the Tark's ship?"

"No, that's not what happened. Trust me," said Tansy. "We must open this panel. Can you–" she reached into her memories for an ancient Earth term. "Can you hotwire it open or something? Ooh, I wish Glindel was still with us!"

"Glindel may be a tech, but I also know something about basic mechanics." said Camp. He pulled the captain's comwatch from his pocket. "I wonder if this is good for anything besides sending messages?"

"You think it might work?" Tansy edged closer.

Camp swiped it over the car panel.

The lights on the smooth round surface pulsed from blue to green. *"Special command detected."* The top section clicked open.

"Wow," Camp stared at the comwatch. "Where have you been my whole life?"

The car jolted again, much harder this time, then moved faster, still backwards.

Camp gripped the bar in front of the panel. "So many buttons and switches! Anything I touch could make it go faster or I don't know, blow the thing to smithereens. These things are completely automated, there must be a special switch."

"You'd think they'd show it to the people riding in the tubes!" shouted Tansy. "Some kind of instructional class!"

Camp fumbled through the panel insert with his free hand. "I don't see anything. We've got to do something before we collide with the tether wall and get thrown into space! Pretty sure we're on an outer tube!"

Tansy scrabbled at a side compartment, her fingernails breaking and bleeding. Finally, it flipped open. "Look here, someone partially severed this wire. The car's movement must have completed the breakage and caused it to malfunction."

Camp peered over her shoulder. "Yeah, that's what happened all right." His eyes widened. "How could you possibly know that?"

The car accelerated.

"Can you just try to fix it?" Tansy yelled.

Camp reached inside and fiddled around. "I'll have to bypass the system, but I think I can!"

The next jerk sent Tansy to her knees on the floor. "Any time!" she yelled.

Sparks flew and Camp howled, shaking his hand and blowing on his fingers. The car came to a shuddering halt. The lights blinked out. They were enveloped in utter darkness and silence.

Camp sank down on the floor beside Tansy. "Are you all right?" he said quietly.

Her fingers were sticky with blood, and she couldn't stop her teeth from chattering. "Y-yes."

He wrapped his arms around her shoulders. Warmth and a sense of perfect safety covered her. She didn't pull away.

"I shorted the whole thing out." he said softly, and his heartbeat thudded through his coat. "Better than crashing into the tube. Someone will come for us any minute. We won't get in trouble. The forcebots will show what happened."

"Sure." She buried her head in his shoulder, breathing the scent of leather and mint.

He pushed back her hood and stroked her hair. "Hey. Everything's going to be okay. It's over now."

Tansy wasn't sure how long they stayed on the floor of the car. Perhaps ten minutes, but it might have been an hour when the door was finally wrenched open and Nimcy, the Embroid tether operator, entered the car. Her comwatch light shone in their faces.

"Goodness, what happened? Are the two of you hurt?" she said.

"No, we're fine." The tips of Camp's ears were bright red. He rose. "I'm afraid I had to mess up your control panel pretty badly to get this thing to stop."

Nimcy went over to the panel and beamed her light around inside. "You aren't lying." She swiveled, a hand on her hip. "What happened?"

Tansy climbed to shaky feet. "Severed wire, Nimcy. I'm almost positive it was deliberate."

Nimcy gasped. "Why would anyone want to do that?"

"I don't know," said Camp. "But I intend to find out."

"If that's what happened, I'm sure the forcebots will show the culprit." Nimcy pointed to the broad, black lens staring down at them like a disapproving eye from the car's ceiling.

Camp staggered to the lens and poked around at the wires that hooked it up to the wall. "Wouldn't be so sure. This thing's been dismantled."

###

The tether tube's maintenance door slid open, and Tansy and Camp went into the Embroid station.

"What a day." Camp touched his head, which had been bandaged by Nimcy.

"You want to come to my house? I can supply you with herbs that will help it heal faster," said Tansy.

Camp gave her a smile. "As much as I'd enjoy spending more time with you, I'd better head back. Need to check on the family at my house and make sure Smirk hasn't pulled out everyone's hair."

"Could that happen?"

"You never know with Smirk."

They put in their security numbers and walked into the Embroid community space.

"At least Nimcy was able to find out the forcebot had been dismantled several hours before we boarded the ship," said Tansy.

"Yeah, that's a level one infraction. I have no desire to spend the rest of our journey in the brig," said Camp.

They traveled through the grid paths, meeting few people, as it was time for last meal.

Tansy stopped a few homes away from her dwelling. "Have a fair evening. Give Smirk a pat for me."

Camp snorted. "He's cute, but he can be a stinker. Last time I left him for a day he emptied every drawer and closet in my house into a big pile in the middle of the floor. Took me three days to clean it all up."

Tansy wrinkled her nose. "Doesn't sound fun."

"Nope." Camp gave her a slow smile. "Take care of yourself, Tansy. I suppose we'll be meeting again sometime soon." He held up his comwatch. "Call me if you have any ideas, or if, you know, you want to talk about anything. Just call me."

"Okay, I will. Camp?"

"Hmmm?"

"I'm glad you were with me today."

"Me too." When he grinned, a boyishness flooded his face, for a brief instant washing away years of hardships.

Tansy watched as he walked down the gridline, past the Clarity Hall, his dark dreads bouncing on his shoulders.

12
Fishing Party

Camp knocked on his own door, frowned, and tried the hasp. *Locked? Weird.* He pulled his passkey from his pocket and waved it over the small panel.

He entered the silent house with caution, his gaze running over every surface. Everything was spotless; clean as the day he'd moved in. The kitchen was scrubbed to perfection and even the comscreen in his living area sparkled.

The travelers' bags were still in his bedroom, neatly stacked. But when he inspected his supply closet, he discovered his fishing pole was missing, along with his favorite tool pouch.

Why would they choose those things? They were his most used and therefore most valuable possessions, but why would they take a risk and steal them? Wouldn't that only bring unwanted attention to themselves?

Camp poured himself a glass of water and chugged it. He wiped his mouth with the back of his hand. *What do I know of Dashner?* The hint of deception that had pricked his palm when he shook his hand was unmistakable. Ignoring such sensations in the past had almost cost him his life. *But what man doesn't have secrets? Especially someone who is trying to protect his family.*

Camp's family members had been gone for years, so he hadn't had to worry about protecting someone in quite a while. Beyond his pet of course, but Smirk could take care of himself.

He raised his head and clicked his tongue. "Hey, Smirk, come get a treat." But there was no scrabbling response. A quick check of the pet's favorite hiding places turned up nothing. *Where is Smirk? Did they take him too?* He chuckled. He pitied the soul who attempted to steal a full-grown mootrat. Unless you bonded with one as a pup, you'd never have the upper hand in the relationship.

Smirk would escape from wherever they'd taken him and find his way home. The tool kit though, he couldn't afford to lose. Many of the tools had been passed down in his family and were impossible to replace. The polished metal and wooden implements were obsolete to most, but he used them every day.

His hand shook around his water glass. Where could Dashner and his family have gone?

Calm down. They wouldn't have journeyed far without their belongings.

He stepped outside and stood by his fence, still, listening.

A child's laughter floated over the barrier between his house and the dwelling that belonged to Candy and Frank. *Raven.*

He pushed through the gate and entered the neighbor's back area, where they kept the only aquaponics system on the Cholter's ship.

The odor of slightly muddy water hit his senses. A large metal structure filled the backyard area. Elaborate stands held shimmering green plants on the top, and a giant fish tank beneath. Water pumped up from the tank, spraying over the plants in intervals.

Dashner and Raven sat on the edge of the giant tank, feet dangling in the water. Dashner held Camp's fishing pole while he and Raven watched the line intently.

Smirk perched on Raven's shoulder, chattering, as usual, about nothing.

Jayne and Candy rested in two chairs by the garden, sipping blue liquid from repurposed glass bottles.

A twinge of homesickness pinched Camp's soul. If it wasn't for the infinite ceiling of lights and the constant hint of plastic and metal in the air, he'd almost believe he was in his old Cholter neighborhood. To outside Kindreds, the Cholter city was a dark and dangerous place. But many families hosted suppers at night, complete with stringed lights hanging from the trees and an occasional uncle or aunt who'd coax a tune from some ancient instrument. *Will we ever have that again?*

"Hello there." Candy patted a chair next to her. "Everything go well?"

"I suppose," Camp settled in and took the drink Candy offered him.

"They didn't say anything about us?" Jayne asked. Her glass shook in her hand.

"No, they didn't mention you at all. They wanted to–hire me for a specific task."

"At all?" The words came as more of a whisper. The crease that had been on Jayne's forehead since Camp had met her smoothed out, and she leaned back in her chair.

Candy's lips twitched, but she didn't ask for further information.

Camp appreciated her grace. *Curiosity is probably eating her up inside. I'll explain everything when this all blows over. IF it blows over.*

Dashner turned from his perch. "I found your fishing pole when I searched for a cleaning device for Jayne. Candy offered to let us catch dinner the old-fashioned way, and I thought Raven would enjoy it. I hope you don't mind. And I used your tools to fix a hole in her wall. I left the bag over there." He nodded to a small table.

Camp spread out his hands. "I don't mind. Hope they're biting. A fish dinner sounds great."

"Sure does," said Dashner. "I haven't had fresh fish in years."

Candy stood and put her hands on her hips. "We received a new batch of fingerlings from the headship a week ago, so Frank just restocked. We keep a careful record of what's caught, but there should be a few dozen big ones left, at least."

As she spoke the line grew taught and the tip of the fishing pole dipped down sharply.

Raven jumped off the side of the tank, upsetting Smirk from her shoulder. "We caught one! We caught one!"

Dashner pulled in a gleaming fish. The tilapia twisted and flopped, its bright scales shining in the main lights. "What do you think? A good dinner?"

"I'd say it's a start," said Candy. "Catch another and we'll fry them, otherwise we'll throw it in a cooker and make fish stew."

"My mother used to cook with a big black pot over a campfire," said Candy. "Of course, we used the ancient ways. Earth ways, with a horse and wagon." A faraway look came into her eyes. "I miss horses."

"I heard they have a dozen or so on the Tark's ship," said Camp. "Maybe you can visit them sometime. I'd like to see a raffi, myself."

Jayne shook her head. "I'd be scared to death. Raffis are so dangerous."

"Eh, the Tarks know how to handle them," said Camp.

Another cry of delight came from Raven. "One more fish!" she squealed, clapping her hands.

Camp found himself smiling despite the situation. *Good to have a child around.* Raven's joy over small triumphs was infectious and her trust in her parents was inspiring.

What were Tansy's plans for the future? Could she be betrothed to someone? He searched the recesses of his mind for everything he knew about Embroid culture. He'd never heard of them participating in arranged marriages. *But she could be engaged to someone. Wouldn't she have told me?* He shook his head. *Even if she wasn't promised to someone else, would she ever want to be with a Cholter?*

Periwinth's feet drug across the floor beneath her ceremonial gown. *Bradstorm is right, as always. I've overdone it today.*

The three Solstice members huddled together at the end of the table. Dread clawed at Periwinth's stomach, and she wondered again why she'd agreed with the council's decision to make her captain. Was she capable? *My heart is sincere.* She truly wished the best for all to find a safe and happy home at the end of this journey. Was it possible for her to accomplish this? *Could anyone?* Though she disliked two out of the three members of the council-appointed Solstice, she was forced to work alongside them. Each had powerful friends, undercurrents of support they'd built their entire careers. If she tried to cut one off, the hemorrhage of rage from their factions could devastate the unity of the ship.

Marrow was speaking in low tones.

Crenth bent in, listening, his eyes fixed on Marrow's face.

Platmoth stood to the side, a finger pressed against his lips. His uniform spanned his broad shoulders as though still on the hanger, immaculate and perfectly pressed. Dark hair gleamed under the lamps of the meeting room. A goatee sprouted from his sharp chin, so perfectly angled that she wondered if he measured it when trimming.

Periwinth suppressed a groan. More than anything she wanted

to go home and sleep. But the three Solstice members appeared alert and invigorated, and she didn't want to show a sign of weakness. Lately her unease had been growing, as though they were cats waiting to pounce. Platmoth, for certain, would want nothing more than an opportunity to carry her off to her chambers, his perfect damsel in distress.

I'd sooner die.

Marrow glanced at her and rose, along with Crenth.

"At ease," said Periwinth, waving a hand. She sank into a chair, unable to contain a wince as her ribs hit the armrest a little harder than she intended.

Marrow regained her seat and frowned. "Periwinth dear, I mean, Captain Zephyr. We assumed you'd decided to stay in your quarters and rest and would send Commander Helms in your place. We have already been here an hour. We have other duties." She glared at Bradstorm, who held out his hands, mutely. She glanced back at Periwinth. "Shouldn't you go home? We can handle the rest of these matters within the circle."

"We've received news of another happening, and Commander Helms and I agree that it must be the result of sabotage," said Periwinth. "A malfunction of a tether craft between the Tarks and Embroids caused the craft to be sucked backwards, almost resulting in complete destruction."

Crenth frowned. "How is such a thing possible?"

"That's what we must find out," said Periwinth. "Miraculously, no one was hurt, and the repairs will not take long, but the craft will be offline for some time, maybe more than three days."

"Troubling, but not surprising." Platmoth stroked his goatee, which somehow made his facial hair even more revolting. "But Captain, though radiant as always, you look positively exhausted."

Crenth pulled out a cloth and wiped his sharpened nose. This feature, along with rounded cheeks made him look like a carved puppet. "Poor girl. That encounter with the forcebot must have been terrifying for you." He leaned closer. "The handlers have been told about the sabotage situation, but they have been sworn to secrecy."

"Really, Crenth?" Periwinth knew better than to push the matter with the man, but she rarely listened to her inner voice when it came to keeping quiet.

He blinked and bit his lips. He'd never quite forgiven her for retracting his self-given title of Grand Vizier.

She continued. "Would you really say that all twenty-five of the people working on that deck will keep quiet? And let's not forget the crew from level 10 that witnessed the whole incident. Marrow has informed me that you shared the information with the leaders from the other ships, so please don't stand there and try to convince me otherwise."

Platmoth placed a hand on her shoulder. His smoldering brown eyes lit up with a smile that would have seemed warm and kind if not for the extra effort forced into it. "Now Captain. Periwinth. We felt the leadership needed to be on the lookout. Who knows what this evil, destructive person will choose to do next?"

Periwinth's skin crawled beneath his hand, and she shrugged it off her shoulder. "You should have consulted me. Everything we share must be handled carefully. The tiniest thing could spark a mutiny. We've discussed this to death."

Heat snapped into his eyes. "The leaders promised confidentiality until we alert them of the proper time."

"Have you no knowledge of the human spirit?" She looked at each one of them in turn. "The only thing that could keep so many souls from telling of such danger would be dire threats or immense bribery."

A smile twisted up Crenth's face, causing further contortion. "And what makes you think something along that nature wasn't contrived?"

Anger burned Periewinth's throat, and she clasped her hands together to keep them from shaking. "Again. This wasn't discussed with me. This isn't how I do things and we will regret policies built on threats."

"Again, dear," Marrow said, "you were unconscious. We had to act quickly."

A dull cloud of pain settled over Periwinth's head. Keeping her chin above the table suddenly took immense concentration.

Crenth's eyes narrowed. "This shouldn't remain a secret. I think it prudent to send human teams to each ship. Armed guards must be on patrol to watch for this saboteur. I've been saying this since it happened."

Periwinth gasped. "We can't send blasters–we can't send–"

Marrow clicked her long, white fingernails together. "I believe the captain is trying to remind us that unleashing groups of armed guards would suggest that individual Kindreds no longer possess strong leadership. The stirring among the ships would be too great, and the loss of morale irreparable." Her glance darted to Periwinth. "That's what you were getting at, isn't it, dear?"

Periwinth tried to speak, but her mouth seemed full of cotton, or marbles, her tongue incapable of forming words. With all the strength she could muster, she rose from her chair. "We need–to discuss–the chain of command–"

Pain stabbed her side, and she lurched forward.

Bradstorm's strong hands were instantly on her shoulders, preventing her from face-planting on the table.

"The captain has had a long day," she heard his firm, comforting voice floating somewhere outside her psyche.

"What's wrong with her? I'll tend to her," came Platmouth's voice.

Please. Please, no. She clutched at the tablecloth, bunching it in her fist, silverware and dishes sliding her way.

"That won't be necessary." Bradstorm's strong arms gathered and lifted her.

She buried her face in the silkiness of his dress uniform. *Why are the men's dress uniforms so much softer?* was her last thought as she drifted off to sleep.

13

Home Turf

Tansy rushed past the Clarity center and straight for home. Most of the Kindred would be gathered for the Waiting. *I must check on Mother. I've been gone all day, and she looked so weak this morning.* Spirit would understand, but would Father Sharood? The old man didn't miss much.

When Tansy stepped into the house, the scent of freshly cooked tomato sauce hit her nose. Aunt Cora sat on the couch, rubbing her rounded belly. An old movie from Earth, some kind of talk show, played on the comscreen in the living space. People in strange clothes mixed what Tansy figured must be types of food in oddly shaped containers on a stage.

"Hi, Aunt Cora," said Tansy. She peeked over at her mother's usual corner cushion. "Where's Mother?"

"Hello there," said Cora. "I convinced her to shower and sleep in her own bed instead of the cushion pile. Poor darling."

Tansy's shoulders sagged, and she sank down in a chair. "I'm glad she's all right for today, but she hasn't been looking well."

Aunt Cora pursed her lips. "Didn't she go to the clinic last week? What did the healer say?"

"The healers haven't been much help. They've given her the customary herbs and oils. The head herbalist told her to seek foods that she could stomach, but she hasn't been able to keep much down." Tansy picked at a loose thread on the arm of her seat. "I'm not a little girl anymore. I know we don't have much time left."

A strange, hungry glint entered Aunt Cora's eyes. "What do you mean?"

The last few times Tansy had visited with her aunt, she'd noticed this strange attitude. Of course, as her mother's twin, Cora knew of the family legend. The rare times she'd mentioned it had been when speaking of her grandmother.

Everyone knew the most gifted Embroids in the group possessed heightened awareness, the ability to catch brief futuristic glimpses, and an occasional ability to discern feelings. Both Aunt Cora and Tansy's mother were members of this group.

Has Mother told her of my intense visions that have all come true? Of my thought-reading abilities? No. The danger was too great. *Maybe she discerns them on her own.* A chill swept down her spine.

"I mean, I've read everything I can find about this cancer," Tansy said. "I know what the end stages look like. You've seen her, she's a ghost of herself. She barely eats. She sleeps all day. I've joined the Wait for many extra hours and counted my memory beads until the ridges have worn from the edges. I've accepted that Spirit might wish to take her home."

Aunt Cora patted her arm, but her touch was cold. "It is very hard. I remember when I lost my mother, your grandmother. I couldn't understand why Spirit would take her away from me when she was so happy here. As all Embroids must, I celebrate that she is with Spirit in a land we can only imagine. Along with your father."

A lump grew in Tansy's throat, and she brushed away a tear. "Something smells delicious. Did you make supper?" she said, trying to sound cheerful.

"Yes. Our garden has exploded with tomatoes, so I made sauce and baked it with zucchini. Very nourishing. Try to get your mother to eat a few bites when she wakes up."

"I will," Tansy said, though tomatoes were far too acidic for Lanis to stomach. Cora should know this, but pregnancy always gave her brain fog.

"How is little Samuel?" Tansy said, nodding to Cora's belly.

"Should arrive any day, and I am ready to hand him to someone else to carry," said Cora. "My other two children were much smaller and lighter, but the doctor said it's normal for later babies to cause more weight gain. And you wouldn't believe the healthy things I've eaten. How I've longed for cakes!"

"I'll be happy to help you once the baby is born," said Tansy. "I appreciate you being here for Mother so much."

"Of course. After all, she is my twin," said Cora. She sighed and rubbed her stomach. "Oh! If my skin stretches another centimeter, I'm afraid it will pop like Grandfather's shirt buttons on feast day years ago."

"Do you think little Samuel will have red hair like Jenso and Bennet?" asked Tansy.

"Who knows? Maybe he'll be blond like your mother and me. And you." Cora sighed. "We are happy for boy number three, but it would have been nice to have a little girl this time." The hungry look came into her eyes once more.

She rose and grabbed her satchel from the table by the door. "Let me know how everything's going. If you need me, I'll come back. It's nice to take a break from all the men in my home." She rested a hand on Tansy's arm. "Trust Spirit. Your mother is a faithful servant. He will delight in her homecoming when the time comes."

"I know," said Tansy. Her lips and face felt numb, like when she'd taken a bite of a dish with too many spicy peppers. "Thank you for coming."

She closed the door behind her aunt and sat back in her chair, rubbing her forehead. *Aunt Cora would never let anyone hurt me. Right?*

She'd been ten the first time she'd replied to her mother's unspoken request. The color had drained from Lanis's face.

"Never do that again," she'd hissed, her fingers and lips curled in a wild fierceness Tansy had never beheld from her mother, before or after that day.

"Do what, Mother?" Little Tansy had bit her tongue so hard it started bleeding.

"My poor darling." Her mother pulled out a handkerchief and dabbed at the blood. "I've long suspected, but ... you shouldn't be able to do that, be able to read my thoughts so clearly. You knew my request word for word."

Tansy had started trembling, though she didn't know why. "I thought you spoke to me, Mother."

Her mother lowered her eyes. "You must learn to tell the difference. Watch for people's lips to move before replying. Never, ever answer unless something is spoken. Better to act like you didn't hear at all. Do you understand?"

Tansy had nodded mutely.

"Responding to thoughts could bring great danger to yourself and our house. And if you see visions, no matter how awful, you must only tell me or your father. Never anyone else. Not even Father Sharood, or one of the elders. Promise me!"

The wildness bit into her mother's voice, pushing it until it swelled into a scream. "Promise me!"

"I–I promise," Tansy whispered, staggering back.

Her mother had run a trembling hand across her eyes. "In the darkened days, girls died for such things."

Tansy had struggled to grasp such a terrible thought. "But why, Mother?"

"Because it was a belief that if the Emergent was killed before her twenty-first birthday, the gifting would pass on to the next oldest girl in the family. The family of the Emergent received much power and money for the use of her skills. These girls were sought after, prized, and pampered by kings and leaders. Your great-grandmother was the last of them. The other girls in the family only possessed the normal Embroid gifts, so the Emergents were considered extinct."

"Why don't we tell everyone?" Tansy had asked. "Maybe I can help someone with my gifting."

Landis had stroked her hair and gazed into her eyes. "Nothing is worth your life. I would never use you in that way, my love. You understand? You must hide these gifts. Hide them forever. From everyone."

Tansy's eyes fluttered open. She went to the cooking implement and turned off the heat. Sauce bubbled through the glass sides of the dish as she pulled it from the baking device, and the delicious, spicy aroma intensified. *My aunt would never hurt me. She loves my mother, and she loves me. My birthday is only a few days away. After that, I'll never have to worry again.*

Still, she was thankful her aunt was expecting a boy.

After eating the delicious food left by Aunt Cora, she cleaned up the kitchen, moving through a measure of a Waiting dance and singing snatches of an old folk song about a girl who followed her true love through a magical realm.

What of Camp? The thought stopped her in her tracks, and she froze, a half-folded linen in her hands. The Cholter was devastatingly handsome. And kind. And generous. But she needed more time to process her feelings, and with her mother's sickness, her aunt's strange behavior, and the meeting she'd attended today, her mind was far too cluttered to sort it all out.

We're in the group together, so at least I'll see him again. Hopefully soon. She turned to the sink to tackle the pile of dishes her aunt had left behind.

A vision floated into her mind like an early morning dream, the kind that jars you awake the moment it ends. *Kafla.* The Tark Princess lay on the ground in a pool of blood, her dress torn open, a jagged wound running across her throat. A snorting raffi stood next to the girl, pawing the ground, blood dripping from its gleaming tusks.

The force of the vision was so strong that Tansy went to her knees, dripping dishcloth still in her hand. Her own throat burned, and bright lights winked in and out behind her eyes.

Kafla. Of all the people on their little group, she seemed the most capable of fighting her own battles. But as a part of this special team, wasn't Tansy's job to help where she could, as unwelcome as that help might be?

"Tansy? Is everything all right?" Her mother peered down at her from hollow, bloodshot eyes. "Did you slip and fall?"

"I'm not sure what happened, but I'm fine." Tansy stood shakily. "How are you? Aunt Cora left a meal, but I'm afraid it might not settle well. I'll get you a slice of bread and the plumquats I gathered this morning."

"I believe I will eat something." Lanis moved to the table and fluttered into her seat like a browning leaf. "It's good to have you home."

"I may have to leave again." Tansy thought of the communicator in her pocket. The Tark princess didn't seem like one to use such a device. Even if she did answer, Tansy couldn't warn her without tipping her hand. A problem she'd dealt with her entire life.

I'll have to go talk to her. Maybe I can stop the attack somehow. Spirit gave me this vision for a reason. I must find out why.

Just then, her comwatch, the one the captain had given her, glowed from the counter. She hid it beneath her robe and slipped into her room.

"Tansy, where are you going?" her mother called.

"I'll be right back." Tansy slid her door closed.

The captain's symbol blazed across the tiny screen.

"Hello?" said Tansy.

"Hello, Tansy Pellum," came Captain Zephyr's voice, sounding thinner and much wearier than she had at the meeting earlier. "We are all here. Please switch to holographic mode."

Everyone? Tansy pulled out her small rectangular holo screen and set it beside the com. The image appeared from the watch, much larger. The faces of the captain and the six other members of the new group peered back at her from separate beams, including little Halsey in the far corner.

"I was informed of the tether car incident a few hours ago, but I wasn't aware until Camp told me just now that you were aboard when it happened. I wanted to check up on you two. Are you unhurt?"

"Yes," said Tansy. "Shaken up a little, but I'll live."

"Understandable." The captain rested her chin on her fingers. "Did you see anyone else in the tether car? Anyone in the stations you didn't recognize?"

"Like I said, Captain," Camp's face was stony. "We were alone."

"I bet you were," said Tracer. "Alone so you could tamper with the wires."

"Never!" said Tansy, grabbing at the covering on her bed; bunching it in her fingers. "Why would we put ourselves in danger like that? We've been told the tether car was a few yards from slamming into the wall."

Suspicion flitted over the faces on the screen, except for Captain Zephyr.

"We will not start with accusations," she said firmly.

"But Captain, he's a–" said Falstaff. His voice trailed off, and he closed his mouth firmly, his face reddening.

"What? A Cholter?" said Camp. "Is that what you were going to say?" He pressed a fist against his mouth. "Captain Zephyr, I'm sorry but if this is how I'm going to be treated in this group, I don't want any part of it."

Tansy's heart sank. *No. Don't leave us, we need you!*

"I don't want to hear talk of this kind from any of you ever again," said Captain Zephyr. "Do you understand me?"

Everyone nodded, though Tracer and Falstaff folded their arms and scowled.

"Good," said Captain Zephyr. "Now, what I am about to tell you absolutely must remain between all of us. Do you understand?"

The row of lit-up faces nodded again.

"I have reason to wonder if members of this group are being specifically targeted. We can't rule it out."

"Us?" Glindel ran a hand through her hair.

"Commander Helms has informed me of further signs of sabotage on the ship." Captain Zephyr pursed her lips. "Most have been intercepted, but these attempts point to much more dangerous outcomes than before. I need you to keep your eyes open and report anything you find." She gazed at each face in turn. "The fate of the seven ships could rest in your hands."

14
Tansy Calling

Camp tossed and turned in his hammock. For the fourth night, he'd made his bed out in the 'yard,' with Dashner, Jayne and Raven occupying his home.

Hosting the family hadn't been much of a problem. He slept in his hammock well as anywhere else, and Jayne was a wizard in the kitchen, making delectable meals that he could never have created with his ordinary rations. She'd mentioned being a chef at a top restaurant in the main city, and Camp believed it.

Smirk lay curled up in the crook of Camp's arm, tail curled over his face. He looked like a fluffy fur hat.

"You sure are cute when you're asleep and not getting into trouble," Camp murmured.

His thoughts drifted to Tansy, his favorite thought escape lately. He wondered what she was doing. *What did the inside of her dwelling look like? What did she do every day?* Most Embroids worked to create healing balms, in gardens, or as artists. *She has a greenhouse, so she definitely tends plants. But that might be because of her mother.* What did she enjoy doing in her free time? He went over the day they'd first met. Her lips, slightly parted, while she stared at the hummingbird in wonder. Her eyes, softening, as he'd introduced her to Smirk.

He sighed. He could lose himself in the profundity of those eyes, far more infinite than the deepest recesses of space.

He flipped open his comwatch, the special one the captain had given him along with everyone else. Captain Zephyr had said they could, and should, contact each other. *Dare I try? What would I say? Can the captain listen in or play back our conversations?* The hint of deception he'd noticed surrounded the captain and Commander Helms in a dark haze.

Every leader had to keep some matters to themselves, it was part of the weight of leadership. His own father, at one time the Cholter leader, had explained this when Camp was a young teenager. "Leadership is the heaviest burden a person can possess," he'd said.

The conversation with the group last night irked him. *How dare they accuse me of sabotage?* But no matter how open-minded people said they were, eventually something would happen, and they would resort to old lines of thinking. *Present lines of thinking in many cases.* But Captain Zephyr had stood up for him. And Tansy–her look of quiet trust, even over the comwatch holo, had been the most encouraging experience he'd had in years. *Of course, she was there with me. She knows I couldn't possibly have had time to do such a thing. How did she know what the problem was, anyway?* He thought back to the legends he knew about Embroids, how very few were rumored to have extraordinary abilities. Could Tansy be an Emergent? He'd read about them in an old book from his school library. Most of the books had been committed to the database. Maybe he should try to find that one.

His stomach rumbled, and he longed to enter his home and find a snack. But he didn't want to frightrn little Raven, who would still be sleeping on his couch. Tomorrow he'd speak to Dashner about talking to the magistrate. Several dwellings remained empty and were being used for storage. If he and Dashner and Jayne worked together, they could prepare a home for the family within a few days. They needed to get on the roster for extra food and supplies. His meager reserves were dwindling despite Jayne's brilliance.

They must check in with the big ship. Every time he'd mentioned this, Dashner's eyes had flashed, and he quickly changed the subject. *It's unavoidable. Why is he making such a big deal about it?*

He sighed and turned over, carefully moving Smirk so as not to wake the furry creature.

Suddenly, his comwatch lit up. Tansy's face wavered into view, bathed in a halo of light. Her hair hung around her face in soft curled wisps.

"Hello, Camp?" she murmured. "Can you hear me? Are you there?"

"Hey, Tansy," he tried to push down his astonishment and keep his voice level. "Are you having trouble sleeping too?"

"Um, yes, I suppose I am." She squinted at the screen. "Are you in an–outdoor enclosure of some kind. Do Cholters not possess dwellings?"

He sighed. "It's a long story."

"Okay." She drummed two fingers against her lips. "I have something to ask you. It's a strange request and I need your silence."

"Yeah?" He straightened up, spilling Smirk from his resting nook. Smirk opened one eye and gave a sleepy growl.

"Yes. I've decided to visit the Tark's ship tomorrow. I want to visit Kafla."

"Kafla? Really?" Camp gulped. *Why in the world would she want to talk to the Tark princess?* Maybe they'd hit it off as friends and he hadn't noticed? He shrugged. He'd never understand women. An absurd picture of Tansy braiding Kafla's hair floated into his mind, and he suppressed a chortle. *Cut it out, Camp. Something else is going on here. You're not giving Tansy enough credit.*

"I have an idea I want to discuss with her." Tansy stuck out her chin in a determined look he was beginning to recognize. "Like Captain Zephyr said."

"You want to plan a party or something?"

"Something . . ." Tansy leaned closer to the screen, her eyes two pools of weary desperation. He didn't need to touch her hand to know she was hiding something. "Look, I need to see her, okay? In person. Please, can you trust me and come along? I don't have anyone else to ask. Otherwise I'll have to go by myself and I might need help."

Camp sighed. "Yeah, I can do that." *Doesn't she realize, I'd probably do anything she asked. Even braid hair. If I knew how to braid.*

Tansy blinked and smiled. "Thank you. Can you be here at first lights?"

"How about half an hour past?"

"That would be wonderful." Tansy paused, wrinkling her nose in a way that made her even more adorable. "Camp, again, please don't tell anyone about this, okay?"

"I'll need to let the family who is staying with me know I'm going somewhere, and we must have a story for the tether guards in each place."

"Well, then maybe you could have a delivery? For the Tarks?"

"They never want anything from us. But I'll think of something."

"Okay. Goodnight, Camp."

"Goodnight, Tansy." He pushed the button and watched her face melt away. *You beautiful, wonderful person.*

Tomorrow. I'll see her tomorrow. He could scarcely believe his luck. No matter what crazy mission she had in mind, he was there for it and would welcome the adventure.

15
Visiting the Tarks

First lights glimmered from high above in the vast recesses of the ceiling, and once more Tansy longed for the real, warm, glowing sun. She hadn't realized how much she'd miss the land with real air and trees. *Would anything be the same in Fortress?* Would she experience the freshness of spring, or the first crisp taste of cool air to signal the beginning of fall? She tried to remember the material given to every person aboard the seven ships. The reports had been composed by Captain Zephyr mostly, in addition to the printouts from the droid ships sent out to scout for viable planets. She didn't remember any mention of seasons. *Surely there must be something like what we know, otherwise, how could the flora and fauna of the new planet survive?*

She peeked back through the door. As usual, her mother was still sleeping. With any luck, she'd still be asleep when she and Camp returned, but she'd left her a note just in case.

Doubt clouded her mind. When visions came like this with such intensity, they generally occurred within twenty-four hours of the reception. *How am I going to explain myself to the Tarks?* They were already so suspicious, and she and Camp hadn't exactly endeared themselves to Kafla. She'd filtered through a hundred excuses but had yet to come up with a feasible-sounding reason.

Suggesting a party was a laughable idea, especially to Kafla. Maybe, just maybe another member of the team would have fallen for it. *Perhaps that child-like girl. What was her name? Halsey.* But not Kafla. Her idea of a party probably involved roasting entire beasts over a bonfire and everyone throwing spears at each other.

Perhaps she could mention a vague premonition, or sense of danger. Most Embroids possessed these light giftings. *She will probably laugh in my face.*

The look Captain Zephyr had given her at the meeting was so direct, so pointed. *I can't risk giving her more reason to wonder.* For all Tansy knew, this whole 'team' thing was a ruse to flush out people with special abilities. She shrugged. *Unlikely. Who else would have special abilities? Now I'm the one acting prideful.* These were desperate times, and thousands of lives were at stake.

As she wrapped her cloak around her shoulders, something bulged in the side pouch. She slipped her hand inside and found the smooth, round object the old woman at the Tark market had given her. When she held it up, the flower inside glowed a fiery red. *Maybe they will understand if some of their people also possess giftings. Perhaps we have more in common than anyone realizes.*

Why did I ask Camp to come along? She rubbed the back of her neck. Now two people would witness her as she hopefully, somehow prevented disaster. How would she explain this?

Does it matter? I can't let Kafla die because of my fear.

She knew better than to ignore such a dire vision. Sometimes her premonitions were about things that caused little trouble, like a run-down land speeder or a robbery of a substation back home. When she'd run to her parents with these stories, they'd shushed her and told her the risk was too great.

The worst time was the elderly man she'd seen at fourteen. He'd been a Grimshim, caught in machinery at a container factory. In this vision, she'd seen his widened eyes and heard his horrible screams.

That day, her father had actually locked her up in a storage closet. She'd rubbed her hands raw trying to pry the door open. When he'd let her out that evening, he cried along with her as he tended to her wounds.

"Yes, you were right, my darling," he'd said. "A Grimshim man did die in a factory, just like you said." He'd taken her by the shoulders then, his eyes piercing hers. "I hope that someday you will forgive me, my little Tansy-tan. I can't lose my little girl."

She'd always wondered what would have happened if she'd stopped the old man. Perhaps she was safe from those who would use her for power and personal gain. But what of the family of the man who had died?

From then on, she'd begged Spirit every day not to show her premonitions of death. And until now, she'd never recieved another. Which meant she hadn't known, hadn't been able to warn her father of the vehicle malfunction that took his life as he came to the Embroid ship when he was working on the art in the Clarity Hall, five years before.

She pursed her lips. The chance to save a life would never escape her again. If she received a foretelling, she would do what she could to help. She'd made that silent oath at her father's Ascension Ceremony, when the Kindred had released his soul to Spirit.

Someone whistled a tune outside the yard enclosure, and she opened the gate.

Camp waited outside, his dreads bound back in a bundle at his neck, wearing a bright blue shirt she hadn't seen before. "Good morning." He gave a strange little bow, then reddened. "Sorry. Customary greeting for Cholters."

"I've seen you do it before. It's nice," said Tansy. "Here's one for you." She gave him a double-handed Embroid salute. "Good morning. Thank you for coming."

"Of course." Camp pulled a small piece of metal from his pack. "Delivery for the Ortemps. Replacement chip for a mech."

"Oh, you managed to scrounge up something. That's perfect."

"We need a good reason to pass through the Tark's ship. They're not supposed to interrogate people who take the journey, but it hasn't stopped them yet." Camp's gaze was steadfast. "As for Kafla, we could tell her we've agreed to come in to check with her regularly. Perhaps weekly? Not that she'll be happy about it. And she'll wonder why we didn't call first." He shrugged. "Let her speculate, right?"

Relief flooded through Tansy, followed by pinpricks of fear. *He's got to suspect something. If I'm doing such a bad job of playing cool with him, who else will figure it out?*

"Good thinking," she finally said. His idea was far better than any she'd thought up. That, at least, brought scant relief.

She squared her shoulders. *I'm going. If something happens to me, my aunt and uncle will care for my mother. They might grumble about having the responsibility, but they're family.*

Camp touched her shoulder. "Are we ready?"

"Yes, yes, let's go."

They moved down the grid paths, towards the tether at the opposite end. The route was becoming familiar to Tansy.

"What do the Embroids use the main building for?" Camp asked, pointing to the Clarity Hall as they passed by. "Ours is partially a big marketplace and partially workstations."

"That's our Clarity Hall. Where we wait," said Tansy.

He folded his arms. "Wait? Wait for what?"

"For Spirit to speak with us. For peace of mind."

"Huh." His brow furrowed "So basically, a fancy place to pray?"

"It's much more than that, but yes. When you boil it down to basics, that is its main function."

"Where are your workstations located?"

"Mostly in our homes, but we use some of the secondaries to make the bigger batches of healing balms and medicines. The weavers generally work in the yards, since they have no fear of rain and the looms are so large."

"Did you weave that?" He touched the sleeve of her soft lilac robe, embroidered with golden flowers.

"Oh no." She laughed. "I'm not a weaver. I grow herbs. I'm learning to extract the juices and seeds to make poultices."

"Cholters use many Embroid medicines," said Camp. "Always have, since we don't always get access to the best medical supplies."

Tansy stopped short. "What do you mean?"

Camp stared at her. "Exactly what I said. Cholters have always received the barest of help when it comes to government distribution. My great-great-great grandparents served in a janitorial position on the first ship from Earth, you see. Our family took up the scrapping trade on Gyron and as the Kindred grew, became more solitary and outcast by the decade. Over the years, when our lowly village did receive medical supplies from the head cities, they'd be mostly spoiled, contaminated, or broken. That's why we rarely accept handouts. We trust Embroid medicine because it's not free. We pay for it."

Tansy swallowed. The Embroids were valued for their medical expertise, and respected by the head cities. "I can't imagine how it feels to live in such mistrust, warranted as it is."

"It's the warranted part that makes it so bad," said Camp. "I will say things have been better for our people under Captain Zephyr's watch, but if anything happens to her position in leadership … I fear for us."

Tansy walked along in silence until they reached the tether tubes. Embroids chose a simple life, but they had always received adequate medical care when they needed a treatment that was beyond their herbal and homeopathic knowledge.

"Here we are." Camp said as the double doors of the tether tube entrance slid open.

Nimcy glanced up from her comscreen. "Tansy, I wasn't expecting you here again after the other day."

"No other way to get to the Tark ship," said Tansy, giving what she hoped was a casual shrug. "Did the tech team come through and repair the damage?"

"Yes." Nimcy tapped the screen, frowning. "But I'm keeping that tube shut down for the time being. You can take one of the other cars."

"As long as we reach the other alive and in one piece," said Camp.

"And you're here as well." Nimcy glanced at Tansy and raised an eyebrow.

You barely know my name. Why would you care who I spend time with? "Thank you, Nimcy!" Tansy said brightly as she and Camp climbed into the tether car.

Camp settled back into his seat. "I'm sorry about that."

"Sorry for what?"

He gave her a half-smile. "Sorry you have to be seen associating with me. I would hate to ruin your reputation."

"Don't ever speak to me like that again," said Tansy hotly. "It's none of their business. Besides, I'd rather be with you than any of my kindred besides my mother. My aunt and uncle are too busy with their children to care about me and I've had few friends since I left school. Caring for my mother and the herbs does not give me much time for socialization. And my Kindred–can be indifferent, at best."

The tips of Camp's ears turned red where they peeked out through his dreads. "Sorry," he mumbled. "But why wouldn't they be nice to you? You're a great person."

"It's complicated," said Tansy.

Her stomach wriggled and twisted, as though an octopus was trapped inside. *Will the Tark princess even listen to me? What if nothing happens?* The very thought brought a flood of faux relief. *If only this gift would go away, and I could be like other people.* The notion that this burden could be removed from her shoulders was intoxicating.

Camp leaned back and closed his eyes.

Poor guy. Thinks we're heading off to issue a party invitation. He probably had a million things to do besides gallivant around other ships on crazy missions.

On the other hand, she hadn't heard any great ideas from anyone else. Maybe the other team members had already hidden their special comwatches away and forgotten what the captain had asked of them. It would certainly be easier. But that would mean the weight of the mission would rest on her and Camp's shoulders. She shook her head. *Spirit, please don't let us be the only ones. At least everyone was on the call the other night. Of course, now most think*

Camp is responsible for the sabotage.

As they stepped through the tether tube, Camp patted her hand. "Everything's going to be okay," he whispered.

Gratitude flooded through Tansy. Much time had passed since she felt such care from someone besides her mother. Because of her lineage, her people treated her to stares and scrutinizing looks when she ventured from home. Camp's feelings were heightened by his general attraction to her, but within those waves were genuine care and concern. She found herself soaking in these emotions like a thirsty flower.

As before, a tribal guard stood at the door. Braids with beads and feathers hanging from them had been woven throughout his long, silver-blond hair. A cloak made from a furry animal hide, most likely an Amulet, a cross between a zebra and a camel, had been draped loosely on his shoulders. Rows of necklaces created from clay beads hung from his neck over his bare chest.

"Why are you here?" he said with the same kind of frown Tansy had been met with on her earlier journey through the Tark's domain.

"I have business with Kafla," she said, trying to keep a tremor from her voice.

His frown deepened. "Kafla? Why would she want dealings with an Embroid and a Cholter? She is far too busy for the likes of you."

"Aren't we all." Camp rolled his eyes. "Look, Mr.–uh, Tark Guard. If you had an identification tag or something–"

"Garbo," the guard growled.

"Okay, Garbo." Camp gave him his easy grin. "I'm on my way to take a chip to the Ortemps, but this lady needs to see Kafla first. I'm sure it won't take long. It's extremely important. The Princess knows us and I'm convinced she'll agree to see us. Be good enough to let us by." Despite his pleasant words, a micro-thin edge sharpened his tone.

"I told you." Garbo's voice had more of a growl to it now. "Kafla is with her beasts and cannot be disturbed."

Tansy's pulse quickened, and a sense of urgency bloomed inside her mind and filled her with new courage. "Seems to me like Kafla is a woman of her own will. Am I right?"

The guard blinked, and strangely enough, a spark of pain came into his eyes. "I would say she is," he mumbled.

"Don't you think she'd like to hear why we came, then? To choose for herself if our mission is worthy? I can contact her if you like; she might wonder why you kept her from important business."

Garbo grunted and mashed a button on the control panel before him.

Another guard entered the control room.

"Lankin, watch the tether station. You two, come with me."

He walked out the door.

Tansy glanced at Camp, and they followed him out together.

16
Raffi

As Tansy remembered from her last journey through the Tark ship, the smell of the beasts filled the entire craft, despite the air filtration system, which had been especially equipped for the stench. Tansy's nose wrinkled despite herself, but she held back the desire to cover her face with her shawl. The last thing she wanted to do was offend Garbo and have him change his mind.

Camp turned to her. "Quite an odor, isn't it? Reminds me of the Gork farm near my house when I was a kid." He waved his hand towards a large corner building to the far side of the grid. "I think that's where most of the animal waste goes. Some of the stuff is flash-dried, and the fertilizer is utilized throughout the ships."

Tansy nodded. "And a good portion will be saved for Fortress. From what I hear, the scouting team found helpful nutrients in much of the soil, but sections were sorely lacking in vital growth components, which is true for any planet."

Camp snorted. "In other words, there's no such thing as too

much manure."

Garbo gestured to the left side of the grid. "All the beasts are kept in these buildings," he said. "Except for smaller ones owned by individual families."

"Like turkeys?" Camp asked.

Garbo scowled. "Few Tarks would desire to own such stupid creatures."

"So they were given to other ships?" Camp shrugged and kept walking. He leaned towards Tansy. "They were smart enough to escape my pen, so I suppose they're more intelligent than he thinks."

Tansy giggled.

Garbo turned and glared at her. "Shrill noises disturb the beasts."

"Sorry," Tansy whispered.

She remembered why they came, and was instantly sobered.

Garbo halted in front of the largest building at the far edge of the grid, close to the outer wall. The stench intensified as he punched the panel and the large metal gate slid open.

The door opened to a small room, with hooks and shelves holding harnesses, gloves, and other implements.

"Princess?" Garbo said in a low voice. "Are you here?"

"Who dares to burden me?" came an irritated growl from an alcove.

Princess Kafla stepped out on a gleaming metal ledge. Tight, interlaced braids haloed her head. Her only clothing was a simple white shift that clung to her like skin, along with high leather boots.

A few wisps of hay stuck to her clothes, but Tansy wouldn't have brushed them off for all the hummingbirds on the headship.

"What is the meaning of this, Garbo? I gave strict orders that I was not to be disturbed." Kafla folded well-defined arms. Light scars criss-crossed her tan skin, gleaming in the light.

Tansy stepped forward. "Hello. We met at the captain's gathering the other day. I'm Tansy and this is Camp. Do you remember us?"

Kafla stared at Tansy, her crystal eyes glittering. "I remember. Do you think I'm a baby or an Old, to forget so soon? I hoped not to glimpse your common faces again. Ever." She opened the inner panel that faced them, went through, and slammed it behind her without a backward glance.

Garbo looked back at Camp and Tansy with a satisfied smirk.

A line of birds marched past the outer door. Tansy recognized the full-headed crest along with the sweeping tail feathers.

"Whoever decided to mix turkeys and peacocks had to be a special kind of crazy," Camp muttered.

"Peakeys? Yeah, pretty wild. I hear they produce more meat and eggs," said Tansy.

"So few of those bizarre morphs exist anymore. I'm glad the mootrats stuck around though," said Camp.

They both stared at the closed panel.

"Should we even try?" said Camp.

Tansy sighed, a deep breath she felt down to her toes. "I suppose."

Camp reached for the door, but Garbo grabbed his arm. "The princess said to leave her alone."

"We're here on Captain Zephyr's orders," said Tansy in the firmest tone she could muster.

Camp stiffened.

It's not really a lie, Tansy justified to herself. *Captain Zephyr did tell us to keep in touch and watch out for everyone else.*

"I'll ask you nicely this once. Unhand me. Now." Camp spoke through gritted teeth.

Tansy's eyes widened as Camp's fingers stretched towards his boot.

He's got a knife. Of course he does. She moved in front of Camp. "Mr. Garbo. Sir. I assure you, when we tell the princess why we are here, everything will be fine. And we'll take full responsibility for any wrath that might incur. Not that she'll be angry once we can speak to her." She focused all her thoughts of trust and goodwill toward him, hoping he'd pick up on her intended manifestation. A twinge of guilt came over her, she hadn't tried something like this since she was a very small child manipulating her parents. The tactic hadn't worked on them, and she'd been punished severely. *The princess's life might be at stake.*

Garbo raised an eyebrow. "Any—wrath?"

Camp's fingers relaxed. "Sure, any wrath. Will be on us."

"And look. I have this token . . . a lady gave it to me last time I came through here." Tansy held up the flower object.

Garbo snatched it from her hands. "Where did you get this? It belongs to Hempsa. She's the wisest and most respected of our prophets."

See, they do have giftings Tansy rubbed her eyes and concentrated good thoughts once more. "Yes, Hempsa. She gave it to me. She trusts me. And you should trust me as well. Please let us in."

Garbo blinked, and the hard lines on his forehead softened. "Why not? Might as well let you in. Only for a moment." He handed the object back to Tansy.

Tansy let out a sigh of relief. *Creator, please forgive me for my manipulation. I will never do it again, unless it means the difference between life and death.*

The animal smell hit full force as Tansy and Camp followed the guard into a long hall. Light tubes, suspended from the ceiling by wires, illuminated the walkway. A mesh mat the Tarks had developed to replace hay covered the floor, as it did in all the animal cages and holders in the other ships. Waste was sprayed with an antibacterial wash absorbed through the sponge-type fibers and separated from the water in tanks below the floor.

Despite the odor, the walls and doors were scrubbed and gleaming. Supplies hung in neat rows along the walkway.

Goats pressed their noses against thick plastic slats as Tansy passed by, pink tongues sticking out as they opened their mouths to bleat.

"Sorry, I don't have any food for you," she said to a tiny brown and white kid.

"What a cute little guy," said Camp. "Wish they'd given me a few of these fellows instead of turkeys. Fresh milk wouldn't be a bad thing."

The next stalls held horses. The majestic animals shoved their faces through windows and snorted at them.

The odor grew even stronger, and Tansy covered her nose with her hand. She hated to be impolite, but the smell was overpowering.

"Gorks," Camp whispered as he waved his hand towards a line of metal bars.

The massive pigs, bred to be bigger than cows, squealed and snorted behind their metal prisons.

Tansy rubbed away the tears smarting the corners of her eyes. "How can the Tarks bear the smell? The stench will only get worse as time passes."

Garbo turned and gave her a hard stare but said nothing. He swiveled back around and kept walking, his shoulders stiff.

Near the middle of the facility was a stronger enclosure, made of thick steel walls with plexiglass windows. Towards the top were barred openings.

Camp turned to Tansy. "Must be the raffi enclosure. I know they're supposed to be dangerous, but I'm a tiny bit excited."

An icy fear pressed against the back of Tansy's mind. *What if Camp gets hurt?* She hadn't even considered such a thing when she'd asked him to come, she'd been so concerned about the princess. The few books she'd been able to find about past

Emergents held dire warnings. If you chose to use your gift to save a life, someone else could die to take their place. Trying to change fate could be a risky affair. *If you believed all that.*

"These barricades are intense." Camp slapped the wall. "I didn't realize the animals were so dangerous. Don't they use them to pull carts and such?"

"If I'm mistaken, they have to be handled by special trainers and they can be temperamental," said Tansy. "Their tusks are razor sharp and cannot be removed or even shortened without killing them."

"Strange," said Camp.

"Well, anytime humans try to mess with genetics, weird things happen," said Tansy. She rested her hand on Camp's shoulder. "Look, I appreciate you coming, but why don't you wait out here? Maybe Kafla will be more willing to listen if I'm alone."

"Stay back and miss the epic discussion?" said Camp. "Not a chance."

"Argh." Tansy clenched her fists at her sides. "I wish you'd listen to me."

Camp said nothing, just set his mouth in that thin firm line Tansy was beginning to recognize.

Garbo halted at the wall. "This is where I leave you," he said. "The princess can think you broke in for all I care." He darted off towards the front entrance.

"Won't she blame him for not watching us better?" Tansy asked.

"That is the least of our worries," Camp replied. "For now, we must decide how we'll talk to Kafla again without being immediately thrown out."

They circled the enclosure.

"There's the gate," Camp pointed to a panel in the wall. Like the rest of the pen, it was made from reinforced steel and shut tight. "Even if we could open it we wouldn't want to risk letting out the animals."

"Yes, I'm supposing that would lessen our chances of any progress being made today," said Tansy.

Banging noises came from inside.

Beside the door was a large red lever with bright red lettering over it. The words were in the Tarkeen language, but the lever stood out to her. *I wonder what that's for.*

"Do you think anyone else is in the enclosure with the princess?" Tansy asked.

Camp shrugged. "Who knows?"

Tansy lifted a timid hand to knock.

"What are you doing?" came a voice from above them. Kafla looked down through the bars with a scowl so dark Tansy almost expected a bolt of lightning to follow.

"Like we said before, we need to talk to you!" Tansy shouted back.

Kafla uttered a particularly nasty-sounding oath in Tarkeen. Her head disappeared, and in a moment the large steel panel opened. She stormed out, shoulders hunched, and slammed the door behind her.

She glowered at them, her eyes glittering with rage.

"Look, I'm sorry we've bothered you," said Tansy. "But we're supposed to be working together, Captain Zephyr's orders. And I needed to connect with you today. I knew you probably wouldn't have your communicator. . ."

"Hacked into it and used it to repair a cage manipulator," said Kafla, a glimmer of a smile crossing her lips. "I became tired of associating with the commoners." She crossed her arms. "I tire of you."

Tansy swallowed. "Yes, well, I had a feeling. But we won't make it out of here unless we work together. I really want to feel the firm ground beneath my feet again someday."

She glanced at Camp, whose eyebrows were drawn together over his nose. Waves of confusion radiated from his mind. *I don't blame him. I'd be wondering what was going on right now too.*

To Tansy's supreme amazement, Kafla's shoulder's sagged, and the steel in her eyes melted. "Yes, I do miss the real, bare dirt. And the beasts, I worry for them. They have given us much trouble in these two months."

"What are your concerns?" Tansy asked, still hardly believing the turn of conversation.

Kafla sank down heavily on a wooden bench beside the door. "We are a proud people, as everyone knows. But I see fear in the eyes around me. This unknown land ... how will we live? How will our beasts survive? And we must reach the planet in the first place. These acts of sabotage are troubling."

She lowered her voice, and Tansy and Camp leaned closer to catch her words. "My mother, the chieftess, threatens to untether many times a day. But the captain is correct. We must stay together with the other ships. If any of us untether, we will die. Even if somehow our ship could navigate to Fortress alone, we would not make it to the new planet without the help of the headship. I do not like to say this, but it's true."

Camp and Tansy nodded. "I've had the same thoughts," said Camp.

Kafla's eyes narrowed, and she leveled her gaze at Camp. "I do not think you are responsible for the problems."

"Well, I'm glad to hear you say that," Camp mumbled, lowering his head.

"You would be an obvious choice," said Kafla. She snapped around to Tansy. "But you—no one would expect you, would they? Perhaps the captain really called the meeting because we are all suspects."

Tansy gasped. "How can you even say that?" But her thoughts had been such a swirl on that day during the meeting. *If other Kindreds have giftings, perhaps Captain Zephyr had a way to block her suspicions from me.*

Kafla smirked. "Don't worry, Embroid girl, I'm only teasing you. No way you'd be able to plan and pull off something like that."

"So now we're idiots," said Camp.

"I'm not sure," said Kafla. "You continue to pester me with your presence, though I commanded that you leave me alone. That is a foolhardy action. You must have a compelling reason. What do you really want, anyway?"

Crashing and banging came from within the animal enclosure.

Kafla leapt to her feet. "Solsha. She's our biggest Raffi. She's been moody today. I'd better see if the handlers need help."

"Don't go…" Tansy tried to grab the tall girl's wrist, but Kafla pushed past her to get through the door, almost knocking Tansy flat.

Tansy righted herself and squeezed in behind her.

Camp followed. "Want to give me a clue about why we're going in after her? Especially when she said these beasts are dangerous?" he said between puffs as they darted through a long, low path between fences.

"Can't now," said Tansy. "Trust me."

17
Hempsa Returns

The raffis rose up behind the fence, twice as tall as the Clarity hall. The beasts' sheer enormity took Tansy's breath away.

The animals roved around their pen, sticking their long, horselike muzzles through the openings above. Gold spots glowed on dark brown skin.

As the raffis caught sight of Tansy and Camp, they snorted and rammed their heads against the bars. Their tusks gleamed in the ceiling lights.

"They don't look docile to me," said Camp. "Aren't they supposed to be dosed with a calming drug for the trip?"

"I don't know," said Tansy. "I thought so."

Kafla whirled around. "You two need to leave. Now. The raffi enclosure is not a good place for you. I don't have time to walk you out." She slipped through a gate, and it clanged behind her. More bellowing and crashing came from behind the wall.

Camp whistled. "That's one brave princess."

A twinge of jealousy hit Tansy as waves of admiration swept from Camp's thoughts.

She shook her head. Negative ideas would impede her visions. *I must focus. I can't be sidetracked. Kafla's life is on the line.*

The banging inside the enclosure continued.

Tansy moved down the path between fences, listening for Kafla's footsteps. *Where could she have gone?*

The crashing noises came from the left this time, and the thunks grew louder and louder. Intermingled now were human shouts and screams.

Tansy moved through a doorway and into an open pen.

Four people stood in a corner, while the raffis milled around the pen, snorting. As Tansy watched the largest one reared up, higher than any living creature she'd seen, its long neck arched and wide, horse-like nostrils flared. Cloven hooves the sizes of human heads cut through the air. The beast's barrel-like sides heaved and rippled.

Kafla stepped away from the wall, holding out a feed bucket. The ice princess spoke, the normal steel gone from her voice. "Solsha, all is well. Come get something to eat."

The enormous Raffi shook her long, flowing mane and snorted, pawing the ground.

"I'm no expert, but she doesn't look very happy," Camp whispered. "Why is everyone still in there?"

"I don't know." Tansy's chest tightened. *What do I do? How can I help? Spirit, would you send me here just to watch helplessly?*

A picture burst into Tansy's mind like a shooting star. *The front of the cage.* She tore back away from the enclosures and down the path to the door panel.

Camp ran after her. "Tansy, where are you going?"

She faced the large red lever. *What if something terrible happens?* She swallowed. Nothing could be more horrible than that vision of Kafla getting hurt, maybe even killed. Grabbing the top of the lever, she slammed it down with all her might.

Something crackled in the air, like the low lightning Tansy remembered on hot nights in the mountains of her home village.

The lights flickered, then pulsed to full strength again.

The sounds of animals braying, mooing, and neighing filled the enclosure, echoing through the walls. Then the crashing began. Sounds of large objects in the cages surrounding them slamming to the ground.

Tansy and Camp pressed their hands against their ears.

What did you do? Camp's thoughts roared into her mind, but he said nothing, only stared at her with widened eyes.

Tansy pulled her hands away and looked around. The bellows of the beasts were gone. Now they could only hear the shouts and calls of the humans.

"Get to the princess!"

"Is she all right?"

"What happened?"

Camp led the way back to the enclosure and they peered

through the plexiglass section. The beasts lay in giant, shaggy heaps, like bundled area rugs.

"Did you kill them?" Camp whispered.

"I don't think so." Tansy pointed, as relief flowed through her. "See? They're definitely breathing."

Camp exhaled loudly. "Well, that's all right at least." He reached for the door's handle and raised an eyebrow.

"Yeah, we'd better go inside," said Tansy. "I mean, at least I should. Whatever happened, it's my fault."

"No way I'm letting you go in by yourself." Camp squared his shoulders. But his doubts came through clearly. *Why'd you do that?*

"I'll explain later," said Tansy.

They walked in. Three Tark men and women surrounded Kafla's crumpled form. One man with very broad shoulders and a streak of black through his long white hair kneeled beside the fallen girl. He grasped one arm with a leathered hand and shook her, speaking to her in Tarkeen.

Tansy craned her neck for a better look. No sign of blood or a cut anywhere. *At least I prevented that.*

"Is she alright?" she asked.

The woman looked up and grimaced. "Others! What are you doing here?"

It was the chieftess, with her hair in a much simpler style than before and a wearing a common shift like Kafla's.

"Oh, Chieftess, please forgive us," said Tansy. "Please tell us that Kafla is alright."

Chieftess Lalani rose and brushed off her hands. "I believe my daughter is fine. She moved to get out of the way of the raffi and tripped. I think she got the wind knocked out of her. But see," She indicated the girl's still face. "She's opening her eyes."

Another woman put a hand on her hip. "Someone must have pulled the emergency lever that sedates all the beasts through chips in their skin. Our people are forbidden from doing that without the order of the princess. I don't know who would disobey our law, but it was good timing. Solsha was going to charge."

Kafla sat up. "What–what's going on?" she said weakly.

"Apparently all madness has broken loose." Camp crossed his arms and glanced at Tansy.

Kafla stiffened her shoulders and attempted to rise. She sank back down. "Solsha charged . . ." she looked up sharply. "Solsha. Where is she?"

"If my guess is right, she's sleeping like a baby," said Camp. "Along with all the other beasts on this ship."

'What? Someone hit the tranq-lever? Couldn't have been one of my–You!" she glowered at Tansy.

A young boy hastened to the small crowd gathered around the princess. "Chieftess! Your husband has been injured!"

Kafla succeeded in rising to a sitting position this time, ignoring Camp's offered hand. "Quince, what happened?"

The boy bit his lip. "I don't know, it looks bad. He was in the stalls with the horses. One of them kicked out as it fell and hit him."

Tansy's chest tightened, and tears sprang to her eyes. *Is it as the legends say? Did I save one soul, only to destroy another? Am I to play with fate like a god?*

The voice of the Spirit rose in her spirit. *"Trust me, daughter."*

Kafla's guttural scream filled the enclosure as she struggled to her feet. She staggered towards Tansy. "You. You will die for what you did!"

Tansy's mouth fell open, and Camp flew in front of her, shoving her back so she landed on her knees. His hand flew to his boot-top once more.

Oh, have I only saved Kafla to kill Camp? "Spirit, please help us!" she croaked.

"Wait, wait!" called the voice of an old woman.

Everyone froze. A tiny crone in ragged clothes pushed through the group and somehow jostled herself between Kafla and Camp.

"Honorable Hempsa." Kafla stepped back, lowering her hands. "How did you find your way in here? It is too dangerous for a sightless one."

The old woman grabbed Tansy's arm. "Get up," she whispered.

Camp offered her his hand, and Tansy rose, her chest heaving beneath her traveling robes. Her head swam from the change in atmosphere.

"Hempsa, you can see pneuma movement," said the cheiftess. "What have you seen today?"

"This girl." Hempsa patted Tansy's wrist. "I have given her my token. She is gifted and special, and the act she chose today was, in her mind, to bring life."

"She has interfered with our beasts," Kafla said through gritted teeth. "And my father has been injured."

"We must leave the Raffi enclosure before these animals rise from their slumber," said the chieftess. "And let us help my husband get to medical care before we kill anyone else." She gave Kafla a leveled gaze. "Come, my daughter. We must sort out these matters elsewhere."

Tansy and Camp followed the crowd out of the raffi enclosure.

"I hope those beasts stay asleep awhile longer," Camp whispered to Tansy.

Tansy pulled the token from her pouch and flipped it over and over in her hands, finding strange comfort in its smooth, cool perfection. *Spirit, please. Let Kafla's father be okay.*

After what seemed like an eternity, two guards passed them, carrying an older man on a makeshift stretcher they'd formed from two boards and a blanket. The man was motionless except for his thick white beard, which spilled over his chest and rose and fell in an erratic pattern.

At least he's breathing. But did I do the right thing? Kafla will be fine, but what if her father dies? They'll probably throw me in the brig for tampering with that lever. I will never be able to explain why I did it.

###

Tansy and Camp sat outside of the building that served as the

Tark's clinic. Piles of medical equipment Camp recognized as from the headship lined the outside walls. He remembered seeing quite a bit of it come through the trash tubes. The Cholters had been mystified as each batch of brand-new equipment dropped into the rufuse heaps. Why would any of the ships dispose of that? They'd decided the equipment must have been faulty somehow and set it aside to examine when they had time. But now he knew: The Tarks rejected the headship's technology, the same way the Cholters refused, well, almost everything. Their Kinship had managed without big city medicine for almost a hundred years on the last planet, and they'd survive without it on the ship.

Garbo emerged from the clinic. He nodded to Tansy and Camp.

"Is the chief going to be alright?" asked Tansy.

"Yes," said Garbo. "His leg was broken but will soon mend. He will live to fight another day."

Fight who? Camp didn't care to say this out loud, but Tansy's lips quirked up into a smile. *She* can *read my thoughts. I knew I wasn't imagining things.*

Tansy jerked her head to the side, her eyes widening.

Don't be afraid, I'm not telling anyone. Camp hoped she caught that. He reached for her hand and she allowed him to take it. Her fingers folded around his and she exhaled loudly, leaning her head on his shoulder.

Thoughts raced through his mind. So many questions, and he only hoped she'd trust him enough to answer them when they had a quiet moment.

But where is it safe to talk? The forcebots are everywhere.

She shrugged against his arm. "We'll figure it out," she whispered. "I'm hoping I won't get thrown into the brig for flipping that lever."

"Why *did* you flip the lever?" Camp murmured.

"I can't tell you. Are you okay with that?"

Will you ever trust me? Could you? "Will you be able to tell me someday?"

She sighed. "If I didn't trust you, I wouldn't have asked you to come with me. I will gather my courage, Camp. I will try to tell you eventually. Can that be enough for now?"

"Sure," he said, trying to keep his voice and thoughts level. But pain slipped an icy knife through the cracks of his mind and he worked, as he always had, to keep it from changing into anger. *She has her reasons, probably built from years of fear. Now it's your turn to trust.*

"Please," she whispered.

"Of course," he said, fighting the temptation to kiss her forehead.

Kafla came through the door, her ever-present scowl covering her face, though the expression could mar her great beauty. "Embroid girl," she growled. "My father will live. Fortunate for you. Very fortunate. And Hempsa has spoken. Her words are to be respected above all."

Tansy sagged against Camp's shoulder. "Thank you very much. I hope you know I was trying–"

Kafla held up her hand. "We will speak no more of this. My anger is at rest for now, and it is best for you that it is not stirred up again."

She nodded to Garbo. "You may go now," she said to him.

He walked off, not looking back.

Kafla gave a little smirk. "He was my betrothed. I was promised to him from childhood."

"When's the wedding?" Camp said, attempting to lighten the dark mood that had settled in the air.

Kafla lifted her chin and folded her arms across her chest. "I could not find affection in my heart for him and did not wish to bond myself to him. My people have a custom. If the woman has no desire to marry the man chosen for her, the suitor she does wish to marry can fight for her hand. Or she can fight for herself." Her emerald eyes locked onto Camp's. "I won."

"That's . . . um . . . great for you," said Camp.

"Yes." Kafla beamed. "It was a triumph. Now." She slapped her hands together. "My father wishes to speak to you. Come inside."

Tansy stared up at Camp. "At least I can apologize."

Camp walked into the room, Tansy still holding his hand.

Flames cast dancing shadows on the walls of the clinic. Instead of the normal artificial lights, the Tarks used strange little oil lamps for illumination. Camp recalled that the Bloomwraiths also used these lamps, though he wasn't certain why. *Not like we're hurting the environment. All our electricity comes from recycled water and star solar power.*

The chief lay on a bed exactly like the narrow white cots Camp had seen in the Cholter clinic. Burly shoulders bulged from beneath the standard blue blanket. His braids had been partially shaved and covered with a neat bandage.

He smiled as Camp and Tansy approached his bed. "It seems I have you to thank for saving my daughter's life. Solsha was mid-charge when you pulled the lever, and she most certainly would have hurt Kafla dreadfully."

"But you were injured because they pulled the lever." Kafla folded her arms against her chest and scowled.

The chief patted her arm. "My dear, I'll be fine. Nothing a scan-heal can't take care of. I'll be up in a day or two."

"I thought you said we weren't going to use the headship's medical devices," said Kafla.

The chief sighed. "Only in times of great need. I can't lay here for six weeks to mend. The beasts need each one of us. Especially Solsha. Her calf will be dropping any day." He glanced over at Camp. "That's why she's been so moody."

The chieftess, who had been standing to the side, stepped forward. "And who can blame her? The last days of carrying a child are most uncomfortable."

"You threw a spear at me, if I recall," said the chief.

"Lucky she missed," said Camp.

"Oh, she didn't," said the chief. He pointed to a thin white scar on his shoulder and gave a low, guttural laugh.

The chieftess gave him a light slap on the arm. "It barely caught you. And didn't keep you from bellowing for your breakfast the next morning."

"True, true," said the chief. Love poured from his deep green eyes.

Doesn't look like he held a grudge for long. Camp smiled.

"Your father needs to rest and heal," The chieftess patted Kafla's arm. "Please see our guests out."

"Don't you need rest as well?" asked Tansy, pointing to the slash on Kafla's head.

Kafla's fingers fluttered to the wound. "This? This is nothing. Let's go."

They went back outside, blinking in the artificial all-ship lights.

Camp moved towards the Embroid's tether station.

Kafla swung around. "Weren't you headed to the Ortemp ship for a delivery?"

The remaining color drained from Tansy's already-whitened face. "Um–"

"I think we've had enough for one day," Camp said to Tansy. "How would you feel about going home for now?"

"That would be good," said Tansy.

Kafla bent down low to speak to them. "Embroid Girl–"

"Tansy," said Camp.

"Tansy." Kafla sighed. "It is obvious you foresaw my danger. Otherwise, why would anyone do such a foolish thing? And why would Hempsa defend you and give you her token? I don't understand, but I thank you." Her face darkened. "But if my father had died, we would have fed you to the gorks."

"You're welcome," said Tansy. Her face reddened and she lowered her voice. "If the headship asks about what happened, do you think your people could tell them I was curious and foolishly flipped the lever?"

Camp squeezed her hand. Her fingers shook within his grasp.

Kafla drew herself to full height. "Yes, Tansy, Embroid daughter. I will command my people to keep this secret." She gestured for them to follow. "Let's go to the tether tube before you get any more crazy notions into your head."

Camp felt as much in the dark as he had when he'd agreed to come on this little expedition, but he also had his hunch confirmed. Tansy was much more than she appeared to be. And she didn't want anyone else to know. *And I'm going to find out why.*

18
Matchsticks

Periwinth strode through the double doors, into the workstation. Two dozen men and women rose from desks and tables, snapping to attention. She glanced over the eager faces. Most were barely out of the highest grade forms, but a few were older than even Marrow. These scientists were the best and brightest from the fleet. The majority were Ortemps and Grimshims, with some headship crew members scattered in.

"At ease," she said. Would she ever get used to being treated in this manner? Even when she'd captained her first little ship, the crew had come to an informal arrangement. They'd lived together, laughed together. *Mostly died together.* She shuddered. A young cadet with a blond pixie cut gazed at her with child-like blue eyes. *How many of these people will die?* She couldn't allow the thought to creep into her mind. They'd spent years strategizing, creating solutions for the horrible obstacles they'd encountered on the first mission. *We must succeed. Failure can't happen.*

Everyone relaxed and settled back into their work.

Periwinth walked around the first station, eyes flitting over a modular grid of proposed garden structures. Ten tiny towers with cascading plants lined the grid, created with the same sturdy plastic-like material that almost everything in the ships were constructed from. This material was stored in liquid form on the underside of the ship in gigantic barrels. Thus far, they hadn't detected the components for the same mixture within the new planet's natural resources, but what they had was greatly compressed. When infused with air any shape created would expand by up to a thousand times.

Bradstorm remained by the door, his arms folded across his chest as usual. He caught her glance and gave her a quick smile.

She smiled in return. Having every movement scrutinized had been another difficult custom to deal with. Bradstorm never made her feel uneasy, though he did sometimes make suggestions for 'wiser safety choices,' as he called them. But the members of the Solstice were also always on the watch. Marrow tended to bring her rebukes like a tidal wave. "You shouldn't move through the ship without at least four officers." "You need more forcebots on the third level." "Do you think it wise to speak with Magistrate So-and-So in such an informal manner?"

Glad none of the Solstice members are here today. Especially Platmoth. Periwinth frowned and trained her eyes on the project occupying the second table.

Three students, a Grimshim woman and two Headship men from the original city of Predica, worked on a white modular structure, fashioned from three-inch hexagonal plates.

"What are we looking at here?" asked Periwinth.

"Hello, Captain," said the woman. "I am Telna. This building is designed to combat the extreme cold and withstand attacks from the Gronther creatures you encountered on your first mission."

She pointed to two model mechs. "The Ortemps have been constructing these bot-sentries and will have them ready to assemble once we reach the surface of Fortress. We assume we'll need at least ten to start off with, twice as big as any we have in our service as of now. They will be manned by pilots and released from the ship to scan the land mass and set up a force perimeter before anyone else moves out of the ship. Each one will be equipped with powerful stun blasters to incapacitate any living creatures so they can be captured for study."

Periwinth sucked in a breath. The Gronthers had been the most terrifying beasts she'd ever encountered. Walrus-like creatures the size of elephants, but with mouths full of long, jagged teeth. Despite their size, they moved like lightning across the ice. She could still hear the first fated crewman's scream as he was taken down to the icy depths, before any of the others could so much as pull out a blaster.

She placed a hand on the woman's shoulder. "Do the Ortemps have the space to create such massive forcebots?"

Telna tapped her chin. "They have utilized the maintenance shafts below their ship's gridlines for construction thus far. The spaces are hollow and large enough for machines twice the size needed in some areas."

"Will these machines be tied in with the main system?" asked Periwinth, thinking of the forcebot battle she'd survived only a week ago.

Telna shook her head. "Ortemp techs advise against it. They won't be powered up until the last few weeks; right before we arrive. They've requested additional supplies to continue their construction, but I need your signature for them."

Periwinth took the offered screen and pressed her thumbprint in the sign-box. "Telna, this plan is the best one I've heard so far. If the Ortemps can construct these mechs in time. Since the ice region is the only known source of fresh water on the planet, we must have stations there until we can explore further areas. The work you're doing is absolutely vital. I am thankful for you and your team."

Telna's eyes shone. "You're welcome. I want my family to be safe. I have two children."

"Yes," said Periwinth. "We all want to be safe."

She'd spent countless hours strategizing how they could travel the full year, with all the ships tethered along. The idea of forcebots going rogue or some source of energy being depleted had never occurred to her. In all the madness, she sometimes forgot the people would still have a fight for survival when they reached Fortress. And she knew, more than anyone on Serpentine, how tough that fight would be.

It'll be better than burning up from a supernova. I hope.

But horrors awaited, the kind that kept her waking, covered in sweat, most nights. And the team had only explored a tiny part of the planet. Who knew what other obstacles awaited them? The probes could only show so much.

But there could be wonderful things. Where there's life, there's hope.

The double doors to the room slid apart, and Platmoth entered. He gave Periwinth the customary salute, flattened hand against the side of his face, and smiled. "Captain. I take it you are finally feeling better?"

Her soul thudded to the bottom of her belly. "Yes, I have returned to full health, thank you."

Bradstorm edged closer, like he always did when Platmoth was anywhere in the vicinity. Periwinth shot him a look and he nodded. *He's wondering what the Visier is doing here as well. Usually he's inspecting the forward decks at this time.*

"Captain," Platmoth said, his twisty smile contorting his face as usual. "I have finished my meetings early for today and as I had a bit of unexpected free time. I wonder if you'd care to join me for light supper?"

Periwinth supressed an eye roll. She had no desire to share a meal with Platmoth in the same room, let alone across the table from him. Certain concessions had to be made and he knew it. People would wonder why she wasn't willing to confer with a member of her own Solstice. "Certainly, I suppose we could go for a bite to eat if it doesn't take long. Allow me to finish looking over these models first."

He bowed again, looking for all the world like a marionette bobbing on a string. "I will accompany you on your examinations if you wish."

She nodded mutely, though that was not at all what she wished.

A short hour later, Periwinth found herself seated in the ranking officer's eatery. The dining room, consisting of arranged silver tables and chairs was located at the very top of the ship. Earth art graced the walls, and ancient sculptures and carvings had been tastefully arranged to please the diners' eyes. A dome-shaped skylight opened out to eternal blackness. At certain tables, lone crewmen sat, necks craned and eyes fixed on the void. Periwinth had often found herself in similar practice here. Normally she looked forward to coming to this place, but not today. *Not in present company.*

Platmoth's silverware clinked against his plate. He swallowed a bite of salmon and dabbed at the corners of his mouth with a shimmering gold napkin. "Excellent fish. Fortunate the breeding program has been so successful. It's a species I would hate to lose." His eyes grew misty. "On Earth, my ancestor was what they called a commercial fisherman. My family passed down the tales of the wild swordfish, what it was like to watch them leap from the sea, and how they tasted." He shook his head. "We have no idea what was lost, do we?"

Periwinth smoothed her napkin over her lap. "I hesitate to eat fresh meat of any kind while we're in space. Life is fragile and we cannot predict how our flora and fauna will respond to the new environment. Our records show that when humans landed on Gyron, we had a gradual loss of 17 percent of Earth's native life over the first ten years, with more to follow. What else will we lose on Fortress? Of course, there will be new life forms awaiting us there."

"Is that why you have chosen a … what is that, Captain, if I may ask?" Platmoth waved his fork at her plate.

"Hamburger," she said. "Plant-based and thawed from the freezer. I don't mind."

"Such simplicity," Platmoth stared at her, his lips twisting into a half smile. "But perhaps we will find new types of fish on the planet. The probes gave such limited information."

"We did encounter the Gronthers," Periwinth said. "And though we didn't have the time or means to search for more signs of life, an animal of that size, obviously carnivore in nature, points to an extensive food chain."

"Most encouraging," said Platmoth, though the information couldn't possibly be new to him. He pointed his spoon, pale green soup dripping off the end. "Might I say it's gratifying to see you in such a lovely dress. A woman should feel free to beautify herself at times, even when she's in leadership."

Periwith glanced down at the beaded front of her simple evening dress, heat rising to her face. *Should've worn my training scrubs.*

Platmoth leaned closer, and she caught a whiff of his fishy breath. "Must *he* be with you tonight?" He gave Bradstorm, who stood by the door, a pointed glance. "Surely he knows you're safe with me."

Bradstorm returned the stare, his expression unchanging.

"Yes. He must." Periwinth longed to throw her hamburger in the man's face, but she hated to waste good food. Marrow would give her fits if she abruptly walked out, but she had a good mind to leave anyway.

I'm a starship captain for goodness's sake. She stuck out her chin. *Why can't I stop worrying about the Solstice? They're supposed to be my advisors and nothing more.*

Platmoth gazed at her, his dark eyes murky. He would be devastatingly handsome if it weren't for the sullen, stubborn set to his jaw. She'd felt sorry for him when they first met, for no one obtained a face like that without going through a life of hardship. The same expression had stared at her from the mirror eight years ago when she'd come back from the first mission.

She took a small nibble of her burger and chewed slowly. *That's it.* She simply couldn't eat another bite in the wake of that stare, that expectancy. The need for something she would not, could not, ever, ever give.

Years ago, she'd handed her heart, warm and beating, to another soul. And he'd taken it with him to a star-filled grave. How could she ever retrieve it, even if she did find a new, worthy love?

Bradstorm touched the back of her shoulder, the tips of his

fingers brushing her bare skin below her short-sleeved evening dress.

"Captain, if I may–the doctor recommends early retirement through the week. You still need to heal."

Leave it to Bradstorm to rescue me. "Why, yes, of course." She pulled her napkin from her lap and placed it on her plate. "Please excuse me. Platmoth. I did say my time would be short this evening."

Platmoth gave a childish pout. "Really, Periwinth, I'm surprised you'd continue to show such weakness. The people of these ships need to see you out in full strength, or they might worry about your incompetence."

The irritation she'd been tamping down through the evening boiled over into anger, but she took a breath and worked to keep her voice level. "It would serve you well to address me as captain," she said quietly. "We are not on such familiar terms as you might like to think."

She walked swiftly to the door of the officer's hall, sighing as his boots clattered behind her. He moved with her through the opening at the same time as Bradstorm, so the three of them almost jammed together on the way out in a most awkward fashion.

They moved to the landing, which was empty, to Periwinth's chagrin. She hurried to the lift's platform, but Platmoth was on her tail.

Bradstorm shot her another glance.

She lifted her chin and turned to face her pursuer.

"Your talons are sharp tonight," Platmoth murmured. "But one day you will belong to me, and willingly." He turned and strode away.

"Or perhaps one day he'll find himself floating through space without a suit," said Bradstorm, the muscle on his neck pulsing.

Periwinth clenched her fingers into fists and walked down the hall to the lift. Platmoth's subtle hints had become more intense every time they met, but tonight he'd crossed a line she hadn't dreamed he'd stumble over. *I've been perfectly clear. I'm not interested. Not now or ever.* She dared not open her mouth for fear that the action would unleash an endless scream of rage that she'd never be able to stop. But it burned her throat and tore at her soul.

I am captain of this ship. I should throw him into the brig for such presumptions. But then where would they be? With a solstice missing one cord of the three-fold rope. Platmoth and Crenth had supporters by the thousands throughout the ships. One wrong move against the leaders, and a sizeable percentage of the population could mutiny.

She focused on her breathing until it evened out again. Instead of hitting the up arrow, she pressed the down command.

Bradstorm arched an eyebrow. "Are you seriously heading to the calisthenics range? What about the doctor's orders?"

"I won't sleep a bit if I don't work off some of this rage. You know that."

He glanced her over, his eyebrow arching. "You're not in any condition for physical exercise. If you must do something, throw a few knives, or shoot a bow."

"Oh no, that's not good enough. I'm aching for a round of matchsticks."

Bradstorm groaned. "Absolutely not. Shall I call the doctor down here? He can command you not to fight."

She punched him lightly on the shoulder. "I think you protesteth too much. Let me guess. You're really thinking you might actually have an advantage. Maybe you'll beat me for once."

Bradstorm shook his head. "You need to take care of yourself. You almost died a few days ago." His voice softened to the tone he used only in the rare occasions when they were alone. "Platmoth has no business talking to you like that. You must confront him and have him removed from the Solstice."

"I can't do that right now. The slightest blip in our system could lead to chaos." She swallowed. "I must endure until we reach Fortress. Once we have the land stabilized and can figure out the leadership situation, the structure will be different."

He exhaled loudly. "Have you considered that one of the Solstice members could be behind the sabotage?"

She pressed her fingers against her forehead. "Of course I have. We must consider everything. When I was in pilot school, dreaming of being the captain of my own little craft, I never thought I'd be surrounded by a crew I could only partially trust."

"At least I'm here to protect you," said Bradstorm. "But I can't help much if you don't listen."

Periwinth dipped her head. "You know I appreciate everything you do." The light dinged at the top of the lift. "But now I'm going to have to slaughter you, so watch out."

"Highly unlikely," said Bradstorm.

The lift opened right into the training room, instead of the usual corridor. Boxing rings flanked one wall, along with punching bags and combat dummies. Enclosed rooms for target practice and various sports like tennis and archery lined the other wall.

In the front area, half a dozen crew members exercised with various weight implements.

Periwinth headed for the room at the end, which was her favorite.

Bradstorm followed her. "I thought you were joking about matchsticks. Would you please just shoot a quiver full and go to bed?"

She gathered her hair at the nape of her neck and tied it back. "Twenty percent or forty?" she said over her shoulder as she opened the double doors of the matchsticks hall. Adrenaline surged through her, numbing the aches and pains throughout her body.

"Argh. If I cared about beating you tonight, I'd go for forty, because we both know twenty doesn't faze you in the least," said Bradstorm. "But since I don't want you to end up back in the infirmary, I insist on ten."

"Twenty it is." Periwinth headed to a wall with several dozen sticks hanging from it. These were about six feet long, black with smooth white tips on both ends. She selected the nearest stick, testing the weight. "Pity I didn't have time to return to my quarters for my favorite one, but we both know you would have figured out a way to lock me in." She adjusted the center strength-meter and tossed the weapon to Bradstorm.

He caught it. "I know three different ways to do so," he said grimly. He ran his hands along the smooth surface, balancing it expertly.

She grabbed a stick for herself, and he followed her to the arena.

"Now that we're here, we might as well have fun," she said. She flipped the switch in the stick's center, and it began to hum. The ends glowed a dull orange.

Bradstorm activated his switch and began to circle her. "One more attempt to convince you not to do this. Ma'am, let's not forget I had to carry you to your quarters yesterday."

I wish he wouldn't call me that. The thought hit her for the first time since the day she'd been voted in by the Solstice.

She'd met Bradstorm in tens class, when his family had moved to the city. He'd been a head taller than the other boys even then. Their friendship had been easy, and he'd quickly become her first crush, even though she'd never expressed her feelings. They'd parted ways after graduation, when she entered pilot school and he'd begun training for planet defense, years before the disaster had been anticipated, before Fortress had been discovered and chosen for the final destination. The Serpentine ships hadn't existed. After losing touch, she never thought she'd see him again. In time, she'd given her heart to another.

She hadn't laid eyes on Bradstorm again until six months before departure, when he'd been introduced as her possible second. He'd risen through the ranks of soldiers as fast as she'd advanced as a pilot. Though the crew referred to him as Commander, and he technically held power over all but the Solstice, he'd deferred most of the honor and respect to her, mostly acting as a bodyguard. Every day they moved together. There wasn't a plan or procedure they didn't both know. But any lack of protocol would show cracks in their personal armor. It was as though they'd come to an instinctive understanding. If a leader of any other ship even caught a hint of their previous friendship, both of their positions would be in jeopardy.

Periwinth jabbed at Bradstorm's head, and he stepped out of the way. The ends of the sticks crackled as they both dodged and feinted.

"I wish . . ." Bradstorm slammed her stick with his own . . . "You would listen to me . . ."

He swung at her feet and she jumped over the staff, "for once in your life."

"Once? Does that mean if I listened once you would stop nagging me forever after that?" She whirled around, dodged under his elbow, and hit him in the back with the end of her stick.

He dropped his staff. "Whew, even at 20 percent those shocks sting." He gave her a rare grin. "Feel better now?"

Her hand moved down to touch her sore knee. "Yes, I do," she said. "But I suppose now we could call it a night. I mean, if you're tired and all."

As they headed back to the lift, her second comm watch blinked. "Interesting. It's Falstaff." She turned the watch towards Bradstorm so he could read it without announcing it to forcebots in the lift.

The screen read: "Trouble here. I'll arrive in the morning to give a report."

19
Ascension

By the time Camp and Tansy's tether car landed on the Embroid ship, the lights had dimmed down to the floors. Kafla had insisted they stay for supper, a very long affair filled with speeches, stories, and a battle song or two. Even though the first part of the day had been stressful, to say the least, Camp enjoyed the meal and the richness of a culture he'd rarely glimpsed in the past.

Despite the shortness of the ride, Tansy fell asleep on Camp's shoulder, her delicate features settled into a peace he'd never beheld, each of her breaths warming the skin beneath his shirt.

He sighed deeply. Though neither one of them had breathed a word of commitment, he hadn't felt such a sense of belonging to someone, being needed, for many years. Not even with his pet, since Smirk was an independent creature who only gave him affection when he wanted something.

Is Tansy with me only because she needs me? He jolted.

Tansy stirred. She blinked and opened her eyes. "Goodness,

how silly of me." She sat up and yawned. "I'm sorry, Camp. I must have been more tired than I thought."

"Soothsaying must have that effect." Camp regretted the words as soon as he'd said them. *What possessed me?* He wanted to bash his head against the side of the tether tube.

Tansy's shoulders sank, and she seemed to wilt into the cushioned seat. "I'm not a soothsayer," she hissed, glancing at the forcebot cameras on either side of the car. "You can't breathe a word of this to anyone, Camp. My life depends on it."

"Please trust me," Camp said. "I'm not going to tell anyone. We all have our secrets. Besides that." He touched her hand. "I would never do anything to put you in danger. If you don't believe my words, maybe you can at least sense my thoughts."

Tansy dipped her head. "Do you think anything bad will come of this? Kafla said she'd keep my secret."

"No way to tell. I'm assuming you don't stomp around warning everyone of certain death."

"No. It's too dangerous. My parents kept me from telling anyone about my giftings for my whole life. And I don't always know when things are going to happen. Spirit chooses what to show me."

"Does that mean . . ." he studied her face. "Does that mean you've let people die?"

"Yes." A tear slid down her cheek. "I could have been killed, Camp, and my parents as well. The discovery of an Emergent is never a good thing. Full generations have been corrupted. Some have been taken and enslaved by more powerful kindreds. My parents drilled these warnings into me as a child, and when I was old enough, I studied the ancient stories for myself. Keeping an Emergent a secret is highly unpopular with my people, but I agree with my parents."

Camp swallowed. "Why would Creator give anyone such a dangerous gift?" he said.

"I've thought about this for many years," said Tansy. "He loves His people and wants good things for them. And maybe someday, we will learn how to steward our gifts correctly. I hope that helping Kafla was a turn to the right path."

The doors to the tether-tube slid open, and a tinny recorded voice said "Tether secured. You may now exit the vehicle."

Camp rose and held his hand out to Tansy. "Sorry for the jab about soothsaying. Sometimes I joke when I'm nervous, but that's not a good excuse. We've been kind of thrown together, haven't we? Not that I mind. I want . . .need you to trust me."

Her soft brown eyes widened. "Camp, I do trust you. More than anyone in the world, besides my mother. If I've held anything back, it's for your safety."

"Then please." He helped her from her seat. "Don't hold back."

"I'll try my best not to anymore," she said firmly, though her lower lip trembled.

She's telling the truth. Certain as my name is Campion. Desire swarmed through him like thirsty bees, a need to kiss those trembling lips and share more than words with this amazing girl.

Crimson flooded her cheeks, and she dropped his hand.

Drat. I forgot she can probably read my thoughts. He pressed his palm against his forehead, as though that could somehow stop the flow of information.

A ghost of a smile flitted across her lips. "Look, I appreciate your help. More than you could ever know, really. For me to say our meeting was by chance would be to deny my faith, But I'm marked for trouble, it's passed down through my bloodline. And those who are close to me could be in danger too. I'm not exaggerating." She glanced up, her eyes shining with unshed tears. "I wish I was."

He struggled to find the right words, a way to assure her that all would be well, but nothing came.

An alarm chimed, and the Embroid tether guard peeked through the door. "Everything all right in here? After the trouble the other day I'm a little jumpy with every transport."

"Everything's fine." Tansy lifted her chin, and Camp led her through the door.

A gloomy violet hue from the main lights enveloped the rows of dwellings as they moved down the main corridor. Tansy sucked in a breath. "This isn't good."

"Aren't the lights usually yellow?" asked Camp. "Does the color signify something?"

"Colors are everything to my people," Tansy replied. "Dark purple only means one thing. Death."

She picked up the pace, her long robe swishing around her hips.

They passed through the town, down the path Camp was

coming to know well. In all the modules, dark purple lights flickered from the windows. People raised hands as they came by but bowed their heads instead of smiling or speaking out.

"It's me," Tansy croaked. "A personal sign of respect."

"Can't you ask them what's wrong?" Camp said.

"No need." Tansy stopped in front of her front gate. Dozens of people stood in a misshapen circle around the outside. All heads were covered by wide hoods, looking like the knobby roots that would poke through the ground around certain trees that grew by ponds near Camp's home village. The people remained motionless, even the smallest children. An occasional twitch or shoulder heave brought upon by a deeper-than-normal breath was the only sign of life.

That's not eerie. Camp held back an urge to run up and shake someone's shoulders. Anything to break this unbearable silence.

Tansy whirled to face him, the tears flowing freely now. "My mother must have died while we were gone. She had cancer." She gave a shaky laugh. "She was doing alright. I thought we had more time."

"I'm so sorry." Camp said. He longed to take her in his arms, perhaps absorb the tiniest part of her pain.

"You need to go."

"No." he grabbed her hand. "I'm not going to leave you right now."

"You can't stay here." She wrenched out of his grasp. "I'm sorry. I wish you could, but they won't let you. They will make you leave."

Several hooded heads had already turned to face them. Solemn eyes regarded him beneath the terrible robes. Did they hold only sorrow, or did he catch a hint of animosity swirling within the hollow stares?

He squeezed Tansy's fingers and reluctantly let go. "Let me know if you need anything," he said softly. "I'll be waiting for any word."

She gave a barely perceptible nod, then turned, her long braid swishing over her shoulders.

As he headed home, the collective pain hovered over him like a dreary shroud. He pulled his arms forward in a stretch, trying to physically rid himself of the sensation. He always felt strange when among the Embroids, fuzzy and uncertain, like he was fumbling through walls of cotton. This was different. Sharper, more tangible and focused.

The doors to the tether tube slid together, shutting off the sensation.

He leaned back in the cushioned seat and sighed. Back on the old planet, this wouldn't be so complicated. People from varying groups did intermarry, though he'd never heard of a Cholter-Embroid match.

If we were on the home planet, we probably wouldn't have met.

The words rang in his head as though coming from her lips again. Warm, like her hand slipped into his own.

His comwatch dinged, and he checked it. One word. From her.

Pray.

###

Tansy moved through the robed figures, her legs stiff and heavy, as though she was wading through a muddy swamp. The people parted to allow her through but no one spoke. No tentative hand brushed her shoulder, no arms opened to give her a silent embrace of concern or comfort. But she was accustomed to being treated in this way. The only touch or affection she'd received for many years had been from her mother. *And Camp.*

Father Sharood stood by the door. "We bid you good evening, daughter."

Good evening. She'd uttered this blessing with her own lips, to the families of the dead, but even in those times did not understand why. How could this evening be good when the person most precious and sacred to her was gone? Mother, the keeper of her secret, the solid chain that bound her to safety. Might as well request for release into the dark and void of space, like her mother's body most certainly already had been. She doubted Father Sharood had waited for her return. The Embroids believed death left the body an instant hull that must be disposed of with little ceremony. Only the spirit should be exalted. That celebration would happen at the Clarity and last long into the night.

Tansy would be forced to go. Grief was not a part of death for her people. After the exhaustion of the day, and then with this homecoming, all she wanted was to curl up on her bed and sleep. Deep, dreamless slumber, to pull her away from the insanity of truth, that her mother was no more. That she wouldn't be allowed to touch her hand or see her face one more time, cold and lifeless as it would be.

Tansy shook her head, a fruitless attempt to rid herself of the dull thrumming that filled her from within. The music would play to that very beat, in fact, and the young and the old would sing and join in the Dance of Ascension.

I cannot. I cannot do it. They won't make me.

She slipped open the hasp of her front door and stepped inside. The violet lights cast the shadows of taunting monsters on the walls of the dwelling.

"Tansy."

She almost jumped out of her skin. Her head whipped up, and her hand went to her waist, to the second comwatch concealed there.

Her uncle Tam lounged on the couch, his face in the shadows. His sandaled feet were propped up on the small table, and a vape stick dangled from his teeth. The harsh chemical scent filled the room, making her choke.

She'd never been alone with her uncle. Her mother had always warned against it and now the fear that pricked the back of her neck confirmed those trepidations.

"Where's Aunt Cora?" she said, proud that she'd managed to keep her voice even.

Uncle Tam took the vape stick from his mouth, holding it

between two fingers and blowing another stream of noxious fumes into the air. "Gave birth a few hours ago. Right after she found your dead mother. I think the shock sent her right into labor."

"Oh." Tansy sagged against the door, suddenly more tired, though she scarcely imagined it possible. "Is the baby…"

Uncle Tam raised a thin eyebrow. "Fine," he said. "Cora and both of the babies are fine."

"Both?" Tansy couldn't hold back the tremor this time. *Twins? How could the scans have missed them?* Embroids looked to alternative medicines for many things, but they relied on modern devices for things like gender and fetal health. She'd never heard of a scan missing something this important.

"Yes. A beautiful baby girl hiding behind her brother. She'll be a sassy one. Your aunt is over the moon."

"A–girl?" The drumming in Tansy's head worsened, and she swayed on her knees, glad for her robe's coverage. This was bad. There'd been nothing to worry about, since there wasn't another girl. But now . . . *at least Mother never knew.*

"She's tiny, but strong. A secret twin has only happened once before in this generation that the midwife could recall. Quite surprising, is it not?" Uncle Tam rose and strode over to a picture of Tansy and her mother, taken when Tansy was in sevens. His head snapped back like a bird of prey. "Well. Perhaps you're not so surprised."

"I don't know what you mean," she murmured. "I appreciate you being here since Aunt Cora could not, but I'm sure you must want to be home with her and the babies. And I must prepare for the ceremony."

"Oh yes, the ceremony for your poor mother," he said in a sarcastic sing-song tone. "I told the father I'd stay here in proxy as the closest family member, since your aunt is still in birth care. Figured it would give me a chance to have a bit of a word." His lips curled into a sneer that made his face even more sinister, if that was possible.

"That's kind of you." Tansy straightened her shoulders. "But I don't need a proxy for Clarity. I would prefer to go alone."

He leaned forward, and now she caught the hint of straight rimport rum mixed with the remnants of the vape.

"That's how it's been with you and your mother, hasn't it? All alone. Keeping secrets from the rest of us. Nasty little secrets." He wiped a bead of spittle from his mouth with the sleeve of his heavily decorated robe. "By our law you belong in my care." He gave a twisted little laugh. "For a short time, that is. Your birthday is in what, three days?" He sank back on the couch and jerked his head to her bedroom door. "Go on. Get ready. I'll be waiting."

She stumbled to her room, wishing for the first time the door had a lock. No. Multiple locks. Dozens of locks. She scanned her room, her gaze settling on a Tera-vine growing in a large, heavy pot. *It will have to do.*

Grunting and heaving, she dragged the pot to the door, the vine tearing away from the wall and dragging on the floor. "I'm sorry, little vine," she hissed. "I'll do my best to repair you later."

Quickly she dressed in the dark purple robe, worn only by family members celebrating a death. Her nose wrinkled. Tam wouldn't be bothered to wear his. Of course, he chose to wear his bright green birth robe. She couldn't fault him for that. A new baby was a better celebration, and both ceremonies would occur this night. *A baby girl.* Her pulse quickened, and she sank down on her bed. She'd always thought her uncle suspected her giftings, but did he believe it well enough to push for her execution?

Keeping the secret of an Emergent was payable by death–in the olden days, almost a century ago. But her mother had assured her that no one was this barbaric now. Why, the Embroids hadn't carried out an execution for over a decade, and the last person had been guilty of three counts of murder. "They wouldn't hurt an innocent girl." Her mother's words had been reassuring, but there had been an uncertain glint in her eye. And that glint pierced through Tansy's soul now, a beacon of terror that she knew would haunt her until three days had safely passed and her birthday had come and gone.

Her hand hovered over her comwatch. She wanted so badly to message Camp, to tell him of her troubles and ask for his help. Someone who would at least feel sorry for her if she cried. But the night was waning, and soon the violet candles would flicker out, signifying the six hours it took for a spirit to leave the world, by Embroid beliefs.

Could the old beliefs be true? Would my giftings pass on to Cora's tiny daughter if I died? Is my mother waiting for me in the great beyond, in Spirit's presence?

That at least must be true. I know Spirit lives. Within and around. If He wills my service, He will protect me.

She scooted the plant away from the door and squared her shoulders. No one would dare to hurt her tonight. She would celebrate her mother and the beautiful life they had shared. She would celebrate her mother's freedom from pain and suffering. But she'd keep a watchful eye on Uncle Tam.

###

The night was a bleary swirl of colors, music, and the soft hugs from robed figures that had been so strangely absent from Tansy's homecoming.

Close to half the Embroids attended the ceremony. The rest were sleeping, so they could take the others' share of the tasks for the next day. When the next all-night event occurred, it would be their turn to attend. Attending an ascension was considered a privilege and a blessing, so the people generally took turns when one came about. Of course, family and friends of the ascended would always receive precedent.

Once everyone had taken their places, the song for ascension began. The keening, haunting melody, meant to last through the first hour, served to accompany the soul of the departed to Spirit's Home, and the notes of the songs became a spiritual ladder for the deceased to climb into paradise. If somehow a person died and the songs were not sung in the proper time, it was believed that the soul would wander the skies for all eternity.

Where is Spirit's Home? Tansy's thoughts rambled as she sang the familiar song. *Will Mother really have to find her way there? Will it be harder since we're flying through space?* She tried to sing just a little louder, but sorrow tightened her throat and made even the quietest utterance more difficult.

As the last notes died away, Father Sharood approached the speaking-stand and nodded to her.

Tansy joined him and turned to face the rows of hooded people. Unrolled on the podium before her was the scroll containing the prayers for the dead, but her eyes blurred as she read them. Thankfully, every Embroid was taught the full book of prayers from an early age. The words tumbled from her mouth through rote memorization, but she scarcely knew what she was saying.

Father Sharood handed her a new bead for her necklace, the bead of ascension. Later she would string it next to the one she'd been given for her father, but for now she curled it into her hand, the sharp edges biting into her skin.

She sat back in her waiting place, numb and weary.

A celebration for death generally lasted all night, but because of the birth the time for her mother was cut short. As the notes of the last somber hymn died away, the violet gloom faded to be replaced by bright, harsh white. The congregation threw back their hoods and prepared to join a song and dance of celebration.

Tansy remained kneeling, staring at the jovial faces. *Did they even care about my mother?*

Uncle Tam danced at the front of the hall with his three sons. He glanced her way and gave her another evil smirk. *Maybe he's not capable of sympathy.*

The music intensified, and she clutched her temples, wishing she could hide beneath her robe and fall into blissful slumber. But no. Her kindred would understand that she could not join in the dance. If she gave into her greatest desire and left the Clarity Hall, she would be committing an offense none would forgive.

Finally the music ended, and the line of dancers came to a halt, panting and laughing. Uncle Tan disappeared for a moment. He returned with two tiny bundles. Everyone lined up and approached to give the babies their blessings.

Tansy joined near the end of the line. When her turn came to pass the babies, she looked down at the new little baby girl. *She has Aunt Cora's nose . . . and Mama's.*

The baby stared at her through tiny little slits of eyes, yawned, and snuggled against Uncle Tan's chest.

Such a little person, perfect in every way. Could be my undoing.

Thankfully, the ceremony finally reached its end. In the first lights, Tansy stumbled down the path to home.

She slammed the door behind her and glanced around the dim room.

The space was empty, the cushions and blankets in the corner neatly folded and arranged.

Panic clawed at her throat. *Why isn't Mother here? She should eat something.* She burst into her mother's room.

The hollowness of the space mocked her, like a blown-out eggshell. Her mother's bed, desk, and personal items had been removed.

Her hand crept to her beads, counting them, pressing her fingertips into each ridged surface, remembering, remembering. Her mother's face, smiling, proud, always there when each bead was given and added to the string. With shaking fingers, she untied the string and added her mother's bead to the collection.

She sank down on the bed, sorrow settling over her shoulders, weighing on the skin of her face. *Mother is gone. I will never see her again. At least, not in this world.*

Of course, if it were up to Uncle Tam, I'd see her again very soon. Not a good thought. If he could sway the town leaders to think his way, many of them might lean towards his rationing. Death was considered a blessing, a release into the self the body could not have, the butterfly soul that could fly into a blessed oblivion, to be spent with Spirit forever.

Tansy believed this, of course she did, but she wasn't in a hurry to leave this life. She wanted to see Fortress, wanted to feel the soft breath of true air on her face and the simple enormity of the outside of a world, again. *And what of Camp? He wanted to kiss me. Would I have let him?*

She stumbled into her room not even bothering to remove her ascension robe, and fell into a deep, and mercifully dreamless, sleep. But the fingers of danger were ever there, grasping at the edge of her mind.

20
Fallstaff's Report

Periwinth sipped her cylon juice and tapped her fingers against the smooth glass table. Falstaff should arrive at any time, and he'd better hurry. The Solstice expected her in half an hour and they'd heard enough excuses for her recent absences. Marrow possessed a mind as sharp as her tongue and Periwinth saw no reason to feed her suspicions.

Last night had been a rough one. She'd been forced to use sleeping aids twice, and the soreness from her combat 'therapy' still bled through to the slumbering realm. Shadowed specters of her dead crew members haunted her dreams, silently begging for help.

"Why would you think Falstaff needed to deliver his news in person? Doesn't he trust our private channel?" she asked Bradstorm for the sixth time. She tended to repeat herself when nervous, though perfectly aware the habit annoyed her second in command.

He smiled anyway. "I'm not sure. But whatever it is, we can handle it. We've had fourteen mechanical malfunctions in ten days, including the L4 and the tether tube incident. Grensbeck, in the Cholter ship, reported a scrapped drink carrier suddenly coming to life and running rampant through the street grid. Not sure how a saboteur would get all the way down to the Cholter ship without being noticed. Or why they'd choose a drink carrier for their target."

"Unless the saboteur is a Cholter," said Periwinth.

Bradstorm raised an eyebrow, his mouth creasing down at the corners.

"Don't look so annoyed!" Periwinth crossed her arms. "Of course I don't want to jump to conclusions and blame the Cholters. But we must explore every option."

Bradstorm leaned his head against his clasped hands. "Yes, you're right. But a Cholter would also have trouble reaching the headship without detection."

"They're delivery people. They move as freely and without suspicion in that capacity." Periwinth groaned. "Oh, I really hope not. Of course, my true wish would be that all these instances would be coincidences and such an evil did not exist in this place."

"Yes, I agree with you there," said Bradstorm. "But the techs would argue that one, maybe two incidents could occur, but not all of them. Ten years have been spent perfecting and streamlining every tiny function."

"I know that better than anyone," said Periwinth.

The door light brightened, and a little chime rang.

Bradstorm opened the door. Two hooded figures entered the room.

"Falstaff, welcome. And ..." Periwinth peered into the hood. "Glindel, hello! We weren't expecting you, but I'm glad you came. She gave them each what she hoped was a bright smile.

"Yes, Captain, I apologize for arriving unannounced," said Glindel, pushing back her hood. "But Falstaff and I have been . . . talking and we decided I should come as well."

"She joined me on the last tether tube," said Falstaff in a nonchalant tone.

Is he turning red? Maybe a teensy romance going on here? This thought wove a tiny thread of joy into the picture. Periwinth had never dreamed her plan could help cultivate an inter-Kindred romance. *Calm yourself. It might be your imagination.*

"Please, sit down." She indicated the chairs on the other side of the table.

Glindel and Falstaff sat, while Bradstorm, as usual, remained standing.

Falstaff leaned forward. "First of all, Captain, can you reassure me that nothing in this room will be recorded or overheard?"

Periwinth glanced at Bradstorm, who gave a slight nod.

"We've just done a security sweep, and meetings are only recorded by my authority. Which I have not authorized today," said Periwinth.

"Is the sweep done by bots?" Glindel murmured.

"No. I do it myself," said Bradstorm.

Falstaff exhaled loudly. "You'll forgive us, Captain, for being so cautious."

"We wish we could do as you have asked and bring grand ideas for unification," said Glindel, sweeping out her arm. "Unfortunately, what we have to say has far more dangerous implications."

Falstaff cleared his throat. "We've found more evidence of sabotage."

Periwinth stared into Glindel's bright blue eyes. "Have you heard talk? Do you believe the knowledge of sabotage has spread past the magistrate and head techs?"

Glindel shook her head. "My people designed most of those bots, so they've been fighting against accusations of shoddy workmanship. Some have suggested members of another Kindred are trying to frame us."

Periwinth's shoulders sagged. "In other words, the house of cards is falling faster than we thought."

Glindel pulled a device the size of a lemon from her pocket. "I found this wedged in a door. Of course I have deactivated it."

Falstaff picked it up and studied it. "Typical slight bomb. I've seen these weapons in our Museum of Terror back home."

"I'm not familiar with that place." Periwinth folded her arms. The Bloomwraith's suspicion of tech was a constant source of amusement on the headship. *In this case who will have the last laugh?*

"It's a dark building full of broken machines and gadgets," said Falstaff. "My people brought small children through to impress upon them the danger of such things. I remember a particularly vile exhibit showing the horror potential of an automatic carrot peeler.

Even most of the elders felt the blood loss depicted was excessive."

He turned the item over in his hand. "This type of device was invented long after the Earthen exodus and wasn't designed for wars. On Gyron, these were used to bust through rock walls for small mining projects." He glanced over at Glindel. "Right, tech girl?"

Glindel gave him a shy smile that all but confirmed Periwinth's hope.

"Right," she said. "These are kept under extremely secure storage on the headship for use when we reach Fortress. Only security crew members who were level five and up would even know about their existence. I received level four when I came on board. There's no way anyone below that clearance would have access to tools like these."

"Yes." Periwinth said. "Absolutely no reason."

"If I'm not mistaken," said Bradstorm, "the bombs are Ortemp-made."

Falstaff frowned. "Do you think it might have been someone from that ship?"

"Good thing Tracer isn't here," said Glindel. "He doesn't appreciate being slighted."

"Sorry," Falstaff grumbled. "But it has to be someone. It's not like little fairies flew in from outer space."

Periwinth spread out her hands. "I don't want anyone here to point fingers based on race, community, or ship. Is that understood?" She gave Glindel and Falstaff hard stares.

"Understood," Glindel and Falstaff murmured.

"Good." Periwinth stood and paced the room. She paused in front of the fish tank, watching a beautiful gray ray with white spots soar by on delicate fins. *Another creature I'm responsible for keeping alive.*

Pressing her palms against the tank, she reveled in the coolness and the gentle vibrations from the pump as it pulsed through her skin.

She finally turned around, to see Bradstorm, Glindel, and Falstaff staring at her.

"Thank you for bringing this to my attention." She sat down again and folded her hands. "I will share this information with everyone in our little group. I never intended to ask you to become spies, but the danger has certainly heightened. All I would request is that you stay alert at all times." She nodded to the door. "If there is nothing further, you may be excused. Please use your pass to get supper in the officer's lounge."

Falstaff pursed his lips. "That's generous of you, Captain. But wouldn't it be prudent for us to avoid being seen together?"

Periwinth sighed. "Yes. Thank you for that observation, you are absolutely correct. I'll arrange for food to be brought to the tether station. There's a comscreen outside this room. If you make your selection there, a meal will be waiting for you by the time you arrive and you can eat it on the tether car."

"Thank you, Captain," said Falstaff.

"I'll arrange the meals and guide you to the correct lift," said

Bradstorm. "Your coms should direct you back to the tether tubes."

"Right," said Glindel.

The three left the room, leaving Periwinth alone, though she knew Bradstorm would remain outside the door.

Periwinth sighed and rested her head in her arms. She'd taken countless classes on Kindred behavior to obtain her pilot rank. But even countless books on the subject couldn't prepare her for the day-to-day dynamics she'd had to deal with already. Learning to deal with people groups and how they interacted with each other could take a lifetime. A part of her wanted to be sensitive and understanding, and a part of her wanted to break down and beg them to get along, like a parent at their limit.

I should take this to the Solstice. They should be informed of these new sabotage attempts. But the thought made her pause.

She couldn't name the reason for her hesitation, especially with Marrow, whom she trusted above all but Bradstorm. *Hmmm.* Somehow Bradstorm had risen above Marrow in her subconscious. And now, members of her 'secret council' were rising in the ranks as well.

The Solstice members are busy with other matters. They don't need to worry about this. Whenever she felt the need to inform them of her little group, she'd brought out this reminder. But now she wondered if this was a feeble excuse.

Something twisted in her gut every time she was in the presence of the Solstice all at once, especially Platmoth and Crenth. Maybe it was the way they watched her with their sharp little eyes, all of them.

Constantly criticizing her every move and decision.

But that's their job. They have taken such a risk. Put so much faith in me.

Letting out a deep sigh, she rose from the table. *What else can I do? I must discover who is causing these problems. The next one could destroy a vital machine, or even worse, kill someone.*

She poked her head out the door. Bradstorm waited for her by the lift.

His shoulders rose and fell. "Let's not make any hasty decisions," he said. "We'll spread the word for added diligence. That's the best we can do. At this point, it seems we have a ghost."

21
Tracer's Report

Camp awakened in darkness, snapping upright and almost falling out of his hammock. Despite his swift movement, Smirk stayed asleep by his side.

The hairs on the back of Camp's neck pricked up, and he crept out of his bed, settling Smirk into the deep pouch his body left behind. He crouched, pulling his ever-present knife from its sheath.

There it was again. A rustling in a junk pile. *What was that?* A dim light, bobbing through the pathways he'd created in the refuse.

Can't be a Cholter, or they'd know I'm sleeping out here. How would anyone else be able to get through the tether tubes? Could it be Dashner looking for something? Maybe he didn't want to disturb me.

He crept along the ground, trying to visualize everything surrounding him. *Why haven't I taken the time to clean up? Oh yeah, Captain Zephyr's magical team. Tansy. Right.*

A hand lit on his shoulder and he whirled around, whipping his knife under the stranger's chin. The knife was wrenched from his hand with a super-human grip, and a sweaty palm covered his mouth. "Hang on there. Promise I'm a friend. But I'll rip your head off anyhow if you make a sound. Will you swear to be quiet?"

Camp nodded gingerly and the hand moved away from face, though the hot breath of the stranger remained on his neck.

"That's good," said the man. "Now step back and turn around slowly. I'll put a light on my face for an instant so you can see who I am."

Camp did as he was told and exhaled slowly. "Hey, Tracer," he said in a low voice. "What brings you to the tail ship?"

"Nothing good," Tracer said, snapping off the light. "Can we go inside? Really don't want your Cholter neighbors finding out I'm here."

"Sorry, I have a family staying with me and the little girl is asleep on my couch," said Camp. "I've been sleeping in a hammock in the yard."

"A family? How's that? Did something happen to their dwelling?" Tracer rubbed the back of his head. "Never mind. I don't have time for stories right now."

Camp shrugged. "We can go into the turkey coop. The stupid birds escaped and I sent a cleanerbot in to sanitize the space. It's this way, but there's lots of junk out here, so watch where you step."

"Can't be that stupid if they escaped," said Tracer, following Camp through the yard.

"Yeah. Like my grandpa used to say, they have street smarts, they just don't have brain smarts."

"What does that even mean?"

"Beats me if I know." Camp ran his comwatch over the door panel and went inside the coop, shining his light around. "Yep, no birds, so no poop to worry about."

"Heh. That's a relief." Tracer switched his light back on and sat down on a stool.

Camp closed the door and turned to face him. "This place is as secret as we're going to get unless you tell me how you made it here without being discovered."

Tracer clenched and unclenched his robotic hand. "Yeah, not ready to share that."

"You must trust me to some extent, otherwise you wouldn't have come," said Camp.

Tracer gave him a level gaze. "I didn't really know who to tell about this, but I couldn't keep it to myself. I thought about going straight to our leadership, but I remembered what the captain said about unity. This could be the undoing of everything, Camp."

Camp's stomach tensed, and a chill went down his spine. "What are you talking about?"

"I can't even believe it myself, and even more that no one on the seven ships has discovered it. But when they do, they will feel like fools, for we have all been duped into believing the biggest fallacy to ever hit Gyron. It really makes me wonder how else they've deceived us."

Camp's heart thudded dully against his chest. "Who?"

"The headship and the leadership. Creator knows who else. But not too many. Not the ones who count."

"I'm not Embroid," said Camp, "So I can't read your mind. I'm exhausted, and I'm anticipating a busy day tomorrow. Could you please stop this circle-talk?"

"Sorry, sorry," said Tracer. "I'm dealing with a shock here. I figured it out today. You see, I was taking my shift to maintain the mechs in the Scion station. We have five mech stations, this is the fifth, and it's the closest to our ship's control center. You know what I'm talking about?"

"Sure." Camp sat down on the floor of the coop and leaned against the smooth plastic wall. The cold surface felt good on his back. "Every ship has one. In case we get separated from the main tethers, by accident or by choice of the magistrate."

"Yes, that's the one." Tracer's eyes darted back and forth, and his voice lowered, as though he were speaking to himself. "The stations have controls for life-support, water, emergency power, and the ability to navigate through the slip-stream. And also–" His voice rose to a higher volume. "The ability to break the tether line. The magistrate's code entered, a lever pulled, a button pushed. That's how it was told to all of us, was it not?"

"Yeah. I've been inside our station myself," said Camp. "With the magistrate present, of course." Actually, Persneep had asked him to come along and learn the untethering process, since the old man's vision wasn't what it used to be, and he needed someone else to learn the steps in case the need should arise. Practically every day, another

Cholter complained that they should separate and take their chances, and it had very nearly happened once or twice. Personally, Camp thought it was a horrible plan. A smaller ship in the slipstream would arrive in Fortress much sooner, but they would have no strategy, no one to inform them of the next steps on their own. And there was no guarantee their cobbled-together food systems would sustain them until they reached the planet, though their storage contained piles of disgusting freeze-dried meals.

"Right, so you know. And we have all been told." Tracer took a deep breath. "Well, that's where the lie comes in." He leaned forward. "I decided to test things out. Since I was maintaining the mechs, I thought I'd check the control room. No one goes in there. What if an engine powered down? What if the saboteur broke in and messed something up? So I hacked into the place and walked around, flipping buttons. Lights flashed. Screens buzzed. But something wasn't right. Then it hit me like a mech's fist. Nothing in there is operational. The whole station is fake."

Camp's mouth suddenly went bone-dry, and he fought for words. "What–how could you possibly know that?" His mind raced for an excuse to touch Tracer's hand, to see if he was lying. But he didn't need to. He could tell by his tone and the sincerity in his eyes.

"Yeah, yeah. How could I know? Except I've been working with the mechs since I was a kid. My father taught me everything and he's the best mechanic of our kindred. I could tell something was off, so I carefully removed the control panel cover plate."

"You what?" Camp breathed. "What did you find?"

"Might as well be a child's toy. Completely useless."

Camp slid down the wall a bit further. "If the captain knows . . ."

"Then she's a liar. None of us can trust her." Tracer's ears turned red, and he slammed his cybernetic fist into his palm of flesh.

"Maybe," said Camp. "But what if she believes it's for the best?"

"What do you mean? How could withholding something that important be 'for the best?'"

"I don't know." Camp's mind raced. "Maybe she's been told it's for the good of everyone. Many of the Kindreds would have refused to come if they didn't think they could break off at any time. Especially the Cholters."

Every muscle in Camp's chest tightened. If the magistrates knew . . . *But what could they possibly do?* It wasn't as though they had ships to sail away in. *Does Captain Zephyr even know? She's keeping secrets from the Solstice. Could they have kept this one from her?*

And what a risk. Everyone knew the tether tubes, though strong, could fail. The ships could hit an asteroid field, the navigation system could send them in the wrong direction. *So many variables.*

"What should we do?" Tracer interrupted his thoughts. "I couldn't tell the magistrate yet. I haven't even told my family. Who knows why I'm here with you but I had to tell someone."

"Thank you," said Camp, clasping Tracer's real hand. Confirmation flowed through the touch, everything Tracer said, he believed to be true. "I don't believe we should tell anyone tonight. I'm going to think and pray about this. I'll share this information with Tansy in the morning, if it's alright with you. She's extremely insightful and she might have a different way of looking at things that we haven't considered."

"Yeah… I guess." Tracer rubbed the back of his neck.

"She's part of our group, and I've spent some time with her. No reason to think we can't trust her."

Tracer pursed his lips. "Have you considered that she could be the one behind the sabotage?"

"Tansy?" Camp gave a short laugh. "How could you even consider that? She wouldn't hurt a flea."

"How long have you known her, anyway?" said Tracer. "Didn't you meet her on the way to the captain's meeting?"

"No, we met once before, but it wasn't long ago. Look, I know everyone's been pointing fingers at each other on the team, but there are ten thousand people on the seven ships. Don't you think the chances are extremely slim that one of us is in on some terrorist plot?"

"Perhaps," said Tracer. "Unless that's why the captain picked us for the team in the first place."

22
Remains

Camp stared at the turkey eggs, perfectly crisped on the edges, that Jayne had fried for breakfast. "Blasted birds came back, then?"

"Found 'em roosting in Candy's supply shed this morning," said Dashner. "Raven collected the eggs. Guess they'd been hiding out. They made quite a mess of the place. I sent the cleaner bots out there, but I didn't move them back to the coop because well," she spread out her hands. "I'm not sure how to handle large birds like that."

"I completely understand, the old tom can be intimidating," said Camp. "Thanks for cleaning it out. I'll move them back this morning and try to figure out how they escaped."

"Sounds good," said Jayne. "The fresh eggs are nice."

"Sorry about being gone so much," Camp spread a pat of synthetic spread on his toast. "It's been a weird week."

"You're fine," said Jayne. "I wouldn't expect you to halt everything in your life on our account. We're the ones inconveniencing you."

"Not at all," Camp mumbled, picking at his food. He was glad the turkeys had been found, since they were his responsibility. But Tracer's visit and the news he'd brought weighed on him, along with other issues. He still hadn't figured out what to do with his houseguests. Dashner and Jayne had begged him not to inform Captain Zephyr yet, but if he intended to keep the trust of the team, he should have told them by now.

The other problem outweighed the first two by a million. Still burned into his brain was Tansy's face when he'd left her last night. Not only was her mother dead, with maybe no one to comfort her at the funeral, or whatever those people did to mourn their deceased, but the way some of the other Embroids had stared at him gave him the creeps. Many seemed downright hostile.

Maybe that's how they always act when someone has died. But he hadn't sensed normal grief or bereavement. He felt something– accusatory. Sinister. As a Cholter, he was used to these vibes. But they weren't directed at him. *They'd been focused on Tansy.*

Jayne sat down across from him. "I'm glad you've returned. We've been meaning to talk to you. We've decided . . ." she nodded to Dashner, who had his face buried in one of Camp's repair manuals.

"We've decided to present ourselves to the captain," said Dashner. "She's welcome to throw us in the brig. It doesn't matter. All bets will be off when we reach Fortress anyway."

Camp poked at the last bite of egg. "If you would share your fears with me, I might be able to help."

Dashner's frown deepened. "It's still so difficult to comprehend, let alone talk about. Camp, you don't know what happened on the surface at the end. It felt like the ancient story of Noah and his ark. People screaming. Begging. Very few zoomers were left in our village, only the richest owned them, and as you know they're only meant for small crews and short distances."

"But everyone was given the chance to leave with the Serpentine," said Camp. "I'll never understand why so many thousands of people stayed when certain death awaited them."

Dashner stared at his coffee mug. "Like I told you, we couldn't leave Jayne's father behind, and he refused to go. He'd given us everything, you see. He was a wonderful man, but he didn't believe in the disaster. Just like many other people.

"The day came when no one could deny the truth any longer. Terrible upheavals began. Blood ran on the streets in our village." He ran a hand over his eyes. "I've never imagined such horror. Jayne's father–we told you he died three days before we left. He was killed by a lifelong friend who was trying to steal our zoomer. And then I–I–"

Jayne rested a hand on her husband's shoulder. "You defended your family and did what had to be done to save us. To save Raven."

"It doesn't make it any less terrible," said Dashner. "Not to me."

Camp swallowed. Everything he knew about war had been read in books or learned in school with videos saved from the Earth archives. In fifteens he'd taken a few lessons on the Tark and

Ortemp upheaval of fifty years ago. But Gyron was a large planet, and apart from a skirmish here and there, the Kindreds had chosen to stay in their own places and keep to themselves instead allowing the relatively small numbers of their groups to be destroyed by petty arguments.

"I'm sure the captain will be sympathetic to your situation," he said finally. "From what I've seen, she's a reasonable person." *And I have information she'll want me to keep to myself. If she even knows. Argh, would I really resort to that? Not for myself, but for Raven, maybe.* He glanced over at the little girl, who was in the corner of the dwelling, arranging her dolly's few remaining hairs with a brush he usually used for Smirk.

Smirk perched on the arm of the couch; his eyes bright.

"You can brush Smirk too, if you like," said Camp to Raven. "He's taken to you pretty well."

"Okay," said Raven, her gaze trained on her dolly.

"There's that then," said Jayne briskly, picking up a stack of plates from the table. "We must get Raven into school. She's already missed half of fours and she's such a bright child. I want her to make friends."

"If you're planning a trip to the headship today, you might want me to come with you," said Camp. "Getting through the Tark's section can be tricky but I've built relationships with some of their people, including the magistrate, whom they call Chieftess."

"If it's not too much trouble for you," said Jayne.

"Naw. And as for your fears, I doubt you'll end up in the brig.

Captain has enough on her plate without worrying about a few stowaways."

"About that." Dashner wiped his mouth with a napkin and leaned back in his seat. "If we're planning to present ourselves to the captain, don't you think we should know why you were asked to that meeting the other day?"

"Look." Camp slid his remaining breakfast across the table. Smirk jumped from the couch and pounced on the food with a delighted trill. "I understand your concern, with your family and all, and you have every right to ask. But I've been commanded not to talk about it. I'll let you know as soon as I'm given clearance."

"Should we be worried?" Jayne's eyes widened. "After that horrible two months in the zoomer, I'd hate to think that these ships aren't safe."

"We are always in danger here," said Camp. "We're hurling through space to a largely uncharted destination, and I'm sure you're aware of what happened to most of the exploration team." He drummed his knuckles against the table. "Not to be pessimistic."

Jayne swiped at an empty spot on the table with a damp towel. "I have a child. I think I have a right to know specifics."

Dashner rose and put an arm around her shoulders. "Now honey, Camp has opened his home to us and asked for nothing in return."

"I know, I know." Jayne's big brown eyes welled up with tears. "I'm sorry. I'm just . . . this is terrifying."

Camp rose and slid his chair back. "Whelp, the best thing to do to remove fear is to uncover the truth. I was planning to check on someone on the Embroid ship today anyway, so a trip all the way to the headship won't matter much. I'll put in a notice with the captain to allow us through. Once we get to the headship, I'm sure they can arrange some kind of board or petition for your family. There's plenty of space on every ship, you can probably have your pick of places. Of course, you'll probably want to live on the headship, they have better schools for sure."

"I'd like to find a place here, on the Cholter ship," said Dashner. "Everyone has been so kind. But I get the feeling they'd be more resistant to the idea of a neighbor than a short-term guest."

"I'm really not sure about that," said Camp. "No one has ever requested it. Most people would choose the headship."

"You think Raven could stay with that nice neighbor lady while we go?" Jayne asked. "We'd make better time if she stays here."

"I'm sure they won't mind at all," said Chance. "I'll send a message to the captain."

###

Captain Zephyr smiled at Camp through the comscreen. "Good morning, Campion. You're the third member of the team I've spoken with in the last twelve hours. Is it too much to hope that you have good news and are not bringing me word of more sabotage attempts?"

"Not a runaway tether car this time, Captain." Camp returned her smile. "Actually, I need to bring some guests to the headship, and I'm not really sure how to go about it."

Captain Zephyr's eyes narrowed. "Ah hah. You wouldn't be referring to the family that docked on the Cholter ship last week?"

Camp exhaled slowly. "I figured you knew about them already."

She folded her arms. "Yes, of course. We knew zoomers with stragglers could arrive for the first few weeks, but I thought we'd passed that window of time by now. I'm amazed at the family's tenacity and relieved they reached us safely." She lowered her voice, though no one else was visible on the screen. "We've been too focused on the sabotage to address the refugees, but I promise you, it's been my intention to do so at the soonest opportunity. We were aware the first day they docked on the Cholter ship. Since no one brought them up, I put it on the bottom of my priority list." She pressed her fingers against her temples. "Please assure them it's not a slight on my part."

"Happy to help," said Camp. "I'm positive they'll understand."

"I was going to contact the Cholter leader today regarding the situation, so your timing is impeccable," said Zephyr. "A disturbing report accompanied the zoomer's discovery. I'm not surprised to hear it, but it might be the reason your family has been so hesitant to announce their arrival."

"Yes. they did mention a battle for that particular zoomer at the end," Camp said. "They've been staying with me, and the couple have been on edge, even mentioned the brig."

"Why am I not surprised that you were the one to open your home?" said Zephyr, her voice tinged with amusement.

"I'd like to hope anyone else would have done the same," said Camp, his ears burning at the tips. "They do have a child."

"We'll do our best to learn the true story before any axes are hefted," said Zephyr. "But when the ship was scanned, the forcebots reported organic material on the hull of the ship. Though most was burned away in the atmosphere, a trace amount was still captured."

"Organic material?"

"Yes. Human remains."

An hour later, Camp stood with Dashner and Jayne at the Cholter's tether station. An insistent tapping noise came from the floor beneath him. Annoyed, he looked for the origin and realized it was his own foot. He stilled the errant appendage and gave Dashner a sideways glance. *Human remains. What could have caused that? Do I want to know?* He bit back the questions as they rose to his tongue. Zephyr would get to the bottom of this. It wasn't his place to ask.

"How long does it take for a ship to travel through each tube?" asked Dashner.

"Eh, about twenty minutes," said Camp. "Six round tubes create a honeycomb shape, with a tether car for each, with a seventh tube in the center for water and air. The bottom tube has no car, in case of dire emergency and repairs. But the cars crawl slowly. Something about the inertia factor in the flexi tubes. The arriving car clicks into place at the tube's entrance. Complicated, but it works."

Through this normal banter, Camp's thoughts continued to race. *Were people actually hanging on the outside of the zoomer, begging to be allowed inside when Dashner took off? Would they have turned people away because of food shortage concerns? Would I have done the same thing for my wife and child?*

Jayne stared at the door. "I remember them talking about the tether cars in the briefing when we were first told of the ships–and the supernova." she closed her eyes. "I wasn't paying much attention because I didn't think we'd need the information. We'd made our peace with staying behind." She blinked. "Perhaps it would have been better."

"But Raven." Camp protested.

"Of course, yes," said Jayne. "But again, we'd made our peace. But like Dashner said, when the temperature began to rise, and I looked down at my child's face–we had a means of escape and we took it. Camp, you just can't imagine."

"Yeah, I really can't," Camp said.

Dashner patted Jayne's hand. "We're here now, and everything's going to be fine."

The car's door opened, and they walked in and sat down.

"Cushy seats," said Dashner, bouncing slightly in his chair.

Camp studied the faces across from him. *The amazing sacrifice it must have taken for them to stay with a family member, knowing that they would all die together.*

The rest of the journey was spent in silence, with only the whooshing of the tube surrounding them. Jayne rested her head on her husband's shoulder, while Dashner stared straight ahead, his mouth in a firm line.

When Camp stepped from the tether station into the Embroid ship, he noticed the violet hue was gone. Normal daytime lights lit the ship grid, and the community was bright and vibrant once more. Women tended their gardens, and children regarded them with solemn faces as they went by.

Not many people out this morning. I wonder where everyone went. When they passed Tansy's grid lane, Camp considered stopping by, but he changed his mind. *I'll give her space for now. I can always check on her when we return.*

The Clarity building rose before them, glass from the colorful mosaics winking in the bright lights.

"I thought all the ships were the same except for the head," said Dashner. "Don't the Embroids use their main building for a marketplace like the Cholters?"

"No, that's the Clarity building," said Camp. "Their place of worship. I think they mostly sit inside and wait."

"Wait? Wait for what?" asked Dashner.

Camp held out his hands. "God, I guess. At my church, we mostly sang and listened to sermons. But everyone has their own way."

Jayne studied the bell-shaped columns on either side of the

massive door, which was shut tightly. "That doesn't look like any church I've seen."

Chants rose from behind the door, a stark contrast to the silence that had always hovered around the place when Camp had come through before. Hundreds of voices speaking as one, urgent and even–*threatening.*

"Loud way to wait," Dashner mused.

Camp shrugged. "I'm not an expert on their customs."

He walked faster, attempting to escape notice from whatever crowd was in the building. His hopes were dashed as the ornate double doors flew open, and a large group of Embroids, all in highly decorated robes, spilled out.

Camp, Jayne, and Dashner were jostled to the side, and they rushed behind a building to avoid the surge. Camp edged out and peered around the wall. *What is going on?*

The Embroids stood in two rows outside the doors, chanting and yelling in a way most uncharacteristic. A cluster of people marched between the throngs.

"Not our business," said Dashner through gritted teeth.

Camp scooted out further, standing on tiptoes and craning his neck. "Wait a minute."

A man led the marching group, blood-red robes swishing over bare feet. His ornate headdress, white like polished bone, bobbed above the crowd. *Must be the highest of their religious leaders.* Eight, no ten, men and women in yellow and white robes followed the first man, also wearing headdresses that weren't quite so tall.

Between the last two robed men staggered a woman, hands tied behind her. Her curly blond hair flowed down her back, free from the normal braid, but there was no mistaking who she was.

"Tansy," he breathed.

The girl twisted her head to look behind her, though the chance of seeing him from her position was small.

One of her captors gave her a shove and she stumbled forward.

Camp's soul dropped to the pit of his stomach and his hand went to his knife-hilt. He rubbed the smooth handle. *Even if Dashner and Jayne helped me rush the crowd, we'd be completely outnumbered. These people have the right to carry out justice any way they see fit. But what did Tansy do? I've got to find out.* He ran his hand over his face. *Maybe there's another way.*

"Look," Camp turned to Dashner. "There's something I need to take care of here. I'll get you to the tether station. When you reach the Tark's ship, ask for Kafla. She'll keep you safe until I get there."

Dashner nodded towards Tansy. "Does it involve some sort of crazy rescue plan for that girl? She must be special for you to risk the wrath of an entire Kindred."

"You'd do the same for Jayne," said Camp.

"In a heartbeat," Dashner replied. "Get us to the tether ship, and we'll figure it out from there."

23
Trial

Tansy's breaths came in short gasps as she stumbled through the crowd. She passed the silent faces of her neighbors, the workers in the herb-houses–even her cousins were there, scowls plastered on their small, freckled faces.

She'd walked into the daily Wait and had been instantly surrounded by white and yellow-robed Opulants. They had clapped restraints on her wrists and ushered her to the front of the Clarity Hall. None of the thoughts she sensed involved any kind of good will.

As one, the people surrounding her erupted into a singular chant. She glanced around wildly.

Every mouth was open wide, as though they wished to consume her and rid the world of her wickedness. Eyes glowed, not with religious ferver, but with hate.

In the early morning, in her still, lonely home, the knowing had come. But even as her feet had plodded to the Wait, she'd hoped.

Hoped they might understand her parents' fear. Hoped that perhaps they'd realize that though her gifts were real, much of the legend wrapped around them was unverified superstition. Above all, she'd hoped for mercy. *Maybe I will still have that.* But as the urgent, ugly voice of the crowd rang in her ears, these hopes were engulfed by a tidal wave of doubt that almost sent her to the ground.

Through the ugliness, one sliver of kindness broke through, like light through a crack in a darkened room. Just as it came, it was gone, snuffed out by negativity. She wondered who possessed a shred of goodwill toward her. Certainly not Aunt Cora or Uncle Tam.

Now Father Sharood led the procession of the Opulents. They threaded their way to the stone garden and the column of reckoning.

Of course, this wasn't the true stone garden that had been left back home and burnt to oblivion. The leaders had placed stone benches in a semi-circle around a wooden podium they'd built and painted resemble the natural rock column they'd used for ceremonies like this in their old city.

The original garden had been used for weddings and the most holy events, weather permitting. The Embroid Kindred had very little need for trials, but a few had occurred over time, mostly from small disputes or custody discussions. These had also been held in the garden, though Tansy had never attended one.

This makeshift ceremonial ground hadn't been utilized since the Serpentine had launched. For one thing, only a small percentage of the Kindred could comfortably assemble there.

Father Sharood took his place at the podium, adjusting the blood-red robes so they covered his feet.

One man led Tansy to a block made of stone and indicated for her to stand on the top.

She stumbled up and remained there, knees buckling, staring down at the metal plates of the floor beneath her.

Scuffling noises and whispers rose from behind her, where she assumed the first of the crowd fought to find places on the benches. Most would spill out into the grids, scrambling to glimpse the trial from the surrounding streets.

Anger filled the atmosphere like a poisonous fog, and Tansy longed for the freedom to run away, to escape from the toxicity. She tried her usual tricks to block out the thoughts, but they were too dense. Her lips formed silent prayers to Spirit, begging for peace and relief from the madness.

The restraining circlets bit into her wrists, stinging her skin. Hair straggled around her face in errant curls. Somehow the greatest annoyance was not being able to wipe the drops of sweat as they dribbled down from forehead to chin. She wobbled again, feeling helpless and out of balance with her hands bound.

Hate writhed within her, not only an echo from the crowd, but a building frustration at the unfairness, at the helpless state she found herself in. *I knew. Why did I give myself reason to hope? If I'd left early enough, I might have escaped, instead of offering myself up like some kind of sacrificial animal.*

She stared up at Father Sharood, hoping for the least bit of pity or compassion to show on his normally kind face, but his gaze upon her was impassive. She'd never seen any Embroid dress in scarlet, and he seemed a being from another realm, severe and unyielding.

He raised his hands, and the chatter from the crowd immediately stopped as though someone had flipped a switch.

"We have gathered to hear the case of Miss Tansy Pellum," he said in a booming voice that could surely be heard throughout the entire section, though he had no artificial means of amplification. "Who will bring forth their grievances against this woman?"

"I will." Uncle Tam rose from a bench.

"Very well," said Father Sharood. "Come forth and speak."

Uncle Tam strode past Tansy, ignoring her imploring gaze.

When he reached Father Sharood, he whipped around. "This woman." He spoke the words so forcefully that spittle frothed from his lips. "Has kept from us a gift so precious, so sacred, countless lives could have been spared." He scanned the crowd behind Tansy, no doubt making eye contact with as many people as possible. "Think of the loved ones you've lost in the past several years. Think about the opportunities you've missed, the accidents that have occurred. So many of these unfortunate events could have been prevented. Instead of sparing countless tragedies, this woman has selfishly kept this knowledge to herself, as did her mother before she passed to the great beyond."

Father Sharood's eyebrows lifted, though Tansy knew he'd already been briefed on the situation. "Tansy Pellum, are these accusations brought to you by your own uncle, the husband of your mother's sister, indeed, true?"

"Not entirely," Tansy said.

The crowd gasped, and Father Sharood raised his hands again. "I will ask for complete silence. You all know your place. Tansy Pellum, I ask you once more. Are you the Emergent?"

Tansy bit her lip and stared down at her feet, hidden beneath her purple mourning robe. *No point in denying it.* Many Embroids had the gift of truth-seeing.

"Yes," she finally said.

Murmuring rose and grew through the crowd, and Father Sharood lifted his hand. "I will demand silence from you all!"

Uncle Tam's sneer twisted through his lips, and he rubbed his hands together. "See, Father Sharood? This heartless, evil girl has kept her gift–an ability meant to be shared to her Kindred–from even her own flesh and blood. MistEllen," he gestured to a woman in the crowd. "How does it feel knowing your little Scotten could be alive today if this evil thing, this tainted being, had bothered to tell you?"

The woman he'd pointed out covered her face and wailed, her heart-rending sobs rising strong and loud, through to the ship's massive ceiling.

"Wait, that's not how it works!" Tansy held out her hands, tears smarting in her eyes. "I don't always know. I would have tried to save your child in some way, I promise. I'm not all-seeing. Not all the time."

Father Sharood stroked his beard. "You are of the last Emergent line, one of twelve that has existed in the last two centuries. The others were persecuted for their abilities, that is true, and many families paid the ultimate price for keeping the powers a secret. Past Emergents have attempted to shield their knowings and fight against their premonitions. Has this been the case for you, Miss Pellum?"

Tansy bowed her head. "It can be very hard, Father Sharood. But my mother–"

"Was as selfish and wretched as you are!" cried Uncle Tam. "Father Sharood, I beseech you. Do we need to hear more? I beg of you, let us dissolve this evil girl and allow her gifting to be bestowed upon a more deserving child. We will give our child to the Clarity as soon as she is of threes." He gestured to the members of the Opulants. "There she can be taught from the proper nurturers from the beginning, and her gift will be experienced by all. We only have two days until this evil creature turns twenty-one. Then all chances for transference will be lost." He turned back to Tansy. "Let it be known. The blame rests not only on this girl, but also with the selfishness of Lanis Pellum, who has received her just reward."

"No!" Tansy screamed. "You will not speak of my mother that way! She loved her people! She was protecting all of you! Fate should not be twisted. I would have been taken to the city, and unable to serve here as it is." Tears choked her words, and she sank to her knees. "Don't speak of my mother in such a way."

Uncle Tam reached for her neck in a swift movement. Before Tansy could blink, he'd grabbed her memory beads and ripped them from her throat. They dropped to the ground, bouncing on the metal surface.

She cried out in rage and pain. A thin stream of blood ran down the back of her neck where the chain had torn her skin.

Father Sharood bowed his head. "It pains me to know such a thing has happened with my people. That anyone could keep such a thing to themselves, especially in this darkest of times." He raised his hand, then brought it down on the podium, his palm smacking the hard wood.

Any words Tansy wanted to speak flew back down her throat, impossible to utter. She choked and gagged. How could this be? The people hadn't carried out a dissolving ceremony for years. She wasn't even quite sure how the deed would be done. *It will be silent and bloodless. Hopefully painless. Does death hurt?* She swallowed hard, thinking of her mother.

"In respect of the dead, we shall wait twenty-four hours," said Father Sharood. "This will still give time before the hour of your birth, so the power will have a chance to make its transference."

"Why would you follow an unproven superstition?" Tansy cried. She shifted on the podium until she could search the eyes of the people in the crowd. She was met with blank stares, as impervious as the stone benches.

Two male Opulants grabbed her arms and jerked her off the block. The crowd parted as they led her through, to a small, squat dwelling near the far corner of the ship. One man removed her wrist restraints, while another slid back the front panel.

She stumbled inside and sank to the bare floor, heart pounding. Clicks and clanks sounded around her as the doors and windows were locked tight.

24
Escape

An automatic prayer ran through Tansy's head like it always did when she was in trouble or afraid, but the traditional words were followed by hot anger.

Spirit, why would you do this to me? First you take my mother, who lived only to serve you. And now you've turned your people against me. In the name of a superstition that hasn't been proven or seen for as long as our Kindred has gathered.

"Child, do you believe that your destruction is my will?" The gentle rebuke came as a sweet refrain in her heart.

"No, no, no." Tansy sobbed, lying on the cool metal floor of the dwelling. Tears poured down her face, and she rested her cheek on the smooth surface. "You did not do this. You gave me a gift, and I have done my best with it. Perhaps Mother shouldn't have made me hide it. But I did what I could, Spirit. And I have vowed to do better. But I can't see how allowing higher powers to use my giftings for their best interests would be a good idea."

Maybe everything would be better if I die. I will be with Mother and freed from this burden forever. Pass it to someone else.

No one knows if that is true, whispered another voice, her own subconscious. *No one knows if transference is real. It could have been coincidental. A legend made to create fear. So many possible explanations.*

She touched the back of her neck where a scab was already beginning to form. Watching the beads fall had been like seeing everything precious in her life drop away to nothingness. *I will be gone forever. I will be nothing.*

The room was devoid of any furniture, so she wiped her tears with the sleeve of her robe and sat against the wall, her sobs subsiding into shuddering breaths. She rested her head back, her eyes closing.

Slumber had almost brought its sweet relief when something banged on the wall.

She sat up. No, not the wall. *Inside the floor?* She listened again. Very faint, a hollow pounding, coming from a few feet away. *In the other room?* She rose and crept around the room, cupping a hand behind her ear.

The racket was indeed coming from the second room that had a thick, shaggy covering on the floor, much like the bedroom in her own house. On a hunch, she lifted the corner and rolled back the rug.

A neatly cut square in the metal stared back at her, with a folded-down handle on the top.

She pulled hard and the metal square came up in her hand.

Camp smiled up at her, a dim light creating a halo around his face. "They went and locked you up, did they? How come you didn't use your 'foretelling' trick and see it coming?"

Tansy had never been so tempted to kiss someone and slap them at the same time. "Who said I didn't know?" She folded her arms tightly against her chest, attempting to settle her pounding heart. "I thought I sensed you out there. How did you get down under the floor?"

"Maintenance tunnels," Camp patted the smooth wall. "The six smaller ships have 'em. They allow bots to come through and make repairs when needed. All the Cholters know about them and use some areas for storage. Lots of extra space, really. They can only be unlocked from down here on this side, but we found the entrance in the tether tube and unfastened them all ourselves. Kids use 'em for hide and seek sometimes. Great fun. Surprised you don't know about 'em, but I guess your magistrate doesn't share much with the commoners."

"Huh," was all Tansy could think to say.

"Anyway, are you ready to be rescued?" Camp raised an eyebrow. "Because that crowd outside doesn't look like they have your best interests at heart. I know I'm not the brightest, being a Cholter and all."

"Would you just stop with that already?" said Tansy. "You're one of the smartest people I know. But at this point you could be a mootsolstacerat for all I care. Help me down there, will you? This robe is constricting."

"Why don't you leave it behind?" said Camp. "Make you harder to spot."

"Oh, good idea." Tansy slipped the thick, heavy fabric over her head and left it in a heap, leaving her with a simple tunic and pants.

She descended the ladder. As she reached the last few rungs, Camp moved closer. She stumbled on the last rung, falling against him.

As she turned to face him, his face reddened in the glow of the tunnel lights.

"What's the matter?" she asked.

"You know what I'm thinking, but I'll say it anyway. Every time I've seen you, you're swathed in yards and yards of fabric. You just look different, that's all."

"I'm much cooler, that's for sure."

"I like the look," said Camp.

Tansy wanted to say, "I know" in a smarmy tone, but the awkwardness was strong enough already.

She gazed around the tunnel. Dim lights ran along the top, giving just enough illumination for her to see the walls' outlines. The space was close to eight feet in diameter, with a narrow floor and a rounded ceiling with strange cables and tubes running through the ceiling. The tunnel vibrated and hummed, but with different sounds than the ship above. "Reminds me of a grade school trip I took to a water refinery plant," she said. "At least, the tunnels were like this."

"Heh. My school trips usually consisted of visiting the dumps of richer towns," said Camp. "Whoever made the best find of the day would get an extra dessert at lunch."

He climbed back up the ladder, closed the door, and slid the bolt home. "Not like we can cover the door from the top. Hopefully they won't check in on you for a while. The bolt'll buy us a few minutes after that if they try to follow us straight down, but we'd better get going."

"Yeah, not sure if they planned to give me a final meal or what," Tansy said as she followed Camp through the tunnel. "The last time someone was dissolved was ten years ago. I was little so I didn't know much about it."

"So. They *were* going to kill you," he said, a grim shadow falling over his face.

"Yes. They think if I die before my twenty-first birthday, the bulk of my powers will be passed on to my niece who was born on the same day my mother died."

He stopped short and whirled to face her. "Is that true? I mean— do you believe it's true?"

"No." She bowed her head. "I mean, I'm not sure. The gift is known to skip several generations and only seems to come to one person in a family at a time. My mother said when she was little, three families boasted of Emergents in their lineage. Now it's only mine. I'm real, and I do have a real gift. My great-grandmother also had the gift. She served the rulers in a big city and was ultimately killed for it."

"That's terrible," said Camp. "A person shouldn't fear for their life because of how they were born. Do you know why she was killed?"

Tansy frowned. "It happened forty years ago when my mother was a child. But she said the Solstice leader at the time met with some sort of accident and as a result became paralyzed from the waist down. He accused my great grandmother of keeping the prophecy to herself."

"Did she?" asked Camp.

"I don't know," said Tansy. "Like I've said, it doesn't always work like that. Sometimes we know, sometimes we don't."

"I completely understand why your family chose to keep it a secret," said Camp.

He checked his watch again. "We need to move faster."

"I don't think they'll be opening the door quite yet, they just threw me in there," Tansy protested.

"That's not exactly why I'm in a rush," said Camp.

A slight puff of air pulled at Tansy's tangled hair, and she stared down the tunnel. A new, more forceful gust blew past.

"This is what I was worried about. Cleanser vents are opened several times a day to rid the area of mold and bacteria." Camp grabbed Tansy's hand and pulled her along. "Hurry! We've got to find something to hold onto!"

Tansy ran with him as the wind grew stronger, pulling at her clothes and hair.

"Here!" Camp yelled. "These poles are sturdy. Wrap your arms around one and don't let go!"

He demonstrated by hugging one of the poles, which was about ten inches wide.

Tansy held on tight. The suction swiftly became a stronger, almost unbearable force, pulling every part of her being and soul. She closed her eyes, wondering if her very spirit could be sucked right out of her chest. Her feet lifted from the floor. *How much will it hurt if I can't hold on? Will I feel it when I hit the wall, or will I be smashed too fast?*

"Hang on, Tansy!" Camp shouted.

How does this keep happening to us? Except this time, they weren't facing sabotage. *Camp knew we could be in danger, but still he risked his life to help me.*

Tears whipped down Tansy's face and were whisked away by the wind. *No one's ever done so much for me.*

She gripped the pole tighter. Her arms ached, down to the very tips of her fingers. If it grew much stronger, she didn't know if she'd be able to hold on. Sweat poured from her palms, and she squeezed tighter. *I can't let go. I won't.*

The air seemed to weaken a smidge. *Maybe it's my imagination. No, it's definitely less intense.* With one last 'whoosh' the air settled down, dropping Tansy and Camp down to the floor with twin *thunks.*

She lay there, elbows and knees smarting, arms raw from hugging the metal.

Camp rose to shaky feet. "Hope you're not hurt." His brow furrowed as he peered down at her. "We must hurry. The wind won't come again for hours, but your Embroid Kindred might.”

“I thought you said Cholter children play in these tubes,” she said as he pulled her up and they began to move again.

“They do. We haven’t lost anyone yet. They’ve fashioned harnesses to make it easier to hang on. I would have brought some had I known the need would arise.”

Tansy shook her head. “Embroid children would never be allowed to do something so dangerous.”

Camp grinned. “That’s nothing. You should have seen me in the refuse yards as a kid. I was sawing out machinery parts at five with a curser blade.”

To Tansy’s supreme relief they quickly arrived at the tube’s end, where a panel door awaited them.

“Okay, look, this lets us right into the maintenance tether car. I have a master code.” Camp pulled a thin metal square from his pocket. “We won’t have to deal with any of your Embroid brothers or sisters.”

“They aren’t my family. At least, not anymore,” said Tansy with a shudder, thinking of the anger and hatred plastered over the faces of her shipmates.

“We’re going to have to hurry it though,” said Camp. “If we can’t get through the other four ships before they find out you’ve escaped, I don’t know what we’ll do.”

Tansy clenched her fists, her fingernails biting into her palms. “I can only pray.”

Camp didn’t respond, but the set of his jaw told her everything she needed to know. *Don't die for me, Camp. I'm not worth it.*

The panel slid open, revealing a small space with another ladder. This led up into a tether tube, complete with a car that was a third of the size of the other tether crafts, with only six seats inside.

"Come on in, this is a maintenance car." Camp said. "With any luck . . ." He waved his special comwatch over the car's operation panel. The console lit up, and the door slid open. Tansy exhaled and climbed into the car.

Camp settled in beside her.

"Are you sure this comwatch will work on the other three cars?" asked Tansy.

"Nope."

"What if someone is actually using them for maintenance?"

"Then the day will become a little more exciting." Camp gave her his easy grin.

A sigh shuddered through Tansy's lips. "Even if we reach the headship, by the law of the seven ships, the captain will have to turn me back in. Why are we even bothering, Camp? Aren't we prolonging the inevitable?"

Camp looked away quickly. "Every breath you draw is precious, Tansy. I have faith that the captain will find a solution. She doesn't seem like the kind of person that would leave a team member behind."

"That's not what I've heard," Tansy murmured. But it must not have been loud enough for Camp to hear. When she focused, she could hear his jumbled thoughts, one plan after another, quickly formulated and then discarded as though he was flipping through a pack of playing cards.

"You never said how you knew I was in trouble," she finally said.

His head snapped up. "Oh, didn't I? I brought the family that has been staying with me through the Embroid grid on the way to the headship to meet with the captain. We saw you being dragged through the streets, so I sent them on ahead to find the Tark Princess. I figured I'd try to rescue you."

"You really have a knack for finding people in trouble, don't you?" asked Tansy.

Camp reached out and ran his finger along the curve of her chin. "I kind of like it," he said.

"Well, I'm glad you do," she replied.

He bent closer, and this time nothing interrupted the kiss.

25
False Brides

When Camp and Tansy stepped into the Tark's station, Garbo beamed at them from behind the station desk. Camp smiled back, despite their precarious situation. *Nice to have a friendly greeting this time.*

"Camp and Tansy," the man said. "Good to see you again so soon."

"Nice to see you as well," said Camp.

"A man and woman came through here a little while ago, claiming they knew you. They are waiting for you outside the door."

Camp was tempted to hug the man, but instead he clapped his hand on the broad, fur-covered shoulder. "I am in debt to you, Sir. We will travel through quickly and try not to give you any trouble today."

The man shrugged. "Trouble seems to ride on your shoulders, Cholter. But we can handle anything here. Not like those half-mechs and their machines. We heard one of their smaller crafts went berserk today and smashed a dwelling. No one was hurt, but still. Be careful when you go through their ship."

"Right. Thank you again." Camp grabbed Tansy's hand and they marched through the station and into the Tark ship.

Jayne and Dashner waited for them on an ornately carved bench. Dashner smiled when he saw them.

Jayne held out her hand. "You must be Tansy. So happy to see you are safe. I'm not going to ask how Camp got you out."

Tansy studied the woman's face, then took her hand. "Yes. Glad to be free. For the moment."

Camp tugged on Tansy's sleeve. "Speaking of which, we need to keep moving."

Dashner and Jayne gathered their small packs without further question, and they set off.

As they moved through the first part of the grid, a trumpet sounded, and the people who strolled through the streets moved to the sides.

A line of three Raffis, led by handlers in ornate gold and white costumes, strode by.

Jayne jumped back, her hand over her mouth. "What are those things?"

The beasts moved on, paying them no mind.

"I guess they're out for exercise?" said Tansy. "Seems dangerous after what happened during our last visit."

Camp shrugged. "I guess they know what they're doing. I don't see Solsha, so she must've had her baby."

Kafla popped up behind the last raffi, guiding the beast's back leg with a thin stick. Her eyes widened as she caught sight of Tansy and Camp.

"Wait for me," she yelled over her shoulder as the parade passed.

The small group stopped. A vein throbbed in Camp's head. *Should we wait? She doesn't know the danger we're in.*

Kafla handed the stick to another person and ran back to them, her white braids slightly disheveled. "Why are you bringing these people through our ship, Camp?"

"It's too long to tell the story right now," said Camp. "Their zoomer docked on the Cholter ship last week. They plan to present themselves to the captain."

"I see." Kafla's eyes flicked to Tansy. "And why is she here? Did the captain ask for her?"

Camp's mouth went dry. "Well, it's like this–"

"My own Kindred wish to kill me, though I've done nothing wrong," Tansy said, her voice choked with tears. "We are going to the captain to see if she can help."

Camp squeezed her hand.

Kafla drew herself up to her full height. "Those with incredible gifts sometimes make powerful enemies, yes?"

Tansy nodded.

"I rescued her through a trapdoor. We made it through the Embroid's maintenance tunnel, but they could find out she's gone at any time," said Camp.

Kafla pursed her lips. "Hurry. Come with me. I might have a way to buy you time."

"But what if the elders begin a search on your ship?" said Tansy.

"My people will not betray you," said Kafla. "And it is our ship. We make our own laws here. Today is the Festival of the False Brides. The final bell has just sounded. This means that no one else will be allowed to travel through the ship until our celebrations are over. It is part of our law. All the magistrates know this."

"When will the festival end?" asked Jayne.

"Six hours," said Kafla. "Of course, if you become a part of the celebration, you will be free to go where you wish."

"To the other tether tube?" said camp.

"If that is what you wish."

They followed the Tark princess through the lanes and byways.

She reached a dwelling and opened the enclosure wall. "Come on in, all of you."

They went into a small house, very much like Camp's in structure but completely different in every other way. The walls were covered with paintings of animals, brushed directly on the plastic surfaces. Tapestries and woven cloths hung everywhere, all created from different kinds of animal fur or skin.

"I'll be right back," said Kafla.

She went into the bedroom and returned shortly, her arms piled with clothing and shawls. "Put these on."

Camp picked out a silver robe and held it up. "You want us to disguise ourselves? There's no way we can pass for Tarks. I mean, your people are so tall." He stared at the princess's bright white hair and dark skin, then touched one of his dark dreads. "And–tall," he finished lamely.

"The festival has begun," said Kafla. "Everyone is wearing crazy clothes. I think you will manage to blend in. And we do have children. Who are not so tall."

"All right," Dashner pulled a shaggy black and white shawl from the pile. "It won't hurt to try. We really appreciate this." He slipped it over his head.

Kafla pressed her hand against her mouth, and her face reddened.

Was she laughing? "What is it?" asked Camp.

The Tark princess attempted to speak, but gales of laughter poured out instead. Camp had never heard a Tark laugh before, and the sound was infectious. Soon the five of them were laughing so hard tears rolled down their faces.

"Why are we–laughing?" Jayne gasped, holding her sides.

"Because." Kafla hiccupped. "The man wants to wear a woman's dress! We don't exchange clothing among our people like some of your Kindreds do. Women wear certain colors and patterns, different from men." She gestured to Dashner. "You would cause a ruckus in the streets with that outfit."

"Well, maybe my disguise will be better than everyone else," said Dashner, wiping tears from his eyes.

"Whew," said Tansy. "Better give me that robe, Dashner."

Soon they had all changed into bright fur and skin clothes. Tansy and Jayne chose veils that would completely swath their bodies.

"In our festivals, the false brides dress like this," said Kafla, waving to their clothes. "Women who do not care to marry."

"Well, that's not the case for me, since I'm taken." Jayne winked at Dashner, then slipped the veil over her head. "But they do make nice disguises."

"For long times, false brides had to wear veils wherever they went," said Kafla, pulling a loose string from a dress. "But now we do not, and that's what this festival celebrates. I'm thankful for that."

"You would be considered a false bride, right, since you didn't marry that one guard?" asked Tansy.

"Oh, yes," said Kafla, with a proud smile. "He married another. They have three children." She waved a hand. "He is very happy now. Much happier than he would have been with me."

"Does that mean you can't marry anyone else, ever?" asked Tansy.

Kafla crossed her arms. "It means I can choose the man I desire to marry, if I ever meet him."

"Sounds like a good arrangement," said Camp. He couldn't help but steal a glance at Tansy. She had donned a dress covered in brilliant turquoise and purple patterns, with gold beads and trim. He stared long enough to see her flush as she slipped on a bright blue mask made of peaturkey feathers.

Kafla opened the door a crack and peered out. "It looks like the festival is beginning. I think you will be safe to leave now. You can leave the clothing in the tether station. If anyone meets you in the street, say 'Blin Tovet.' It's the festival greeting."

"Blin Tovet," said Camp. "Got it."

Camp led his small company into the corridor, their borrowed garments swishing and crinkling as they moved.

Camp stepped close to Tansy. "Do you think you'll make that false bride get-up part of your normal attire?" he asked.

"I don't know," Tansy replied, tilting her head. "Should I?"

Her flirtatious tone warmed Camp's heart. *If only we weren't running for her life, what fun we could have. Someday maybe we'll be able to have a proper date.*

A group of Tarks approached them, dressed in similar wild costumes.

"Blin Tovet!" shouted a woman in a dress trimmed in scarlet beads and fringe.

"Blin Tovet!" yelled a man with a mask made of purple feathers.

Flutes and stringed instruments played beside the grid lanes, and crowds of people danced and moved together. The scent of roasted meats and vegetables filled the air. Streamers flew before colored lights. Children smiled, faces smeared with sauce from foods they held.

Camp moved through the throng, unable to keep a skip from his step. Hard to believe the evil he'd witnessed one ship over.

The crowd parted for Garbo, who darted up to Kafla and

whispered something in her ear. Her eyes widened and she grabbed Camp's arm. "Hey, the Embroids are coming over on the tether ship. I'm heading to the front station to stall them due to the festival, but you need to move faster."

Camp hiked up his robe, took Tansy's hand, and sprinted through the crowd. Dashner and Jayne huffed and puffed behind them, and they wove through the gridlines swiftly.

Camp was jostled and elbowed. An enormous man in a voluminous green cape stepped back squarely on his foot, almost falling into him.

"Behind you!" Camp yelled.

The man stepped forward, and Camp continued to move, limping slightly now. He strained to listen through the crowd, expecting to hear someone call out to them or demand that they stop.

At last Camp's fingers pressed against the tether-station panel. He exhaled and grinned at Tansy. "Made it."

"Should I bother to point out to you that we have three more ships to journey through?" said Dashner.

Jayne punched her husband's arm playfully. "Stop being so gloomy. This is a good omen."

The tether operator, a Tark Camp had not yet met, raised a hand in greeting.

Camp opened his mouth to speak.

The Tark squinted at him. "I don't know who you are, and Princess Kafla has instructed me not to ask. But someone is here for you."

A cloaked figure rose from the bench.

"It is good to see you," Tracer said, pushing back his hood with a robotic arm. "Now get out of those ridiculous costumes. We must hurry."

26
Through the Tube

Tansy's throat tightened as Tracer led them to another panel in the floor, similar to the one she and Camp had climbed down to reach the air shaft. "Isn't this dangerous?" she said. "Can't we take the tether ship?"

Tracer shook his head. "Now that the Embroids know you've escaped, they will have the power to request the tubes and crafts be searched, and none of the ships can refuse. We have an obligation of good will to cooperate if any ship reports a criminal on the loose."

Camp folded his arms against his chest. "Tansy is completely innocent. They want to kill her over a superstition."

Tracer shrugged. "I don't doubt it, but that doesn't matter when it comes to the laws of the seven ships. If one Kindred states that a person is proven guilty by trial, no other ship has a right to interfere. It's part of the agreement signed by each magistrate."

Tansy blinked. *It's like I suspected. Even if we reach the headship, Captain Zephyr might be powerless to help me. Why are we even going?*

"Dashner and Jayne, you should at least go in a different tether car," she said. "You have nothing to do with me and my situation."

"If Camp believes in you, then we will fight for you as well," said Dashner. "We have no family here besides our little girl, so we're creating a new Kindred as we go along."

He climbed down the ladder, followed by Jayne.

"Down you go," said Camp.

She descended into the depths. *Will this be my last act as a free person?*

Camp followed last, closing the hasp and plunging them all into darkness. The lights of their comwatches winked on at once.

"Do you have something to harness us to the poles if the air blasts through?" she asked Tracer as they began to move through the tunnel.

"Oh, I have something better than that." Tracer gestured ahead.

A large machine loomed in front of them.

The mechanical beast, almost the size of a tether car, crouched before them on four metal legs. The vehicle's glowing eyes shone from a cat-like head.

"Is that a felis mech?" asked Dashner. "I've never seen one, only read about them."

"Yes," said Tracer. "Let's get in and get moving before the maintenance blast comes through."

Jayne scrunched up her mouth. "What is he talking about?" she whispered to Tansy.

Tansy remembered the couple hadn't been with them in the previous tunnel of doom. "Believe me, you don't want to know," she whispered back.

They all climbed through an opening in the side of the massive beast. The craft had room for six passengers, plus the pilot's chair at the front. Tracer sat down and grabbed the u-shaped steering wheel-type controller. "Everyone buckle up and hold on."

The machine lurched forward and began to lumber through the tunnel. This area was much larger than the one Tansy and Camp had gone through previously.

Tansy's stomach bunched, and she was suddenly glad she hadn't eaten since that morning. She closed her eyes and hung on to her chair.

"This might get us through your ship," Camp yelled over the clanking and creaking. "But what will we do after that?"

"This baby has her own path through the tubes," said Tracer, patting the dashboard. "She can get us all the way to the headship."

Camp shook his head. "I learn more secrets every day."

"Hopefully Father Sharood and the Embroid leadership are also in the dark about this particular little machine," said Tansy.

Tracer shrugged. "They might be aware of it, but would they consider you'd be allowed passage? Only my Kindred are allowed to operate them. Nobody bothers with the airshafts except for the forcebots. I've already contacted Falstaff and Glindel. They've disabled the few security devices still in place on the Bloomwraith's ship and Glindel took care of everything on the Grimshim's end. We should have a safe journey all the way through."

"I don't know how smooth the ride will be," Camp muttered. But he smiled, reached over, and took Tansy's hand. "Are you okay?" he asked.

"Yeah." She sighed. "Just tired. And I thought I was hungry, but now I'm not so sure." She leaned against his shoulder. "At least I'll get something to eat when we arrive, even if I'm thrown into prison."

"Nobody's going to prison," Camp said firmly.

Tansy glanced at Dashner and Jayne, who were snuggled together as best as possible from their strapped-in seating. Doubt radiated from everyone in the mech, even from Tracer, whose face betrayed no emotion whatsoever.

She settled against Camp's shoulder, and he put his arm around her. "No sense worrying," he said softly. "You are alive, and that's what matters. Maybe try to rest."

Camp's neck jerked forward, and his restraints tugged on his shoulders. His dreads floated away from his shoulders.

Tansy's long curls had also floated up like a bouquet of golden flowers in a sudden spring breeze. "What's going on?" she said sleepily.

His fingers tightened on the arms of his seat. "Tracer, what was that?"

Tracer stared back at them. "We've lost gravity."

Camp unbuckled his restraints and rose into the air. "I thought that was impossible."

Dashner rubbed his eyes, his short hair standing on end and waving gently. "Is it ship-wide or just this area?"

Tracer tapped the viewscreen in front of him. "No way to tell. I turned off communication so no one could trace this mech if they somehow figured out you were with me. I'd like to think this is an accident, but maybe we are being targeted."

"What do we do now?" asked Jayne. Her eyes were wide in the light of the comwatch.

"Can't stay here." Tracer frowned. "With communications out, there's no telling when anyone will find us down here. And we don't know if this failure is only in this area or if it has happened throughout the entire Grimshim ship."

He unbuckled his restraints and floated up to join Camp. "Let's see who we can contact."

"Glindel" Camp said into his comwatch.

Glindel's face flickered on the tiny screen. "Make it quick," she said. "We're dealing with the latest little game the saboteur left for us today."

"Sorry," said Camp. "Have you heard about any parts of the Ortemp ship or any of the other ships losing gravity?"

The color drained from Glindel's face. "Don't tell me."

Tracer grabbed Camp's arm and peered into the tiny screen. "Yeah, we're floating around in my Felis right now below your ship in the mech passage. Almost to the tether door. And we have a bunch of angry Embroids on our tail."

Glindel pressed her fingers against her temples. "I'm not even gonna ask."

"Can you get down here and try to restore the gravity?" asked Camp.

"No way I can leave the grid with this mess to clean up," said Glindel. "Maybe I can get Falstaff to come. I'll try my best."

"Falstaff?" Tracer groaned. "Would he even know what to do with something that uses electricity? Bloomwraiths don't even know how to flip a light switch."

"Don't be uncharitable." Glindel frowned. "He's not like other Bloomwraiths. In the meantime, Tracer, you need to get everyone out of the mech. Pull your way through the tunnel along the sides; but stay close to the floor in case the gravity is restored."

Then it hit Camp. *We're floating above the ground. If gravity comes back before we get out of this thing, we'll go crashing to the floor. Even if we're not killed, we'll certainly be worse for the wear.*

"Thanks, Glindel," said Tracer. "We'll let you know how it goes."

"Yeah," Glindel said. "Don't die."

The comwatch blinked into black.

Tracer pushed himself off the side of the mec, went to the door, and swung it open.

Camp followed him and peered down into the blackness of the tunnel. "Looks like the lights have powered down along with the gravity."

"No," said Tracer, "That is my doing. Remember, the lights weren't on when we first entered the Felis. I've been turning them off as we come through each tunnel in case there were other maintenance workers. I was kinda hoping they would go off to figure out why the lights are out and maybe give us time to get out." He looked up. "All right everyone, better come with me."

Jayne, Dashner, and Tansy all removed their restraints and immediately floated up from their seats.

Tracer surveyed them all. "Best rid yourselves of any clothing or shawls that will hamper movements. The trick to anti-gravity is to realize that no matter where you are, you will stay suspended. You will have no sensation of being the right way up."

He pulled the door open the rest of the way.

"Look, the most important thing," he stared into everyone's anxious faces. "Do not let go. Hold onto the side of the ship once we get out. If you let go with nothing to hold onto, you will hang wherever you are, suspended, until the gravity comes back on. And depending on how high you are or when that is, you could smash to the floor."

"So how are we going to get to the wall?" asked Dashner.

"Yeah, that." Tracer sighed. "I'm taking a rope with me. I'll push off the side of the mech. If I'm lucky, I'll make it to the wall and tie the rope to something. Everyone else can pull themselves to the wall with the rope."

"Isn't that an enormous risk?" asked Tansy. "What if you don't make it to the wall?'

"You'll haul me back and I'll try again. "

Tracer's eyes gleamed in the comwatch light. "We can't stay here." He gave everyone a quick smile. "Let's get out of this thing. Remember, hold on. Don't let go." He went through the door, and Camp followed.

Cooler air hit Camp's face. He couldn't see the walls surrounding him. *This must be a bigger tube since we're almost to the headship.*

"Hey, all of you grab on to this bar," said Tracer. "Dashner, can you come over and hold this rope while I tie it on?"

"Sure. Sorry, Camp, climbing past you here." Dashner climbed over Camp, grabbing at his sleeve. After an awkward scuffle he was over to the side where Tracer waited.

Tansy scooted next to Camp and squeezed his fingers.

"Are you okay?" said Camp.

" I don't know," said Tansy. "What if someone gets hurt? It would be my fault. It's always my fault, Camp. I have this feeling of dread in the pit of my stomach that's been there since my mother's ascension. So many dangerous things have happened. I can't sort them out, and I don't know how much more there is to come."

"You've been dealing with grief and fear," said Camp. "It's a wonder you have any sane thoughts. "I'm just praying hard."

"Me too," said Tansy. "We must believe that Spirit has a plan in all of this."

The tension in Camp's shoulders lessened, despite the situation.

There was something about the feeling of weightlessness, like they were breaking the laws of science, though the opposite was true. He hadn't felt this way since the last summer they were allowed to swim in the lake, before the water had become too heated for safety. His friends, Marco and Ali, were with him that day. Friends he'd left behind. A quick tear flew from the corner of his eye and floated into the air, a tiny, shimmering glob.

"All right, everyone," said Tracer, "It's tied. I'm going to launch myself out and see if I can hit the wall. You all hold on."

He pushed himself off the mech with a mighty heave.

The cat mech began to float in the opposite direction. Camp tightened his grip on the bar he'd been holding.

"I don't like this," said Jayne. "How on earth will we haul him back if he doesn't–"

"I'm here!" Tracer yelled. "Let me get the rope secured."

"Thank the Creator, it's long enough," muttered Camp.

"Alright," Tracer said. "Everyone find the rope and come on over. Don't tug on it too hard, don't want to bring the mech with you."

Dashner went first. "All right, I made it," he said. "Come on, Camp."

Camp dragged himself along, feeling the tension of the mech bobbing on the other side. He chuckled. *Wish the light was better for me to see that massive mech bouncing along like a balloon.*

His fingers brushed against the convex wall, and he found a bar to hold onto. "Okay, I'm here."

He waited for Tansy, his breaths ragged. *Where is she? Why is she taking so long? What will I do if she somehow loses hold?*

Her head poked up beside him. "Here I am. Stop worrying so much. We need our strength to get through the rest of this tunnel."

Jayne came right behind her.

"All here now?" said Tracer. "Good. We need to get as close to the floor as we can. Not far to the end now."

They followed him as he pulled himself to the bottom of the tunnel, his heavy work boots flung out behind him.

Camp imagined the feeling of gravity suddenly returning, of meeting the floor with an unknown force. He'd never paid much attention in physics class, so he really wasn't sure what would happen. *Nothing is going to happen. We'll be fine.*

He looked back at the cat mech, the luminous yellow eyes giving minimal light. They'd gone farther than he'd thought possible in such a short time.

Or maybe we've been here for hours.

As he checked his comwatch, a scarlet light flashed. A loud warning beep sounded from Tracer and Tansy's badges at the same time.

"Low oxygen? How can that be possible?" Camp asked, his heart thudding against his chest.

Tracer shook his head. "I have no idea. Even if someone shut down life support, we should still have plenty of air to make it out of here."

"Mine says two minutes," said Tansy, her voice shaking.

"We've probably been warned several times, but we were too busy getting over here to notice," Tracer said.

"Won't the Felis have emergency oxygen?" asked Dashner.

Tracer glanced back at the hovering mech. "Sure, but we're closer to the exit. We'll have a much better chance of making it to the doors. Move faster, everyone."

"But what if the entire ship is affected now?" asked Jayne.

"Impossible," said Tracer. "Just work on getting to the end."

Camp's head began to swim. *Could the lack of oxygen be affecting me already? Maybe the power of suggestion.* He shook his head and continued to pull himself along, arm over arm, rung by rung.

His movements became sluggish. Hand over hand. *Follow Dashner. Don't stop.* Pressure filled his skull, and he wondered if his eyes were bugging out like a vintage Earth cartoon character. His tongue stuck to the roof of his mouth, but he longed for air instead of water. Darkness closed around him like a fist.

"I'm letting go," Tansy murmured behind him. "What's the point of going on? They want me dead, anyway."

"No, Tansy." The words slurred together, and he wasn't sure if they even made sense. "Don't give up." He couldn't grab her hand, because then he wouldn't be able to move without releasing his grasp.

In the blaring light of his comwatch he saw it; the most impossible thing one could imagine in such a place. A tiny emerald shape, with wings in a blur.

The hummingbird brushed his cheek, making tiny chirps, then flit away.

"Tansy, do you see it?" he asked.

"No, Camp. I can barely see anything."

"It's a hummingbird. Like the one we saw that first day I met you. It's beautiful, Tansy."

"I want to see it, Camp. Please."

"Then come on, you have to keep going."

"What are you talking about?" said Jayne, her voice also slurred.

"Maybe you'll get to see, once we reach the door," said Camp.

The bird stayed in his line of sight, moving forward. Camp veered off from the rest of the group in pursuit.

"What are you doing?" Tracer shouted below him.

"I don't know." Camp mumbled. "I'm following a bird."

One more foot and then I'm done. I'm letting go. It's too hard.

His comwatch light flashed from red to green, and a panel glowed under his hand.

Taking the deepest breath he could muster, he yelled, "Here! Over here! Hurry!"

The panel slid open, revealing the ladder. A blast of air hit his face, and he gulped it in. *Talk about the sweetest thing I've tasted.*

Tansy was right behind him. He pulled her in, and she sank against the wall, gasping and panting.

Dashner popped up, then Jayne.

Tracer was last, and he slammed the door behind him. "Thank

the gods this area wasn't affected by the life-support drainage." He gave them a sheepish smile. "Sorry, everyone, I guess I swerved off course. Good thing Camp found the panel."

"I had a tiny guide," said Camp. "I wonder where it went?"

He scanned the small space, and his shoulders sagged. "I hope the little bird finds a way out."

"A bird? Flying in zero gravity?" Tracer held up his hands. "Must've been a hallucination."

"Maybe," said Camp. "Now let's get out of here."

27
Marrow's Meddling

Periwinth rubbed her temples and glanced at the comscreen again. Dozens of messages from leaders on every ship. More tales of sabotage, but mostly Embroid after Embroid demanding that the captain return Tansy as soon as she was found.

Bradstorm leaned against the console. "What's the news?"

"Oh, it's all bad," Periwinth said. "I'm trying to decide if we should try to fetch this little party of rebels or wait for them to arrive. We must confront the new couple and address what we found on the hull of their zoomer."

Bradstorm ran a hand over his beard. "A disaster in the present is much more compelling than a disaster foreseen. The human mind doesn't always comprehend the truth until it's too late. How much time did we spend begging the stragglers to change their minds? The naysayers, the conspiracy theorists, the people who accused us of power trips. Remember those days we went knocking on doors there at the end? The Solstice members were so angry that we weren't spending our time readying the ship."

"I thought the people would listen to me if I addressed them in person." Periwinth sighed. "It worked for a few."

"Right. And those people are alive because of you." Bradstorm's voice softened. "From what we've been able to gather, this family's supply of food and water would have to be limited in a zoomer of that size. Limited probing capabilities would mean no way to see how close or far away they were to the Sepentine, or if they'd even reach us. Taking on one passenger could have meant death for everyone. We must put ourselves in their shoes."

Periwinth's throat tightened. "I have."

Bradstorm's shoulders sagged. "I'm sorry. Of course."

Periwinth brushed a tear from her cheek and cleared her throat. "Anyway, back to the band of rebels. Wouldn't be so difficult to find them if the Cholters, Embroids, Tarks, and Bloomwraiths hadn't disabled so many of the forcebot reporters in the maintenance tubes."

Bradstorm gave a weak chuckle. "Yeah, they've really helped the saboteur along, haven't they? The ones remaining have been rewired to the ship's local surveillance centers to service the magistrates. Except for the security stations on the Tark's ship, which were, of course, repurposed as animal feed storage. We knew this type of thing would happen when we launched."

"What a waste of time and resources," said Periwinth. "I don't know why the Solstice insisted we install them in the first place."

"Most of their choices tend to boggle my mind," Bradstorm

replied.

A new message from Glindel flashed on Periwinth's screen.

Periwinth's chest tightened. "The gravity system was shut down in the maintenance tunnel in the tether tube. Oh, that can't be good for our little team."

Bradstorm leapt to his feet. "I'll get down there immediately. You think it's sabotage?"

"What else could it be? I'm coming with you."

Bradstorm led the way from the room to the lift, and she followed at his heels, thoughts racing. *If they lost gravity, would the other life support systems fail? Surely Tracer can get them out. Unless the saboteur finds a way to open the airlock.* She moved faster.

As they reached the lift, the door slid open. Marrow stepped out. She arched her heavily painted eyebrows.

"Why, Captain, wherever are you going?"

Periwinth's heart dropped to her toes. *Of all the times to come for a chat.*

She flashed a quick smile. "Marrow, how lovely to see you. I'm heading to the training room for a short run."

"You won't mind if I join you?" Marrow patted her shoulder. "It's been a while since we've had a chance to talk, and I'm wondering what's been going on in that busy mind of yours."

Periwinth shot Bradstorm a glance. Every moment counted, and Marrow would only slow them down and ask questions they weren't ready to answer.

Bradstorm folded his arms. "I've been called to check on a few things below deck. Solstice Marrow, will your guards accompany you to the training room?"

Marrow frowned, her wrinkled lips rippling in a twisted arc. "As always. Are you particularly concerned for us?"

"Why would you think that?" said Periwinth. "Let's go." She nodded to Bradstorm as the elevator doors closed. *Thank the Creator I can trust him with this task.* She truly didn't know what she'd do without at least one person she could trust implicitly. *If he failed me ... I think I would lay down and die from the stress of it all. He carries so much for me.* But in turn, she carried every life on the seven ships.

Marrow gave a sideways glance at her personal guards, one man and one woman. They stared back, passively. "I'm glad you decided to take a little time for yourself, dear," she said. "It's important to build your strength back after the incident."

"Yes," Periwinth said absent-mindedly, wondering what would happen with Bradstorm and the team. *Who would know their route and attempt to harm them? Or is it another random attack?* It seemed a far stretch to say that now, since so many of the incidents had involved members of the group somehow. *They've all risked so much to get Tansy here alive. Even though the Embroids can't prosecute anyone from a different ship for harboring a said criminal, their own kindreds could convict them if they want to play nice with the Embroids.*

She tried to keep her face a mask, devoid of emotion. *Siding with Tansy would risk everything we've worked for with the seven ships. But what can I do?* She'd come to care for each member of her team, especially the sweet and quiet Tansy. And from a practical standpoint, if Tansy possessed even a fraction of the powers held by past Emergents, she could be a powerful asset to the entire operation.

Now I'm thinking like the Embroid leadership.

"Whatever is the matter, dear?" asked Marrow. "It's not like you to be so quiet."

"Sorry," Periwinth blinked. "My ribs are a little sore and I'm suddenly hit by exhaustion. Perhaps I was hasty to plan a training session. I may need to return to my quarters."

Marrow peered into her face, her eyes narrowing. "Or perhaps you should tell me the truth."

The elevator doors slid open. "Guards, leave us," said Marrow.

The guards glanced at each other, then back to the old woman. "Are you sure, Solstice?" said the woman guard.

"Do I look confused?" Marrow barked. "Yes, leave us this instant."

The woman guard's eyes flashed to Periwinth, who nodded. The two guards stepped off the elevator.

Marrow pressed a button with a wrinkled fist, and the door slid closed again.

Periwinth worked to keep her breathing even, and her hands relaxed at her sides. "What seems to be the trouble, Honorable Marrow?"

"Look, Peri," Marrow said, reverting to a nickname she hadn't used since Periwinth was a teenager. "We are the most revered and powerful people of the seven ships. We are the beginning and end of what these thousands of people know, and the only way any of them can hope to survive this journey, and what will come afterwards. But more than that, you and I are family. I have been a mother to you for fifteen years. And I do not appreciate being lied to." Her wrinkled lips trembled.

"What are you talking about?" Periwinth folded her arms tightly across her chest, feeling suddenly like she was being scolded as a teen when she'd returned home too late at night.

Scarlet crept over Marrow's normally composed face. "Don't deny it. I know all about your little group of misfits. Why did you keep it from me? It's not just your lies. My heart is broken that you would deceive me, ME, in such a manner."

Periwinth again had to fight to keep her voice level. "Solstice Marrow, I request that you calm your emotions and remember your station. I am the captain of this ship. I am your superior. If I choose to keep something to myself, you will trust I have a good reason for it."

She took a deep breath. Until a year ago, she would have never dared to speak to her mentor in such a way. But times had changed, and she realized what a select few, the closest people who truly cared, had tried to tell her. *The Solstice is not all-wise and all-knowing. They have been corrupted. Even Marrow. Especially Marrow.* She wanted to continue, to rail about all the times Marrow had gone over her head, made important decisions without her authority, and outright lied to her. But she didn't. *It won't do any good.*

Marrow blinked, and Periwinth almost expected her to try to reach out and do her an injury, such was the level of intensity in her eyes. But she swallowed and smiled.

"Certainly, Captain. Whatever you feel is best. You are, after all, in command."

"Yes, I am," Periwinth gripped the rail inside the lift. "And I'd ask you not to forget it."

She pressed the button and the lift's doors opened. "I suggest we take some time to catch our breath and think."

"Of course," Captain," said Marrow. She cleared her throat and tapped Periwinth's arm with her long, crystal fingernails. "You need rest and re-evaluation. That's for certain."

A man in a medic's uniform stood outside of the elevator, and at the edge of Periwinth's peripheral vision: Halsey.

She only had a second to wonder what the young girl was doing there before something sharp pricked her neck.

"You must rest, Captain," the medic said. "Doctor's orders. We'll be taking you to a quiet place to sleep."

Perwinth's mind struggled for awareness, for an edge of being. But the fight was in vain, and she quickly succumbed to the sleeping drug.

28
Chapel

Camp sat on the bench in the tether station, waiting for some word from Captain Zephyr. *She promised that she'd take care of us. I think a death sentence warrants concern. Oh, and the whole loss of gravity–and oxygen–thing.*

He glanced down at Tansy, who was snuggled against his shoulder. Her luminous eyes were wide, and her lips trembled. She'd been so brave but facing death multiple times in one day was catching up with her. Everything was so uncertain.

She stared up at him. "I'm fine."

"If you say so," he said. "But we need to get to the captain. These tether stations are too much of a neutral zone and I'm worried those malfunctioning bots will suddenly start doing their job again. Father Sharood could make it over here at any moment."

Dashner shifted in his seat. "So the operator won't let us through and into the ship?"

"Nope," said Tracer. "Not until we hear from the captain, and they haven't been able to reach her."

The door flew open, and Commander Helms entered. His uniform was more casual than they'd seen in past meetings, and his hair flowed around his shoulders instead of being tied back in its usual neat braid.

"Welcome again to the headship," he said, giving a swift nod. "I'm glad to see you're all still breathing. I've been briefed as I journeyed here. Of course, if we'd known of your predicament sooner, we would have rescued you. As it was, Glindel informed me of the malfunction a mere fifteen minutes ago."

He pressed his comwatch and lifted his wrist. "Officer Ulder, your team is on standby until further notice. The crisis is averted. Helms out."

Turning back to the group, he smiled. "I've assembled a rescue team, but it appears that we had no need. Tracer, I assume it's you we should thank?"

Tracer shrugged. "Everyone worked together, Commander. But if we'd waited on you, we'd have been floating corpses. Something sucked the air right out of the tube. I'd really like to know who tried to murder us."

"Yes, there are many who would like to know that information," said Commander Helms. "If someone has the capability of shutting down the life support for a maintenance tube—it seems as though the danger keeps growing. We have members of every kindred searching for this dangerous person, but so far we've found nothing." His gaze rested on Tansy. "And then there's you,

Miss Pellum."

Tansy sat up. "Yes, Commander, I–"

He held up his hand. "No need to explain your troubles, we have been briefed. I'm here to represent the captain, she was unfortunately detained but should meet with us shortly. I hope within minutes." He checked the comwatch again, his forehead wrinkling. "I would have thought by now she'd have come up with an excuse to get away." He shrugged and nodded to the couple standing beside Camp. "You must be Dashner and Jayne. You are welcome here on the headship, of course, but we would have appreciated you coming to meet with us sooner. No one would be turned away from refuge here, no matter what sacrifice had to be made along the way. But there will be further conversation about what was found on the hull of your zoomer."

Dashner reddened as everyone turned to stare at him. "There was nothing I could do," he stammered. "I didn't even know the man. He climbed into the fuselage at the last moment. I couldn't have saved him if I tried."

"We're not throwing stones," said Commander Helms. "But you should know we were notified by the individuals who remained on the planet that ten ships were stolen from the city's remaining fleet. So far, you're the only one that's managed to catch up with us."

He WAS *lying. They stole the ship; it wasn't given to them. Must have been quite a battle there at the end.* Camp felt no smugness, only sorrow. *I would have helped them either way, even if I'd known.*

"Please, Sir, could we send out scout ships to search for the remaining stragglers?" asked Jayne. "We don't know how many others made it through the atmosphere."

"In this slipstream, we cannot go back, only forward," said Commander Helms. "We would have to follow the blackcurrant, and the ships wouldn't be accessible there. They'd be several lightyears away. And the lives of everyone would be at risk.

"A few more days remain before any ships would run out of possible resources, depending on passengers and what they could manage to scavenge. It's still possible for someone to catch up with the Serpentine. At the risk of sounding heartless." He sighed deeply. "The people who stayed behind chose their path. They had years to decide whether to remain or go. Our pressing concerns are the humans on this ship." He turned and headed out the tether station door.

Everyone followed. Tansy grabbed Camp's hand and squeezed it tight.

Warmth flowed through him, and he bent to whisper in her ear. "I meant what I said. I'll die before I let anything happen to you."

She gave a long shuddering sigh but didn't reply.

A small person in a shimmering white cloak waited for them in the hall. Camp recognized Halsey. He hadn't seen her since that meeting in the captain's room, except for a few times during group meetings on the comwatches. She'd always been silent, her bright eyes flickering across the screened faces.

She bowed her head. "It is good to see you all." Her eyes darted to Tansy. "You are safe. That is well."

"Why are you here?" asked Bradstorm.

"I came to bring you word from Captain Zephyr," she said in her high, child-like voice. She pushed her hood back. Again, Camp noticed her fingernails, the strange, almost sickly violet hue.

"I should have heard from her." Commander Helms continued to move forward.

Halsey kept in stride. "The captain wanted me to tell you she's tired. She decided to retire to her quarters for the evening. She trusted you to handle the situation with the team."

Commander Helms halted and turned. "She said what?" he said through a clenched jaw. "That cannot be possible. She doesn't even know the team made it out safely from the maintenance tube."

Somehow, Halsey managed to shrink down even further, looking even more fragile and childlike. Camp held back a strange urge to run forward and pat her head.

"I'm only telling you what she said to me, Sir. I believe she mentioned injuring herself in the training room." Tears fringed the pale, almost translucent lashes.

Commander Helms cleared his throat and continued to walk. "That's more than peculiar." He glanced at Dashner. "I assure you; this is very uncharacteristic for the captain. I'm sure there's a reasonable explanation. We'll continue to the meeting room."

Another soldier came through the door and entered the hall, catching them as they all stepped into the lift.

"Commander Helms. Embroids in the tether station." His eyes fell on Tansy. "They are demanding we bring them the girl."

"Detain them in any way you can," said Commander Helms. He closed the elevator door and leaned back against the wall, closing his eyes.

"I hate to be a bother," said Camp, "but what are we going to do? Why would the captain abandon us in such a desperate situation? Doesn't she even care about Tansy?"

The Commander's eyes flipped open. "I'm not quite sure what's going on, but I do trust the captain. We will figure this out."

A strange little smile flitted over Halsey's face but was quickly replaced with her usual emotionless stare.

"Something's wrong," Tansy whispered to Camp. "She's up to no good."

Halsey turned and fixed her snapping black eyes on Tansy's face, even though she couldn't possibly have heard her. Tansy blinked.

Camp gulped. Not for the first time, he longed for the ability to read minds like Tansy, even though she'd assured him that the gift was not as great as it sounded. *There is the prosecuted and sentenced to death by her people thing.* Cholters had their little tiffs, but they'd done away with the death sentence a century ago and never found a reason to bring it back.

A small object rolled around on the floor and landed against his foot. *Jayne's earring.* He lurched forward and picked it up, his face barely brushing against Halsey's hand as he rose.

"Sorry," he said hastily, handing the earring to Jayne.

"Oh, thank you," Jayne said, clipping the silver disc over her ear.

A prickly feeling settled over the back of Camp's neck, and he folded his arms tightly against himself. *Tansy's right. Halsey may seem innocent, but she's a liar.*

Of course, there was no way to inform Commander Helms of this new information while they rode the lift. He glanced over at the man, whose glassy eyes rested on the door.

He must feel completely betrayed. Captain Zephyr wouldn't have retired to her quarters while we were in such danger.

The lift door slid open, and Commander Helms strode into the corridor. "Come with me. I taking you to a place where I think you'll be safe, at least until I can locate the captain and find out her plans."

He led them down several passages Camp hadn't seen. The walls were lined with wooden beams, brightly polished. Pictures taller than men and created with panes of stained glass hung from the walls. One depicted a group of men in a strange-looking ship on waves at sea. Another showed a simple basket with bread and fish. *These pictures are from the Bible.* He met Tansy's wide-eyed gaze and realized she must know these stories as well. *At least the Embroids know the true Word to some extent.*

Commander Helms halted beside a pair of arched double doors, also constructed from wood. Instead of using his comm-badge at the main panel, he simply tugged on a brass handle to open the door. He waved the group inside.

The room was good-sized, filled with two rows of cushioned benches. A wooden podium stood in the front, and a wooden symbol Camp recognized as a cross hung from the wall behind it.

This must be a Christian church. But I've never been inside one like this. Camp's father had taken him to meetings with Cholters who worshipped the Creator. They preferred to meet in small groups and mostly outside. This place had a solemn, sacred, hushed feeling. His soul welcomed the moment of peace.

"Is this like your Clarity?" Camp asked Tansy. He spoke in quiet tones, reluctant to break the tranquil atmosphere.

She didn't answer but gave a swift shake of her head.

Halsey went to the front bench and sat down. "I like this place," she said with a slight, babyish lisp. "I come in here often."

Camp held back a pre-teen inclination to shove her out of the seat. *How can I talk to Commander Helms alone without rousing her suspicions?*

He sat in the pew behind Halsey, and Tansy scooted beside him. Dashner and Jayne stood to the side of the little chapel near the front, staring up at the cross.

Tracer took a seat on the edge. "I'm going to see if I can reach Glindel. Tell her we're safe."

Commander Helms strode to the front as he checked his comwatch. "It would be prudent of me to head to the captain's quarters and find out what's going on. But I shouldn't leave you all here alone."

Halsey rose and touched his arm. "Allow me to go. I'll see if I can find a guard from your team and get him to come here. Surely you can trust one of them."

"Trayford." Commander Helms rubbed the back of his neck. "He'll be on level thirteen, patrolling the observation deck. I'd contact him, but I have reason to believe our communication is being compromised."

"You can consider the task accomplished." Halsey gave him a simpering smile and swept out the door.

"Commander Helms," both Tansy and Camp said together as the door closed behind her. They looked at each other.

"Go ahead," said Camp.

Commander Helms nodded to Tansy. "I'm listening."

"Halsey may pretend to be trustworthy," said Tansy, "but she is not. I couldn't get an exact read on her thoughts, but for someone who looks so innocent her mind is teeming with lies and deceit. I didn't notice at our first meeting because I was still sorting everything out."

Bradstorm sank down on the front pew. "Are you certain?"

Another thought poked at Camp's mind. *Purple.* "Purple fingernails," he said.

"What are you talking about?" asked Tracer.

"Halsey's fingernails are purple. The day we met her, and again this afternoon. Not painted purple, stained purple. And purple is the color of Cliatride, an element used for–"

"Making bombs," Tracer said slowly.

"Get off that pew!" Camp shouted to Commander Helms.

"Everyone clear out now!"

Commander Helms jumped up and ran to the door, with everyone behind him.

He tugged on the brass handle, but it wouldn't budge. "Help me! She must have jammed them somehow!"

Dashner and Tracer ran to the doors and began to shove and kick the wooden panels.

Something very loud blew past Camp's head. He threw himself over Tansy, rolling them under a pew. A blinding flash of light exploded into the air, followed by searing pain that shot through his body. Everything went black.

29
Lift

Periwinth rolled over and touched her face. *Odd, I don't remember falling asleep.*

A tinkling laugh sounded from the other side of the room.

"There you are. I wasn't sure if my dosage was correct. After all, I can't be a prodigy in every way, can I?"

A pale face loomed into her fuzzy vision.

"Halsey?" Peiwinth moaned. "Thank goodness. Marrow–"

"Drugged you with something. Right. Good thing I knew where she took you and what she gave you," Halsey said, patting Periwinth's hand. "And hmm–good thing I knew how to sneak into the medical supply station and get exactly what I needed to counter the drug's effects." She tilted her head. "Makes you wonder, doesn't it?"

"Actually, it does." Adrenaline surged through Periwinth's veins, edging through her mind. Her fingers began to shake. "How did you accomplish all those things, Halsey?"

"Hmmm . . ." Halsey tapped her chin. "We know I'm a smart one, don't we?" She pulled a blaster from the folds of her white robe and placed it in her lap. "We know I studied at the best school in Gyron, thanks to you, dear Captain. But what you might not remember is that my father was a weapon specialist in the final skirmish, so far from the main city that most people didn't even know about it. And his genius was unparalleled until . . . what happened?" she tilted her head to the side. "Oh yes. The city let him die, along with the rest of my family."

"Your family had a genetic disorder," Periwinth said, taking great care to keep her tongue from sticking to the roof of her mouth.

"Yes, they did. One I shall eventually succumb to, if I choose to do so." Halsey's lips pulled back from her teeth in a chilling snarl. "But that could have all been avoided if you and the Solstice had agreed to allow a small contingency of scientists to work on a cure. A minute team, perhaps three or four researchers. But none could be spared. Every single one of them had to work on these blasted ships and the medical stations."

Periwinth shook her head, trying to clear the fuzz, trying to make sense of the words the child-like woman was saying to her. "Honey, I'm so sorry. We have all suffered so much. As you know, very few of my Kindred remain. I think that's why I was drawn to you at first. But you know what happened. At any other period of our history, every effort would have gone towards a cure. But we had no time." The feeling began to return to Periwinth's lips. "The antidote had to be perfected before we launched. Otherwise, almost all of humanity could have been wiped out."

"My humanity was wiped out," said Halsey quietly. She picked up the blaster and ran her finger over the shining red surface.

Periwinth stretched her legs and swung them over the edge of the narrow cot she'd been laying on. "Where are we, anyway? I must try to find Bradstorm. And Tansy." The memory of the past day rushed at her full force, and she sprang to her feet. "Goodness, what has become of the group floating on the mech?"

"That's not for you to worry about now," said Halsy, raising the blaster and leveling at Periwinth's head. "Best to come along with me."

The distant voice in Periwinth's mind that had been screaming of danger hit a higher decibel, and she stared at the blaster. "Halsey, what are you doing? Why would you want to threaten me? I've given you everything you asked for."

"I want my family back," said Halsey in a level tone. "And since that's impossible, I want you to follow me."

Better not aggravate her until I figure out what's going on. "All right, sure," said Periwinth. She rose slowly. She still wore her simple everyday uniform, the one she'd put on that morning, if it even was the same day. Her comwatch was nowhere to be seen.

Halsey waved the blaster at her. "Go on, through the door."

"Halsey, you don't have to threaten me. I'll go with you. You can put the blaster down."

"It gives me comfort to hold it at this time," Halsey said. "Now move." A dangerous edge sharpened her tone.

Periwinth went through the door of the room, which was bare of everything but cot and chair. She scanned the wall for a contact panel. *Nothing. Where could we be? Doesn't every room on the ship have a communication panel?*

They stepped into a dimly lit corridor, the shadowy outline of a lift's panel at the far end.

"This is the underbelly of the headship," said Halsey from behind Periwinth. "Where the lowest of the families live. Except this section is uninhabited. You know why? Because this was the section created for my kinship."

Periwinth swallowed the enormous lump in her throat and turned slowly. "Surely that's not true, Halsey. Your family would have been allowed to choose a floor and section that suited them."

Halsey shook her head, her luminous eyes glowing in the dim red lights. "No. Many families live in quarters such as these. If you don't know this, then you are a poorer captain than even I thought."

"I've toured every living space on this ship," said Periwinth firmly. "While some are small, they are brightly painted with lovely furniture and decorations. None are like this. If your family had been on board–"

"Don't you realize? We would have been put here because no one wanted to watch us die. No one wanted to be exposed to such an uncomfortable sight. But the disease worked faster than even the scientists thought at first. So my family didn't even have a chance to decorate before they succumbed to a miserable death."

"Why haven't you ever talked to me about this?" said

Periwinth.

"Because I knew you didn't have time to listen. Now keep moving."

Where are we going? Periwinth's mind raced. As well as she thought she knew the girl behind her, the facial expression was inscrutable, unmoving. Whatever it was she had in mind to do, it would be very hard to talk her out of it.

But maybe a distraction.

She turned to glance at Halsey. "So how did you manage to follow Marrow and her guards down here without being detected?" she asked, attempting to keep her voice light and breezy. "That must have taken a clever bit of work."

"Yes," said Halsey. The cloud over her face brightened the tiniest shade. She jerked her shoulder, the one that held the blaster, up and down in a lopsided shrug. "See that band? It blocks security signals of any possible surveillance on the ship. As long as I can keep out of human eyesight, I cannot be seen."

That's why we've been having so much trouble with the forcebots. Wait. "You're the saboteur," Periwinth said slowly.

"Took you a while, but you finally caught on," said Halsey.

"Why would you do that? Why would you put everyone at risk? People could have died."

"Oh Captain, don't you see?" Halsey's voice softened, and her eyes grew big again, luminous. She was back to looking like a little girl again. "That's what I wanted."

"To kill people?"

Halsey skipped along, the tassels on the hem of her robe brushing the floor. "Yes! If my family can't make it to Fortress, no one should. It would be fair, right? Except ..." They reached the end of the hallway, and she slapped the panel to the lift. "They've discovered me. Even now, they are searching the ship. And even with my lovely little bracelet here, they'll find me. So, I'll do the next best thing." The lift door slid open. "I'm going to destroy you."

The hairs on the back of Periwinth's neck stood on end, and she fought for words. "Halsey, you don't want to do this. There's still a chance. You haven't seriously hurt anyone. I'll vouch for you."

"Oh, but I have." Halsey's mouth twisted into a cruel smile. "I killed most of the people from your team. And I killed your man."

Periwinth's heart dropped to her shoes. "You mean Bradstorm?" Numbness swirled back into her face, and her knees buckled, threatening to tip her into the floor. *Wait.*

Obeying her body's inclination, she dropped to the floor, catching a glimpse of Halsey's shocked face as she went down. She rolled into the girl's knees, pulling her down with her. The blaster went off harmlessly as she wrestled it from the bony white fingers and flung it away.

Halsey screamed and clawed at her face. "You must die for them! You must die for all of them!'

Peiwinth squeezed her grip tighter and they rolled into the lift.

With an impressive burst of strength, Halsey pushed her away and back outside the lift, while she remained inside. Periwinth grabbed the blaster and popped up, training the weapon on the open lift door. "Come on out, Halsey. We can get you help."

Halsey's pale lips stretched into a grin, her eyes wild, her hair hanging in ragged strands around her face. "Nothing can help me. You see, Captain, three days before I boarded the ship, I found out the disease in my system has ceased to be dormant. I'd never make it to Fortress, even if I desired to go there."

Periwinth stretched her free hand out to the girl, tears streaming down her cheeks. "Let me help you. We'll get a medical team on it. Maybe they can figure out what to do."

Halsey's shoulders drooped, and her head hung down. "Would you help me, Captain?" She glanced up through her long eyelashes, looking more like a little girl than ever. Her lips quivered.

Could she really be listening to me? "Yes, yes. I care about you, Halsey. You're like family to me. Please come out of there and we'll do whatever it takes."

"Whatever it takes?"

"Of course."

"Oh Captain Zephyr!" The pale fingers uncurled. "Please. Help me."

"Yes, yes. Just come out of there."

"Please!" The girl's arms stretched out, but she didn't budge from her place in the lift.

Periwinth's grip on the blaster lessened, and she allowed herself to give a small smile. "Come on, Halsey."

What is that above her on the lift? A small orange light flashed. *Where have I seen that before?*

"Halsey! Get out of there!" Periwinth screamed. "There's a bomb!"

"It's too late," said Halsey. "And if I can't take you with me, so be it. There are plenty of others I can bring instead." She lunged forward and hit the lift's side panel.

Oh no. Periwinth rushed forward, too late to catch the doors. "No Halsey!" she screamed. An image flashed through her mind. Lieutenant Centlon, his eyes bugged out, drug across the ice away from their team, a trail of bright red blood in his wake.

She opened the emergency panel on the side of the lift. "Authorization Zephyr," she yelled. "Stop the power to this unit."

A rumbling came from deep within the ship, and she was flung to the floor

.

30
Father Sharood

Static, dense air hit Tansy's face, stale like the caverns she'd explored near her hometown during childhood. She crept through inky blackness, patting the walls with ginger hands. *Strange.* The spongy surface yielded to her touch, like a carpet of moss. She sank lower to the–*floor or dirt? Where am I anyway?*

Where is Camp? Where is my mother? She had never felt so incredibly alone and lost. *Oh. that's right.* She'd been in prison, awaiting execution. "If this is death, where is my mother?" she said out loud, though she had no reason to believe anyone else existed in this place.

A cold fear gripped her heart. *What if this IS the afterlife? What if I'm meant to be here, all alone, for eternity? Oh, Spirit, please no!*

"Tansy," called a voice from the density above.

Tilting back her head, she strained to glimpse the sky or ceiling, but only darkness met her gaze. "Camp? Is that you? Keep calling! I'm trying to find my way out of here."

"Tansy!" came the voice again, closer, like it was right by her ear.

My eyes are closed. Tansy gave a short laugh. *Maybe that's why I can't see anything.* She opened her heavy eyelids, and suddenly the world was flooded with light.

"There's my girl." A long, ragged breath sounded by her ear, and someone patted her hand.

She turned her head. "Camp?

Bright lights shone overhead, highlighting a white ceiling and shiny, bowl-shaped lamps. Screens flashed beside her with details of what she figured must be her vital signs.

We must be in a clinic like the one on the Embroid ship. Except there would be a bard-healer strumming on a lute in the corner. Instead of the comforting scents of healing herbs, the acrid stench of big-city ointments filled the room.

Camp leaned closer, peering into her face. "How do you feel?" A bandage covered one eye and his arm was in a sling.

She lifted each limb slightly and wiggled her toes and fingers. "I–I'm okay, I guess. My head kind of aches. How are you? You've been hurt?"

"I'll be fine," said Camp. "A few scratches and dings. Everything still works. I'm more worried about you."

Jayne moved to Camp's side. Her old clothes had been replaced by a long white tunic with bright blue embroidery around the collar and sleeves. Small bandages dotted her arms and face. "Tansy. I'm thankful you're awake."

"Commander Helms had the worst of it," said Camp. "And–Dashner. We'd figured out that demon girl had put a bomb under the pew, but we didn't know the door had been laced with 'em as well."

"Are they going to be alright?" Tansy struggled to sit up. A sharp pain stabbed her temple, and she sank back into the welcoming pillow.

"Whoa there, I think you should keep laying down for a while longer, at least until the doctor comes in," said Camp. "Dashner and Commander Helms are both in surgery. The doctors think they'll pull through fine. Tracer was pretty much unscathed, but his cybernetic arm will need repair."

Jayne stared down at her hands but didn't say anything. Tansy's heart went out to her. *How terrible to be on a strange ship, with her small daughter left behind, and her husband injured in such a way.*

Camp pushed a strand of hair back away from Tansy's face. "We're lucky one of the chaplains happened to be heading in to prepare for morrow's service. He heard the blast and got a team to bring us here."

Jayne looked up. "Before he lost consciousness, Commander Helms told the soldiers to keep the explosion and our transport confidential for now. As far as we know, neither the Embroids or anyone from the Solstice knows about what happened."

"No word on the captain," said Camp. "We've all been trying to reach her."

"And Halsey?" Tansy struggled to sit up again and fell back.

"They need to find her. What if she went off to attack the captain?"

Camp's shoulders rose and fell. "We have no idea. We've been here for an hour. My wrist is broken, the doctor said it would take a day or two to mend. But Commander Helms–his healing might be more involved." He leaned closer. "His arm was blown off at the shoulder. The doctor said another few minutes and he would have bled out."

"Oh no." Tansy's hand flew to her mouth. "How awful."

"Chances are they'll be able to reattach it. They can do amazing things here in the headship," said Camp. "But still, yes, pretty bad."

Jayne rose and moved to the other side of the room.

"And Dashner?" Tansy whispered.

"Nasty burns over sixty percent of his body," whispered Camp. "But again, they believe he'll pull through."

Tansy settled back on her pillow. She remembered it all now. Camp leaping over her, flinging her under one of the pews in the little chapel. *If it wasn't for him, I'd have been hurt much worse. Or– dead.*

"We must find Halsey," she said. "I don't even want to think about the next plans on her agenda."

Camp's head jerked up. "I wonder if Tracer ever reached Glindel? Maybe she can come over. No one outside of our group can access our comwatches, remember?"

"No one but Halsey." Tansy groaned. "No wonder Commander Helms thought we might be compromised."

"Wait." Camp pulled out his comwatch, tapped the screen, and breathed a sigh of relief. "Oh my gosh, it still works. My regular one was shattered in the blast. I think I can rig it up to contact one person, and no one else will be able to access our conversation. Let me try."

He fiddled with the glowing device; lips pursed.

Glindel's concerned face projected on the pillow above Tansy's shoulder.

"Camp, where are you?" Glindel said. "Falstaff and I have been going crazy not hearing any news. Last I knew, you were floating in a mech." She squinted. "You're banged up. Tansy, are you on a medical cot?"

"This isn't even from the mech incident," said Camp. "We had a run-in with the saboteur. At least we know who's doing everything. It's Halsey."

Glindel gasped and uttered an oath Tansy had never heard.

"I don't think the Embroids have located us yet," said Tansy, "but we need to find the captain before they find us."

"The captain's not with you?" Glindel's fingers crept up to her lips. "Where is she?"

"Commander Helms doesn't even know where she is," said Tansy. "Or at least that's what he said before the bombs exploded. He's in surgery now."

Glindel gasped. "Planets align! Is everyone alive at least?"

"Barely," said Camp.

The doctor, a young woman with curly dark hair, entered the room. "How is everyone feeling?"

"I've got to put this away," said Camp. "I know you've had a crazy day of your own, Glindel. I can't leave everyone here right now, and I'm still woozy from whatever pain drug they've given me. Can you please come to the headship and try to find the captain?"

Glindel's eyes darted to the side. "I'm already at the tether station, I'll be there as quickly as I can. Keep your comwatch on so I can locate you after I find her."

"Right," said Tansy. "Stay safe."

Voices boomed outside the door. Camp shoved the comwatch into his pocket.

"They're here," Tansy whispered. Her gaze traveled over the room, looking for something to block the opening. Weapons, heavy medical stands, anything. *Even if I were in any shape to fight my Kindred, could I?*

Father Sharood stepped into the room, his blood-red robes billowing around him.

Tansy's breath rushed from her lungs. Her first inclination was to hide under the covers, as if that would do any good.

"And here we find our criminal." Father Sharood pushed back his hood and steepled his long, knobby fingers. He sucked in his gaunt cheeks, making him look even more otherworldly than normal.

Tansy had always had a healthy respect for Father Sharood, perhaps even a bit of awe one would have for a religious leader, but now she hated him with every fiber of her being.

Camp stepped in front of her bed, spreading out his one good arm and wincing as he moved the other. "You won't touch her," he said in a steady tone.

"Boy, don't you see what you're doing?" Father Sharood hissed. "This girl has chosen the path of wickedness. Selfish beyond human comprehension. We are embarking on the most dangerous journey anyone in humanity has ever taken." He held out his hands. "We're a group of souls, striving through an impossible journey of survival. It's unthinkable that anyone would hold back a gift that could ensure the safety of even one extra person. Think of the children. The newest babes." He leaned closer. "Precious lives snuffed out, because of this girl's carnal fear."

Camp didn't move. "How can you speak of someone giving their life so callously? Your people have no evidence the powers will be transferred. And even if they are, the new baby wouldn't be able to help anyone for quite some time, unless Embroids have the power of premature speech, which I don't think they do?" Camp glanced at Tansy. "Do they?"

"No," said Tansy.

"You've been informed of our ways, Cholter." Father Sharood tilted his head. "But you are ignorant beyond belief."

Jayne moved over to stand by Camp. "This girl would be killed because she chose not to be abused by her own people. In the name of a reckless superstition. I thought Embroids were a peaceful Kindred."

Father Sharood's lip curled. "Ah, a Quient. I didn't realize any of your Kindred had chosen to join our little company. A bit late coming in, eh? You know nothing of the Embroid people. I'd thank you mind your own business."

He jerked his head and five members of the Embroid Opulence marched into the room. Tansy locked eyes with her neighbor, Mr. Arnott, beneath his yellow hood. He glowered at her.

"We've come to gather what belongs to us," Father Sharood growled. "You can get out of the way, or we will use force."

Camp crouched and braced himself as the first Embroid advanced. The man was half a head taller than him.

"Camp, let them take me," said Tansy. "Don't get hurt because of me."

"We've already discussed this," said Camp.

"Maybe you should move before I break your other arm," the man said.

Jayne screamed, loud and long. The Embroids' heads swiveled, and Camp swept the first man's legs from beneath him. The man crashed to the floor, his head smacking against the cot's metal frame. He didn't move.

Jayne pulled a taser of some sort from the folds of her gown. Light exploded from the device, and another Embroid was down, twitching.

Camp pulled his arm from the sling and flexed it. "Those healers know their stuff." He jerked another Embroid's head down to his knee, knocking the man out cold and sending him to the floor with a bloody nose.

"I need—help here!" Father Sharood was saying into his

comwatch.

I can't believe they were so arrogant to come unarmed. Tansy struggled to sit up, to grab something and fight, but she was still so woozy.

"Everyone stop at once!" a woman's voice commanded.

Silhouetted in the door was Captain Zephyr.

"Captain Zephyr, finally." Father Sharood moved back, gesturing to the mini-war going on around them. "You have a blaster, please bring some order to this situation!"

Captain Zephyr moved in. "You heard me. Everyone stop and raise your hands." Gone was the kind, calm woman Tansy had encountered in the past. Cool eyes surveyed the room, and the set of her jaw demanded obedience.

Camp released the Embroid he'd had in a chokehold and stepped back. "Yes, Captain." He raised his hands.

Jayne and the one Embroid left standing followed suit.

"Now," said Captain Zephyr. "Everyone who isn't injured will leave this room, this instant. We'll bring in medics to help these–" she prodded an unconscious Opulent with a booted toe. "Unfortunate new arrivals."

A new shade of scarlet stained Father Sharood's cheeks, almost matching his robe. "Captain, I demand that you–"

"There will be plenty of time for demands, Magistrate," said Captain Zephyr. "Until then, I insist that you leave this room. Now."

31
Confession

Strolling couples passed the space lock window, which ran the full length of the twenty-foot wall and provided the best view of the passing inky world. This observation deck had become the most popular gathering area during the day. Some people chose to sit at the provided tables for special dates and holidays, and some wandered by, alone, to gaze into the abyss and ponder life.

Periwinth pressed her hands against the thick glass and stared into the darkness. It seemed infinite. *But the finish line exists, doesn't it?* Somehow, the slipstream would come to an end. In ten months, this ship would reach Fortress. How many souls made it to the end–well, that was up to everyone aboard the Serpentine.

She hadn't come up with the idea for the planet's title. The name she'd called the place in her mind would invoke an opposite sentiment. But once she'd pulled herself out of the dark hole of fear the place had flung her into and had actually been able to share her story, the leadership had marginalized the issues and watered down the danger, blaming her space-addled mind. The people longed for a candle, a brightness. Some sort of peace to swallow down and deliver goodness to their soul. *And who could blame them?* Everything they knew was set to be destroyed by something that was supposed to be a source of warmth and life.

A new decision presented itself to her, another bead on the string of terrible choices she'd had to make for what seemed like a lifetime. And of course, she was the only one who could choose. Responsibility weighed on her heart like a cast-iron skillet, pressing her down until breathing and thinking and being became almost impossible.

And then there was the horrible conversation she'd had with Tracer only hours before. He'd risked everything to inform her of the false control stations. He'd told her, voice trembling, but with hope filling his eyes. That somehow, she'd known. That somehow, there was a perfect plan in place, a reason for this deception.

I can't let them know how powerless I am. They will never let me finish leading this journey, and I must. I'm the only one who knows the secrets that await us.

Bradstorm cleared his throat and she jerked away from the window. "Yes?"

"Captain, Tansy and the rest of the team are in a safe place, guarded by a dozen crew members." He studied her face with his steady gray eyes. His arm had been reattached, though the doctor said getting back the full range of mobility would take a few weeks.

"What are you doing out of bed?" Periwinth demanded. "I heard the doctor's orders."

"Neither one of us pay much attention to doctor's orders, do we?" he said.

"I suppose we don't." Periwinth turned back to the enormous window, wishing she could go back in time, to the day she'd made this trip in a tiny zoomer with a small group of hopeful crew members. Her best friends. They'd been so happy, so excited.

"Periwinth, are you listening?" came Bradstorm's gentle voice.

"I'm sorry," she trained her focus back on his face.

"As I was saying, Father Sharood is furious, but he's agreed to give you a few hours before they 'make a regretful decision,' as he called it."

Periwinth sighed. "What does he plan to do? Come at us in force?"

Bradstorm lowered his eyes. "The Embroids believe the girl's death will release some sort of power back into their kindred. It's all mumbo jumbo to me, but they're dead serious about it."

"Sickening." Periwinth clasped her hands, her knuckles whitening. "And the Solstice?"

He shrugged. "None of the three have responded to calls. I sent a team to rappel down the elevator shaft to search for Halsey, but so far they have not located her body in the wreckage. It's not looking good. On the other hand, you were able to stop the lift just in time, where it caused minimal damage. If the bomb had exploded on the floor Halsey directed it to, the navigational system and life-support for the entire headship could have been taken out. We could all be dead."

"Poor girl." Periwinth ran a hand over her eyes. *Just another person I failed.*

Bradstorm's gaze rested on her lips, then traveled to her eyes."Do you need anything, Periwinth?" he said softly.

Someone to hold me and tell me everything's going to be all right?

"I'm still reeling a little from the day. If Glindel hadn't run into me and led me to Tansy's room–"

"Fortunately, your comwatch was left in the cabinet of that room they kept you in, Captain," said Bradstorm. "But let's not waste energy on what might have been. We've checked the stations. It is as Tracer reported."

"All doubt has been removed?"

"Without question."

"Walk with me. I'm going to my meeting room."

"As you wish."

While they moved through the main hub, people stepped back, most dipping their heads in respect as always. *How many will still respect me, still trust me, once this day is through? How would I feel if my leadership revealed such treachery?*

They reached the familiar wall, where the fish swam in tranquility. Periwinth glanced at them as she moved past, wishing she could be such a creature, completely oblivious to the chaos around them, without worry of how they'd survive the next day. She sighed as they entered her meeting room.

"So." Bradstorm tapped his fingers against the table. "What will you decide?"

Periwinth bowed her head "You know what I must do."

Bradstorm sighed. "You've had an impossible choice. I support you all the way."

"I thought all would be well during this journey. I hoped that everyone would work together for the good of all, just for the short time it took to reach Fortress. That the true challenge would hit once we reached that formidable place." She gave a short laugh. "How naive could I be?"

"You dared to hope, that's all," said Bradstorm.

"Yes, well, hope has made me reckless, and I will not make that mistake again. I will not allow any more innocent blood to be spilled. And I cannot allow people to see the imbalance of power that is obviously in play. We must retain some level of order, or we'll never reach our destination."

"I have faith in you," said Bradstorm. "I always have, and I always will."

Periwinth allowed a small smile to cross her lips. "Thank you, Storm. I must get to work. Please guard the door so no one will disturb me."

He gave a slight bow. "Of course." He stepped through the panel, and it closed behind him.

"Creator, give me strength for what I'm about to do," Periwinth prayed. Sweat beaded on her forehead, and she wiped it away as she turned to the comscreen that took up most of the far wall. She flicked her wrist before it.

"Open frequency 5 2 7 8," she said. "The captain will address all ships at this time."

The screen blinked on, showing a mirror image of herself. She swallowed and smiled.

"Attention, all peoples of the seven ships. If it is safe to do so, please stop what you are doing and listen to me carefully."

"We believe that this ship carries the only humans left in existence of any world and any galaxy. I realize that all of you have separate faiths and separate deities that you pray to. My personal belief is that we have a Creator, and we are here according to His good will. Every soul on the seven ships is precious. Until my final moment, I pledge to fight for each of those souls, without one single exception.

"Governments must adapt and change to the needs of the people. Therefore, I am putting into place a Captain's initiative. I wish I could say this is the only instance I will do such a thing, but at this time, I can make no such promises. I will say much thought and prayer has gone into the proclamation I'm invoking at this time.

"From this day on, any person or persons that seek sanctuary from their own people's laws and initiatives where death is a penalty will be given a fair trial with a jury of their peers, that is human beings from more than one kindred group, on the headship. This goes into effect beginning yesterday. Therefore, Tansy Pellum, under sentence of death from her own Kindreds the Embroids, will be given a hearing before a grand assembly tomorrow morning."

She took a deep breath and exhaled slowly, her hands and toes tingling. The adrenaline she'd harnessed to survive the day's intense events had all but run dry, and she felt she must collapse, fall to the floor and give into the utter weariness that overtook her being. *More must be said.*

"I, as your captain, must make an admission. When we first planned to make this long migration to a mostly unexplored planet, we agreed that one spaceship, large enough to hold all who must be saved, was impossible to bring safely through the slipstream. Therefore, the idea of smaller ships tethered together was formed."

She bowed her head and swallowed. Her hands shook, and she clasped them together. Lifting her head, she stared her reflection in the eye.

"As the person charged with the safety of your very lives, I must share this truth. When we formed this alliance of ships, we assured each of your leaders that the ships, if separated, could function on their own. We trained a crew of each Kindred to learn the controls in your separate station in case this happened. And we informed each leadership team that if they studied the use of a series of controls and switches, they could separate the ships in a great time of need.

"People of the Serpentine collective, you have been deceived. These ships cannot be parted by your magistrates, or anyone else. The only way the tubes could be severed would be by the command of myself and the three members of Solstice and would only be evoked as a last resort. The ships cannot be piloted separately, and they would not be capable of supporting life. You were told these things because the leadership felt that the lives saved by this deception would be worth the cost of misplaced trust. But now I believe for us to persevere and survive these next ten months, truth must be our binding. The only way we will arrive in Fortress and begin a new life is if we work together in full unity."

The door slid open behind her, and footsteps pounded the floor.

"Please know I care for you all deeply, and I hope that we can continue–"

Crenth pushed in front of her and slammed his comwatch over the control panel.

"Solstice 2, authorization 0 7 6 8 2"

The screen blinked away.

He turned to face her, as Marrow and Platmoth joined him on either side of his tall, thin person.

"If you hurt Bradstorm to get to me, I'll have you hurled into space."

"Your precious commander is fine," said Platmoth. "Just overcome by a bit of sleeper's sulphur."

Periwinth swallowed and squared her shoulders. "Is there a reason why you chose to interrupt the captain's address? And how is it one of you has a command code stronger than my own?"

"Do you hear this?" Marrow hissed, her wrinkles drawing down like wet rolls of paper. "This person, the woman we created, dares to question our decisions."

Periwinth stepped back. "You created? What are you talking

about? I worked myself to death to become a captain, and the three of you begged me to apply for this position. I have done nothing–"

She stopped. *No, Periwinth. You're placating and justifying. That's exactly what they want from you.*

Thoughts raced through her mind. Everything was clear. The triad of Solstice had put her in place as a headpiece, nothing more. If she didn't play nice, she'd be thrown down in an instant. Her position was probably already in jeopardy after her announcement. *Then they'll follow their goals to the detriment of all. No matter what they've done, I can't upset the leadership. Everything is too fragile. With my admission, we're already dangerously close to inter-ship war.*

"I demand a meeting of the Conveyance," she said.

"We will do no such thing," said Platmoth. "The Conveyance is nothing but a name."

"No." Periwinth drew herself up and stared into Marrow's beady sharp eyes. "The Conveyance is the captain's last resort, signed by all, that is my privilege to call and assemble."

Marrow's long fingers clenched into fists. "How could you accomplish such a thing? Are you–" A slow, incredulous smile spread across her face. "You couldn't be referring to that group of degenerates you cobbled together. Weren't they all killed in the chapel explosion?"

"None of them died, no thanks to any of you." Periwinth stepped behind her desk and leaned forward, resting on her knuckles. "My intention is not for you to lose your titles or ranks, though none of you deserve to keep anything."

"Jolly well not!" Crenth sputtered. "Do you know what you've done? We barely made it to this room without getting torn to pieces."

"With luck, we will be forgiven. If we'd waited, then we'd have no hope," said Periwinth. "The false stations were already discovered and brought to my attention. Better for me to bring it forth in good faith than for news to spread among the people in secret. I have made this public for the good of all on the ships. In return, the lies must stop. We would be fortunate to make it through this situation. We most certainly wwould not survive another such deception."

Crenth shook his head. "I pity you, Captain. You're delusional if you think–"

"We'll take the deal," Marrow interrupted. "Call your Conveyance. We'll agree to work with them. That is, if any of these people will stand by your side after what you've divulged."

Crenth and Platmoth's eyes bulged from their sockets until Periwinth wondered if they might actually pop out and roll around on the floor.

"The captain is right," Marrow purred. "We must say that we're behind her, that we planned this revelation together for the good of the ship. We each have our supporters. They can be convinced. Or bribed," she added.

"Good. I'll be back in twenty minutes. I trust you all can avoid total ship annihilation for that length of time." Periwinth went through door.

32
Kindred Shift

Tansy waited in her room, pacing the floor and shaking out her hands which still smarted from the Embroid bonds, even two days later. She'd begged for Camp to stay with her, but the captain told her she'd have to be alone until the assembly. As a consolation prize, she'd been allowed to sleep in regular quarters as opposed to the brig.

"After all, you aren't a prisoner," Captain Zephyr had said. "This is mostly to keep you safe from your kindred, as ridiculous as that is. Two guards will be posted outside."

Last night, Tansy had watched the captain's message about invoking the new law. *But how will she protect me? The other kindreds understand so little about my gift. They might agree that I've been selfish to the detriment of all. No one will believe me when I say I've tried to help when I could, with what I knew. I trust the captain, but what if something happens to her?*

Her thoughts flickered to Camp. How she missed his sweet

smile, and that light in his eye when he caught sight of her across a room. He'd gone back through the ships to fetch Dashner and Jayne's little girl so she could be with her parents, but he'd promised to be back before the assembly.

"Of course, you'll be fine," he'd said. "But I'd never leave you to face something like that on your own."

She touched the thin bandage on her forehead. Her skin still ached from time to time, but she'd mostly regained her strength. The clinic worker told her that herbs she'd tended in the Embroid greenhouse had been used to make the ointments to soothe her burns and those of Dashner, who was recovering well.

The room's panel flashed, and the door cracked open.

Tansy rose as Camp strode in, his dreads swinging. The sling on his arm was gone, but the patch over his eye remained. Eyes took longer to heal.

"How did you get through the guards?" she asked.

"Captain's pass." He held up his comwatch.

"Oh. Well, it's good to see you," she said. "What's happening out there? I haven't seen or heard from anyone since yesterday, only the address from the captain earlier."

"So many things," he said. "You're supposed to come with me. Our little group is now what the captain calls a Conveyance. I'm not sure what it means, but everyone's there. We need to hurry."

Tansy pulled on a cloak and followed him through the door. "That's so strange." She stopped short. "Wait a minute. Everyone? Will Halsey be replaced by someone else?"

"A crewman named Ulder. Commander Helms says he trusts him with his life."

"Who can anyone trust anymore?"

"I think we can trust the captain," said Camp.

"Yes. Hopefully she isn't called to step down."

"If that happens, I truly believe we will all be lost."

They walked in silence for a moment, letting the enormity of these thoughts sink in.

"Tansy." Camp cleared his throat as they waited for the lift. "Whatever happens, I want you to know ... meeting you has been ... you're so special. And beautiful. And–" he lifted his hands.

"Thank you," she said. "I think you're pretty special yourself."

"Glad we feel the same way," he said. "Anyway, now that I know about you being the Emergent and all, I figure I should tell you about my gift."

"What kind of gift?"

"When I touch someone, I can gauge their trustworthiness. The knowledge kind of sweeps over me. Like back in our world, when the light dawned, and we knew morning had come."

"How interesting," said Tansy. "In the past, I would say you must have an Embroid in your family line. But now I'm realizing that anyone from any Kindred could possess a gift from Spirit. But why wouldn't we all know about them?"

Camp shrugged. "Maybe, like us, people are afraid."

"Can't blame them for that," said Tansy. "And I understand why you didn't tell me before, but . . . thank you for telling me now."

"Sure," said Camp as the lift opened. "We need to hurry."

He grabbed her hand as they moved through strangely empty corridors. Usually they'd seen at least a handful of people wandering through on some mission, whether crew members or civilians. *Something is definitely amiss.* Tansy reached out to Camp's mind, but he seemed just as clueless.

Camp checked his comwatch as they reached the end of another hallway. "No new correspondence. Helms might be waiting for us outside the assembly hall. I don't know."

"I'm so glad he's okay," said Tansy. "I can't help but think that everyone got hurt because they were trying to save me."

Camp stopped and turned, his eyes blazing. "Don't you ever say that," he snapped. "People were hurt because of a mentally disturbed woman with a bomb. She wasn't just after you; she was targeting all of us."

"Maybe," said Tansy.

Camp turned right, then left. Just as Tansy began to feel like a rat in a maze, they entered a hall with a ceiling that stretched over three stories high., with skylights opening to the blackness of space. Marble statues, brought all the way from Earth two hundred years ago, lined the walls.

Nothing disturbed the silence but the quiet hum of the ship, always with them, that had become like their own heartbeats.

Camp whistled. "I thought I'd seen some amazing things on the headship, but this is beyond my wildest dreams."

Giant double doors filled the wall ahead of them, but Camp

passed those and went to a little red panel, almost invisible, on the side. The top of his head brushed the door frame as he went through. "Come on, this is where we're supposed to go."

Tansy squeezed into the narrow passage. The underground air shafts they'd used to escape the Embroid ship seemed downright roomy compared to the space.

"Come on," Camp said. "Through this little door."

He waved the comwatch over the control panel.

"Welcome, Campion," came the mechanical digital voice that had become a part of their every waking day.

Tansy waved hers in front of it. "Welcome Tansy," said the voice. The door slid open.

They stepped into a small room.

Tansy blinked, her eyes adjusting to the sudden light. Glindel, Falstaff, Kafla, and Tracer met her gaze with stoic faces. No one waved or smiled, and Falstaff looked close to tears. A man wearing a guard uniform sat beside Falstaff. *Must be Ulder.*

Camp joined her as she sat. "Any idea what this is all about?" he murmured to Tracer.

Tracer shrugged. "Falstaff seems to think we're here to receive punishment for helping Tansy escape, but no one knows. The leadership teams from each ship have gathered out in the massive hall. Wait until you see it."

Tansy's heart sank. Captain Zephyr had promised them protection. *But what if the ships revolt?* Once the jury of the headship made their decree, nothing more could be done.

Commander Helms entered the room, his arm bound up in a sling. He smiled. "I see you've all arrived. I've prayed you'd all come, and I am eternally grateful for your bravery."

Camp leaned over. "Doesn't seem like we're in trouble," he whispered.

Tansy shook her head. Displeasure was not what she felt from Commander Helms at all. *One doesn't need to be an Embroid to figure that out.*

Falstaff slouched in his chair. "Can you tell us what's going on, Chief?"

"Yes, we need more information," said Kafla. "Especially after the Captain's announcement. The Chieftess was beside herself."

"Everyone is," said Tracer. He glanced at Camp.

"I think the captain will do right by us," said Camp. "I mean, it's all we've got."

"My family is pretty upset with me." Glindel rested her chin on her hands. "They don't understand why I didn't tell them what was happening. But I believe the captain was trying to do something good."

"She's still a person," Tansy said quietly. "She still makes mistakes. Like all of us."

Commander Helms strode to the center of the small room. "We are grateful for the sacrifices you have made and the trust you've placed in us. As for how things will be settled–I can't get into that yet. Won't be long though." He looked down. "Anyway, the Captain and the rest of our honored guests are waiting for you."

He led the way. Tansy and Camp joined the rest of the group to follow him.

They moved out to a balcony. Most of Tansy's group gasped as they gazed around them.

The room was enormous, almost the size of the main grid on the middle five ships.

Tansy stepped out on the balcony and stared down. A sea of people fanned out before her, their faces mere blobs in the shadows of the bright lights focused at the front podiums.

Tansy figured most of the population of the headship must be there, as well as a good percentage of the Kindreds from the other ships. She saw Father Sharood, his group of attendants, and her Uncle Tam to the far right, and the Tark Chief and Chieftess in the center section. Many of her neighbors and acquaintances sat among the crowd as well.

Captain Zephyr stepped out on stage. The three people that Tansy recognized as the Solstice by their robes and headdresses came behind her.

Captain Zephyr wore a blue and silver robe, and a silver chain circled her shining black hair. She looked regal, beautiful, and strong. But Tansy worried for her. Hostile thoughts rushed from those in the crowd, many with murderous intent.

Longer balconies ran across the sides of the arena, and soldiers lined them, weapons cradled in their arms. But who would they shoot at? The cacophony of thoughts was too great. Tansy couldn't get a clear read on anyone.

Camp took her hand. "Pray to Spirit," he whispered.

The captain cleared her throat.

The crowd continued to make noise, some applauding, some booing, some shouting.

A member of the solstice, a woman Tansy knew as Marrow, came from behind Captain Zephyr and raised her hands. The crowd instantly died down.

Oh, that can't be good. From the frown on Camp's face, Tansy knew he was thinking the same thing.

"Fellow shipmates," the captain said in a calm, confident voice. "I realize you have been given quite a shock. And as I stated before, it was with a sorrowful heart I had to reveal the deception that has been put upon you."

The crowd noise swelled again, and a section of soldiers worked to keep a small group of Bloomwraiths from rushing the stage.

Marrow raised her hands once more and the noise died down, but it took longer this time.

Two more Bloomwraiths were returned to their chairs by soldiers.

Tansy had never witnessed such a mob, except for her trial by the Embroids of course. It was unsettling, being a part of this emotional soup.

"The last two days have consisted of terrible events," said Captain Zephyr. "As you know, we've discovered a saboteur who threatened all the ships and could have eventually, I believe, destroyed us all if she hadn't been stopped. Sadly, she chose to take her own life. We are safe from that threat, at least."

"Before any of these horrible things came to light, I chose random members of your Kindred. Not your leaders, for I knew this would be too unbalanced. But seven among you, to bring me suggestions for ways to unify our Kindreds. These people will become a conveyance, a group of individuals who will gather and discuss what's best for the ships together. They will walk among you, listening to your ideas and sharing thoughts." She nodded to the group in the balcony. "They will work as advocates for all, with a new vision. To bring these ships to the unified state we so desperately need to make it home."

The crowd's murmuring grew again.

Glindel inhaled sharply. "Us? I don't remember agreeing to this."

"Look at the captain's eyes," Falstaff murmured. "She's desperate. This is her last resort. She couldn't tell us. What will happen if we say no? She needs each one of us."

The captain beckoned to them.

"Time to go down," said Commander Helms. "If you don't want to be a part of the Conveyance, you are free to refuse. But all the souls on this ship depend on the unity this moment could bring, and I think you know that."

Falstaff ducked his head, then started down the steps. Glindel followed, then Tracer. Kafla hesitated, then began a stately walk, head held high.

Camp headed for the steps, leading Tansy by the hand, but

Commander Helms grasped her shoulder. "No, Tansy. I'm afraid you can't be a part of this. We will choose another Embroid member for the group."

The captain can't save me. Tansy's head swirled, and her knees buckled slightly. "What will I do?"

Commander Helms bowed his head. "Take courage, I believe all shall be well. But safety might come with a high price. We will discuss the matter later."

Tansy leaned against the balcony, watching while the team of people who had quickly become her friends lined up behind the captain.

"From now on," Captain Zephyr said, "These young people will be your advocates. Embroid Kindred, please know you will not be forgotten, a member from your group will be chosen soon. These people's tasks will be to hear everyone's concerns, from young to old, and bring them before me."

Each person on the stage looked a bit shocked, even Kafla.

The three members of the Solstice sat with their arms folded, unmoving.

"Now, we have another bit of unfinished business," Captain Zephyr continued. "Tansy Pellum. Will you please come to the stage."

Tansy obediently moved down the stairs, her knees trembling so hard she almost stumbled more than once.

Camp watched her as she came, his thoughts rushing up, coaxing. *You'll be fine. Trust in Spirit.*

Captain Zephyr put an arm around Tansy's shoulder and turned her to face the crowd.

Father Sharood scowled at her from the front row, but instead of fear, Tansy felt a sense of peace.

"This girl is accused of treasonous acts. She is a self-proclaimed Emergent, which means she can sometimes see the future and read thoughts. Is this true, Tansy?"

Tansy glanced up at Captain Zephyr. "Yes. Sometimes."

"And because of an unproven superstition, you were sentenced to death by your own people. Is that true?"

Tansy's tongue stuck to the roof of her mouth, and she worked to loosen it. "Yes, Captain."

Captain Zephyr looked out at Father Sharood. "Embroid Magistrate, tell me, this superstition of the Emergent's powers being passed to the next baby girl in the family line. Has it ever been proven?"

He leaped from his chair. "It is our time-honored belief and tradition–"

Captain Zephyr held up her hand. "This is a hearing of facts, Magistrate. Do you have binding evidence that this superstition has been proven in the last hundred years?"

"No," Father Sharood mumbled, sitting back in his seat.

"I bid you all to look at your comwatches," Captain Zephyr addressed the crowd.

Throughout the room devices lit up like tiny fireflies flickering over a meadow.

"I want you to ask yourselves, what if this were your daughter? Your mother? Your friend? Should she die for superstition's sake? And if you were in such a place, would you want someone to be your advocate? Because next time–this could be you."

Captain Zephyr lifted her comwatch, which was also lit up. "We will all have the chance to decide. Right now."

Father Sharood and the elders on either side of him shouted and waved their fists in the air.

"We demand justice!" shouted Father Sharood, veins bulging from his skin. "She is an Embroid. You do not have a say over her life."

"No, Magistrate," said Captain Zephyr. "I have authority because she is a member of the seven ships, one of the few remaining members of humanity. We will put the matter to a human-wide vote."

A deathly silence hung over the crowd as everyone stared at their comwatches. Captain Zephyr also gazed at hers.

Tansy strained to hear the thoughts, to sense the general direction of feelings. Members of the crowd made their selections.

Her legs wobbled beneath her. *It's too much. What if we lose? Will the captain truly hand me back to Father Sharood after everything we've been through?*

Loud chimes rang from each wristlet, shrill if only from one device, nearly deafening from all at once. The crowd's intensity grew and swelled, a roaring emanating from the Embroid side of the room. The bone-hats rose and fell as Opulents checked their comwatches.

The captain's officers surrounded Tansy like an ocean swell, lifting her up and away from her place, and she found herself being bourne back through the tiny passage. She screamed and kicked. "Where are you taking me? What happened?"

Camp's face bobbed through the soldiers. "Tansy, settle down! They're protecting you! Everyone voted. Seventy percent of the people who were present voted for you to live. We've won. You're safe."

Epilogue

Cool, copper-colored liquid bubbled in the tiny glass, and Periwinth sipped it slowly, savoring. Ginger ale was hard to come by and would be impossible to produce until they'd established the Fortress colony.

Tansy sat across from her. Her Embroid robes had been replaced by a standard crewman's uniform, and her long curls were braided up into a simple chignon.

"So, you will be staying here," said Periwinth. "You have left your Kindred for good."

"For now," said Tansy. "With my birthday past, the danger is not so intense, but I am still hated and feared. I can't live in my home. Of course, I'm saddened by it."

She pulled out a chain from around her neck that had been tucked under her uniform. Attached was a small, egg-shaped carbuncle. "I wanted to show you this token."

"That's beautiful," said Periwinth. "I've never seen a flower like that."

"A gift from a Tark woman," said Tansy. "It's a flower from

Earth." She gazed at Periwinth through long, thick lashes. "Gifts are scattered throughout the Kindreds. You've started with your Conveyance, but I believe it would be best for our survival if you discovered more of them."

"Noted," said Periwinth. "I suppose you know mine."

"You are a gift-seer? Or something like that? It makes me wonder what the other members of the team can do."

"It's not for me to tell," said Periwinth. "But I think you will learn them all in time."

The girl's eyelids fluttered, and she stared at something intently, as though an invisible picture had floated before her. "He is coming, Captain. And when he does, you will be faced with more impossible choices."

Periwinth froze. "What are you talking about?"

Tansy blinked, shook her head, and smiled. "I don't know. But I'm sure whatever it means, you'll find a way to handle it."

Periwinth settled back in her chair, willing her nerves to calm. *Creator, help us all.* "If you 'see' anything else, please let me know. That is, if you feel free to do so."

"Of course, Captain Zephyr. This is my place now. You are my Kindred. And I will do what I can for the good of the Serpentine."

THE END

Serpentine Layout
with Kindred Directory

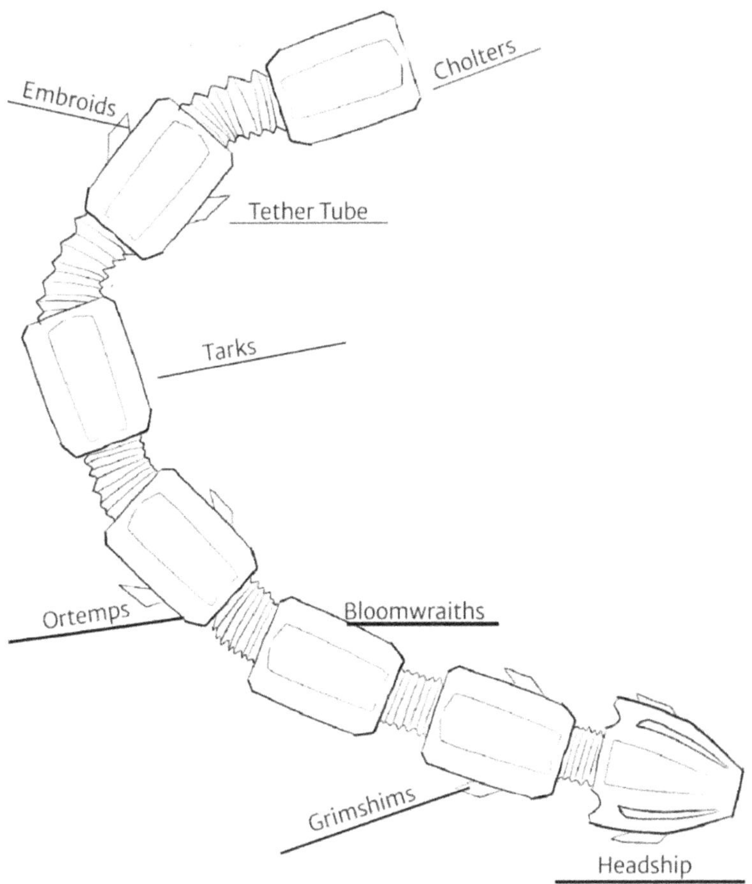

List of Kindred Groups by Ship:

Cholters:

7th ship.

Approximately 750 people. Known for their amazing repair and repurpose skills. They are responsible for collecting and sorting the trash from the other six ships and recycling what can be reused. Sometimes unfairly stigmatized by other Kindreds.

Embroids:

6th ship.

Approximately 1200 people. Responsible for several greenhouses. Produces herbs and poultices for the other vessels. Deeply spiritual and gifted.

Tarks:

5th ship.

About 1800 people. Keep most of the animals meant for the new planet of Fortress. A proud and fierce people who may prefer to reach for a spear instead of having a friendly conversation.

Ortemps:

4th ship.

About 900 people. The Ortemps are responsible for an armory

almost as big as the one residing in the Headship, but their weapons are designed for ground defense, rather than air missiles. Had a 100-year feud with the Tarks, after which they called a draw and now remain in a fragile peace to this day. Many of their people suffer from genetic birth defects that cause them to be born without 1 or more limbs, or even with missing eyes or ears, which is why many of their people are fitted with cybernetic components.

Bloomwraiths:

3rd ship.

About 1500 people. This Kinship is responsible for all flora being transported to the new planet, besides what's being grown in gardens and greenhouses. They have allowed trees and plants to overgrow most of their ship, creating an almost forest-like environment.

Grimshims:

2nd. ship

About 1200 people. These are the tech people who work the closest with the headship. They are responsible for most mechanical systems throughout the tethered ships and will send teams to problem areas to address any needed repairs.

Remaining Kindreds (Headship):

1st Ship

3500 people, made up of 38 Kindred groups.

ABOUT THE AUTHOR

Angela. Castillo has been writing stories since she created
her first tale in green crayon at the age of eight. She's lived all
over Central Texas but mostly hovers around the town of
Bastrop, Texas, which she loves with an unnatural fierceness and
features in many of her books. Angela has four wild children,
a husband who studies astrophysics for fun, and a cat.
If you would like a FREE collection of Angela's short stories, you
can sign up for her newsletter at
https://fairygirlbooks.eo.page/wtkxs

Look for Book 2 in the

Serpentine series to arrive in Fall 2025

"Lord willing and the creek don't rise."

Enjoy the following excerpt
from Angela Castillo's book
"Willow Green 1: Once Upon a Ren
Faire."

Once Upon a Ren Faire

Willow Green
Book 1

1
Green Tresses

The late spring Texas sun beamed overhead, and I studied my silver and green Celtic cloak, spread out over the trunk of Blaire's car. *Probably be a scorcher.* I ran a finger along the elaborate embroidery, shrugged, and put it on. *It's too pretty to leave behind.*

"Hurry up, Keltia!" Marianne called.

I rushed past the costume tents and the sellers who had stalls outside the fences of the faire. Crowds of people dressed as elves, centaurs, faeries, and countless other fantasy creatures swarmed past.

A little boy jumped in front of me, waving a wooden sword and almost catching my shoulder with it.

"Sorry!" he shouted after me.

My three friends had almost reached the ren faire entrance by the time I caught up with them. The gates were made from wrought iron, with serpents and mythical creatures twisted together to form the massive panels. The palatial gates seemed slightly out of place in the rough-hewn log walls, but it was all part of the faire.

The ticket taker glanced at our season's passes and waved us through. "Welcome to thee one and all. We hope you enjoy the last day of the season."

We stepped into the faire. Excitement and color swirled around us like a mixed bag of ribbons. The biting odor of kerosene filled the air as a jester strolled by, juggling flaming batons. A minstrel strummed a mandolin beneath the shade of a giant cypress.

People crowded the little paths leading to various booths and activities. The energy surrounding us teemed with the joy always found at these events, with an added tang of bittersweetness, like the last moments before you fall asleep on Christmas night.

Blaire, the fearless leader of my 'ren fair friend' group, as we called ourselves, stepped in front of me.

"Okay," she said, twisting her straight blond hair into a ponytail as she talked. "Where do we want to go first?" And please don't say somewhere to eat." She glared at her fifteen-year-old sister, Sasha.

Sasha sniffed. "I wasn't going to say that. But I wouldn't mind finding the sweet bun wagon."

"I'll be heading to Chadwick's," I said.

"Not the dagger again." Blaire rolled her eyes.

"My costume won't be complete without it," I replied. "And my parents gave me my birthday money early."

"I forgot your birthday is in three days," said Marianne. "You'll finally be eighteen like Blaire and I."

"We're going to par-tay!" Blaire did a little dance. "We should all go get mani-pedis and hit the clubs in Austin."

"I don't think so," I mumbled. Mani-pedis had never been my thing, and I wouldn't be caught dead in a loud, crowded club.

"Shall we focus on today, ladies?" Marianne held out a paper program. "How about the joust? It starts in five minutes."

"Good idea," said Blaire. She moved forward, the train of her princess dress swishing behind her. "I can't wait to see that hot guy again. You know, the one who won all the matches last month?"

The amount of time I'd spent talking about daggers paled in comparison to how much Blaire gushed about guys, especially since she dumped her last boyfriend. But I did enjoy the joust, so I stomped after the group. *I'll get my dagger afterwards.*

The jouster, Sir Emerson, had been at this faire all year. Blaire had tried to jostle her way behind the scenes to talk to him more than once, but he was always surrounded by possies of 'wenches' and 'maidens' as Sasha called the barmaids and costumed workers.

Marianne chose a bench on the edge of the jousting arena, and I sat next to her.

"This seat is the worst," Blaire huffed from the other end. "The sun is right in my face, and I can hardly see."

"We got here late," Sasha said. "And this is the last day. What did you expect?"

"I'll switch with you, Blaire," I offered, though that meant a further roasting in my cloak.

"Fine." Blaire rose and we swiftly changed places.

Three heralds with long trumpets stepped out into the middle of the ring. An ear-splitting fanfare filled the air, mercifully drowning out whatever further whining Blaire meant to do.

The announcer, a short, balding man in ballooning pantaloons, strode into the ring. "We welcome you today, to the greatest show in all the land." He continued with the same spiel he gave every time we came. The crowd clapped and laughed in all the right places.

Though I'd been here dozens of times, the shows never lost their appeal. Maybe it was my unusual name that caused me to love all things magical and medieval. Perhaps it was because my mother had brought me to this ren faire, which was only a few miles from our little Texas town, for years. As a professor of medieval history, she'd point out unusual costumes and buildings, sharing with me the history of every magical thing.

"Here come the jousters!" Blaire squealed, pulling me from my musings.

The six knights paraded down the fairway on their spectacular horses. Each rider's costume matched their steed's saddle blankets, orange and white, green, and blue . . .

"Sir Emerson!" Blaire jumped up, clapping her hands.

Some people swiveled to smile at her, but most were screaming and clapping as well.

No wonder the knight was a crowd favorite. He hadn't donned his helmet yet, and his wavy light brown hair was tied back into a short ponytail. A confident smile curled beneath his neatly trimmed mustache and goatee. His colors were black and red, matching his gorgeous black stallion's saddle blanket.

The fanfare continued, and the cheers thundered throughout the arena.

"Now, our fine, jousting friends," the announcer said. "Would you prithee be so good as to stand at your stations?"

Each jouster obediently dismounted and led their horses to their designated areas.

I sighed and fiddled with the ribbon at the end of my braid. I'd rather watch the jousting itself than these silly little add-ins. But the crowd always ate them up.

"Now, would each knight please choose a lady?" the announcer said.

The men stepped through the fence and out into the stands in six different directions. They shaded their eyes and scanned the crowds with roguish smiles.

The women went wild. "Pick me! Pick me!" echoed throughout the stadium, from eight-year-old faerie maidens to matriarchs with white curls piled high on their heads.

Sasha and Blaire yelled louder, and even Marianne waved both her hands. Our entire bench threatened to turn over. I gripped the edge of my seat and planted my feet on the ground.

Emerson picked our section, then turned down our row. I'd never admit it to Blaire, but he *was* handsome. Prickles moved up and down my arms. The knights had never come this close to us, no matter where we'd sat.

"Oh my gosh!" Blaire grabbed Sasha's arm. "He's coming our way!" She leapt to her feet. "Pick me, pick me!"

Emerson's eyes lit on Blaire, and he gave her a smile. But he passed her by and headed in my direction.

I became very still, like the time a deer had approached me in the forest. The knight's leather armor really was something, hand-tooled and stitched. I'd never seen anything like it, not even in the best booths.

"Kindly, ma'am, could I beg you for a favor?" he asked in a soft voice. "T'will bring me luck in the arena." His copper eyes fixed on my red hair ribbon. "Perhaps your ribbon? Those bonny emerald tresses would look lovely unbound."

My cheeks warmed. I'd dealt with unwanted attention from my green hair for most of my life, but it still embarrassed me sometimes, especially when called out in a crowd like this.

"Sure." I untied the ribbon and handed it to him. When our fingers brushed, my skin tingled. *He's a man like any other. Probably has a new girlfriend for every fair. Or ten.*

"I thank thee kindly, milady." His intense gaze held me captive. "I will win for you."

"Sounds good." I shrugged to break my momentary lapse of sanity. *How very Knight's Tale of him.* Probably said that to every girl at each ren faire. But despite everything, a fuzzy sensation washed over me. *Wow.* He was charming.

Emerson strode back to his horse, women reaching out to touch him as he walked by.

"That's it, I'm dying my hair green!" Blaire plopped down on the bench and pouted.

It's not that great. I pushed back my now unraveling braid. Few people knew my hair color was natural. My mother had, bless her heart, covered my little baby head with hats and hoods. For a while she'd resorted to wigs and color treatments until I'd finally put my foot down. By then, unusual hair colors were common. People constantly asked me where I'd had mine done, and when I smiled and said, "at home," no one believed me. I'd never met another soul with natural green hair. Well, except for one person. And he was only in my dreams.

The knights lined up. Up first was Herbert; in brown and gold, against Archibald; in yellow and orange.

I clapped and cheered along with the rest of the crowd. After all, it was my renfest duty.

When Emerson reached the post, he winked at me and pointed to the fluttering red ribbon, tied on his jousting pole.

"Oh, I'm so jealous, I'm never speaking to you again." Blaire folded her arms.

"Good grief, it's not like Keltia did anything special to be picked," said Marianne.

Sasha wiped her forehead with the flapping sleeve of her faerie costume. "Can we get something to eat now? I'm hot."

I sighed. Blaire and Sasha were the daughters of my mom's friend, and we'd been pushed together since kindergarten. Years ago, when Marianne and I had decided to go to our first renfest,

Sasha and Blaire begged to tag along. Now they expected to be invited whenever we went.

Next time, I'm going without the drama sisters.

A roar rose from the crowd as Emerson unseated his opponent. He trotted his horse around the ring, lance held high.

Emerson trounced each opponent soundly, then went on to win a game that involved knocking watermelons from pedestals.

The knights lined up again and bowed. Emerson locked eyes with me once more, mouthing a 'thank you.'

Blaire shot me a dirty look.

The crowd began to exit the sidelines.

Blaire gathered her skirts and slid down the bench to me. "Don't forget to get your favor back from him," she said, pointing to the swarm of women around the jousters. "We actually have a chance to talk to Emerson again."

"He can keep the ribbon, I have others," I said.

Blaire clutched at my arm. "You can't be serious! I guess you don't care, but I've always wanted to meet him. How can you do that to me?"

"You can fetch it for me, if you like." I stood and smoothed down my tunic. "I'm off to buy my dagger. I'll meet you at the baker's stand."

"Come on, Sasha." Blaire headed down to the fence where the knights were signing autographs and talking to the crowd.

Sasha followed, protesting about sweet buns the whole way.

"Keltia, do you want me to go with you?" asked Marianne. She bit her lip, and her eyes darted to the fence.

"No, you go meet the hot knight." I waved her away and headed for the path that led to the rows of shops in the center of the fair.

The aroma of freshly roasted corn and turkey legs filled the air. My stomach rumbled, but I shook my head. "First my dagger, then the feast." I giggled. Something about the ren faire always made me feel like a different person. But I'd be disappointed if it didn't.

Even Mom, the stalwart college professor, dressed in full costume and talked 'medieval style' as she called it, when she came with us.

That's it. Next time I'll ask Mom to come instead. I'll say it's a special date and then I'll have a break from Blaire and Sasha.

"Girl with mermaid tresses!" a shopkeeper called out. "Does the Mermaid need a pretty trinket?"

"This mermaid is off to the blacksmith shop," I shot back.

"The mermaid wants teeth!" a second shopkeeper yelled.

"Exactly." As I continued to a wooden building with a bright red roof at the end of the row, the silly banter sang out around me. All part of the ren faire fun.

As I passed the stalls of merchandise, I checked for details; an embroidered pattern on a dress; detailed carving on a staff. Most items at renfests were cheaply made for impulsive buys during the day, but a few shop owners were master craftsmen who meticulously researched everything they created.

Over the last few years, I'd saved babysitting money, and now tips from working at a coffee shop, to put together the most researched and authentic costume I could afford. My tunic, leggings, cloak, belt, and greaves had been purchased at various fairs, all hand-made and ridiculously expensive. The only thing I wore that hadn't been bought at the fair was my cloak clasp, a brass brooch with entwined tree branches.

I reached the store and stepped inside, taking a deep, shivery breath. *Now to choose my dagger.* The air in the shop was heavier than outdoors, and musty. Rows of swords lined the wall, and showcases of smaller weapons filled the center of the room.

Leaning against the counter, I studied the gleaming row of daggers and short swords. I'd had my eye on three. A blade sporting a dragon hilt with ruby eyes, a cudgel with amethyst stones, and a smaller dirk with a single opal on the sheath.

Chadwick, the blacksmith, came in from the back area where he had his bellows set up for crowd demonstrations. His coveralls hung loosely on his tall, thin frame, and his bright blond hair was cropped short, showing off costume elven ears.

"Keltia, how lovely to see you! By the smile on your face I'm guessing today is the day."

"Yep, Chadwick, finally have the money." I pulled out the leather pouch I kept tied at my waist.

Challah, his wife, came to stand next to me. "We sold that dragon blade yesterday," she said softly. Bright red braids slipped over her shoulders as she reached for a box on a shelf. "But I thought you might be interested in this new one Chadwick finished last week. For some reason, it seemed to say your name."

She opened the top of the box.

I peered inside. "Oooh."

The dagger was the perfect length, about eight inches long, with a sheath made of burnished copper. Ornate leaves and vines ran up the hilt. Flowers dotted the vines, and an emerald gleamed in the center of each blossom.

The hilt had been shaped into a woman's face with long, curling hair. Though young and beautiful, she had a haunted look, like she carried the cares of a world on her shoulders.

"It's a dryad's blade," said Challah.

"Like a tree spirit?" Mom had told me about dryads. They originated in Greek mythology and had originally been considered to be the daughters of Zeus.

I grasped the hilt and pulled the dagger from its sheath. A tremor, like a small shock, went through my arm as I examined the shining blade.

"Yes," I said in a voice scarcely above a whisper. "This is mine."

Chadwick came to stand beside his wife. "I thought as much," he said with a satisfied grin. "And look at that. The vine pattern matches that brooch you always wear."

"Why, so it does." Challah touched the small clasp at my shoulder. "Which merchant did you buy that from, dear?"

"I didn't buy it here. My mother said it was fastened to the blanket I was wrapped in when I was found as a baby. I think I told you about that last time I was here."

"How interesting." Challah gave Chadwick a tiny smile. He raised an eyebrow but said nothing.

With great reluctance I slid the knife back into its sheath and put it in the box. "I love this, but I don't think I can afford it today." The smallest knives in the shop ran in the hundreds. Even though the emeralds on this dagger were tiny, they had to be expensive.

"If you want the knife today, we will sell it for one hundred dollars," said Chadwick.

I gasped. "I can't take it for so little!"

"You must," said Challah. "He made it for you. We can't sell it to anyone else."

"Wow." I studied at the beautiful hilt. I'd never wanted any item more, and my heart pounded with the realization that it could actually belong to me. "Okay, but I'll be plastering it all over social media. You'll have people beating down your door next year."

Challah glanced at Chadwick. "I'm not sure we'll be here next year."

"Oh no!" I counted out five crisp twenties from my pouch. "Why not? Did you not sell enough this year? You're not charging enough. I will pay you more for this!"

Challah opened her mouth to answer, but Chadwick put his hand on her shoulder and spoke instead. "We might be moving. Um, out of state."

"Oh. Well, good luck, wherever you go," I said, not wanting to imagine the ren fest without them.

The floorboards squeaked behind me.

"'Tis a fair blade you've chosen."

I started and turned to see Emerson at my elbow.

"Forgive me, I beseech thee." He stepped back, spreading out his hands. "I didn't intend to alarm you. I wanted to return this in person, though your friends did protest much."

My red ribbon dangled from his hand.

He was young, only a few years older than me. He'd shed his gloves, and his hands were leathery and strong, which made sense for someone who probably worked with horses' tack and saddles all day.

I took the ribbon. "Thanks, but you could have kept it."

Chadwick cleared his throat.

The elven couple stared at me, and I met their gazes, expecting amused expressions. To my surprise, Challah was pale. A slight crease appeared on Chadwick's forehead, and his eyebrows drew together.

Challah broke the long and awkward silence. "How can we help you, Sir Emerson?"

Chadwick pulled a handkerchief from the inside of his coveralls and wiped his forehead but said nothing.

"Not meaning to bother you," said Emerson. Was his voice a tad loud? "I needed to return the favor, so to speak. That's all."

What's their deal? Does Emerson have some kind of reputation around here? He certainly has plenty of women around him most of the time. I glanced behind him but didn't see any of his normal entourage waiting in the street.

"I'll bid thee farewell," Emerson nodded to Challah and Chadwick.

"A word with you, Sir Emerson?" said Chadwick.

"Of course, always at your service," said Emerson.

Challah handed me the box with the dagger inside. "Have a lovely day. And thank you for shopping at Chadwick's Smithy."

"Th-thanks," I said, stumbling to the door. A lump filled my throat. I'd been dismissed. But why?

A small porch bordered the smithy, and I stood outside as voices rose and fell from the shop, but I couldn't make out what they were saying. I shrugged. *Must be ren fest stuff.* People in the fair had their own culture and rules. As long as it didn't come to blows, I certainly wouldn't interfere.

Maybe I should stick around and make sure everything's all right.

An empty puppet stage stood a few yards away from the smithy, and I jumped inside, scarcely daring to breathe. *My friends are going to laugh their heads off if they find out about this.*

I busied myself by removing the dagger from the box and fastening the sheath to my belt. It was the perfect size and weight.

A few moments later, Emerson emerged from the shop. He began to whistle as he sauntered along with that confident air of his in the opposite direction of the arena.

See. What was I worried about? What a strange last day of the fair. At least I had my dagger, and at an unbelievable price.

When he'd passed out of sight I began to emerge from the stage, but quickly ducked back inside as a group of men came towards my hiding spot. They were dressed as barbarian soldiers, but even in my hiding place I could tell that their armor was mostly leather and chain mail instead of cheap metal or flimsy plastic. I longed to ask where they'd bought them, but the scowls on their faces seemed as genuine as their costumes.

Must have had too much mead.

"Any sign of him?" asked a tall man with bright black eyes and a bushy beard.

A muscular, Viking-like soldier with a shock of reddish hair shook his head. "No, Sire. But he can't have gotten far."

The leader cursed. "I'll kill that Emerson."

The group continued past me and I gagged. They smelled of sweat and mead and something stronger, like they hadn't bathed in weeks. *They might be campers. But would it hurt them to shower?*

They'd mentioned Emerson. Could this be part of a skit they were doing for the fair? During the day, the actors participated in ongoing plays and sketches based around a theme, like Robin Hood or King Arthur. Sometimes they acted out skits in the middle of crowds, out in the streets of the faire. But where was the audience?

Could Emerson be in danger? Maybe I should warn him.

Huddled in my stage, I waited until the troop marched away–in the opposite direction from Emerson's path. I crept out and began a hunt of my own.